W9-BXY-006

The STRANGER'S SECRETS

The STRANGER'S SECRETS

BETH WILLIAMSON

KENSINGTON PUBLISHING CORP.
www.kensingtonbooks.com

BRAVA BOOKS are published by

Kensington Publishing Corp.
119 West 40th Street
New York, NY 10018

Copyright © 2010 Beth Williamson

All rights reserved. No part of this book may be reproduced in any form or by any means without the prior written consent of the Publisher, excepting brief quotes used in reviews.

All Kensington titles, imprints, and distributed lines are available at special quantity discounts for bulk purchases for sales promotion, premiums, fund-raising, educational, or institutional use.

Special book excerpts or customized printings can also be created to fit specific needs. For details, write or phone the office of the Kensington Special Sales Manager: Kensington Publishing Corp., 119 West 40th Street, New York, NY 10018. Attn.: Special Sales Department. Phone: 1-800-221-2647.

Brava and the B logo Reg. U.S. Pat. & TM Off.

ISBN-13: 978-0-7582-3473-5
ISBN-10: 0-7582-3473-2

First Kensington Trade Paperback Printing: January 2010

10 9 8 7 6 5 4 3 2 1

Printed in the United States of America

Prologue

May 1863

The smell of dirt and rotting vegetables filled the room, while the tang of fear coated her tongue. Sarah Spalding pushed herself into the corner, as far as she could, pushing past the cobwebs and insect carcasses. She ignored the whispery touch of the tiny feet as they scuttled over her in a panic.

Her heart thundered in a crazy rhythm as she sucked in short gulps of the stale air. Footsteps, shouts, and crashes sounded from above her. They were destroying what was left of her home.

Tears pricked her eyes as she imagined what they were breaking, destroying, or perhaps stealing. There went Father's favorite pipe against the wall in the study, then Mother's glass vase in the parlor. By the time they were done, there'd be nothing of her former life but the ghosts left behind.

Sarah hugged her knees, pressing her face into them. She knew what would happen if they found her downstairs. Even if she was only seventeen years old, she was smart enough to know what drunken Yankees would do to a young girl hiding in the root cellar.

When she heard her mother scream, Sarah had to bite her lip to keep her own from escaping. God only knew what they were doing to her. All the servants had abandoned them within a year after the war started. She and her mother, Vivian, were the only living souls on the Spalding Plantation.

Now they may both end up as spirits haunting the very ground that had nurtured them.

Sarah had no idea how long she hid in the cellar, but it was long enough that her legs began to cramp right along with her back and shoulders. She daren't move, though, because even the slightest scrape might be overhead. As it was, the men could search the house and find her room, deduce there was another female in the house, and tear it apart looking for her.

She fingered the hilt of the knife tucked into the sheath in her sleeve and vowed the first man to attack her would be the bloodiest. Her brother, Micah, had taught her a thing or two about defending herself. After he went off to war, she never went without that small knife he'd given her. She even kept it sharpened, just in case.

There were no windows in the cellar; therefore, no light permeated except when the door was open. So when a flood of bright light splashed over the gloomy room, Sarah almost cried out in pain as her eyes stung from the sudden change. Yet she kept it in, swallowing the howl that threatened.

"The door leads to a root cellar," one man said as boots thunked on the top step. "And it's dark as hell down here."

"There food?" another asked.

"No, the vegetables are all gone. Without anyone to plant and harvest crops, we have no foodstuff to speak of." Her mother's voice was still as elegant as ever, but Sarah heard the underlying hate.

"You ain't lying, are ya?" The first one sounded cold and vicious. "'Cause I'm gonna go have me a look and if'n you were lying we might have to punish you."

"Go ahead and look. There's nothing to see but empty barrels and crates and spiders." Funny her mother didn't sound worried about them finding Sarah. No, in fact, she sounded annoyed the man would question her honesty.

"I'll do that." The boots came down the stairs slowly, giving Sarah ample time to panic.

Sweat coated her face and ran down her back. The fear

turned to terror as the unknown man made it to the bottom of the steps and walked straight toward the corner in which she hid. She prayed to God to help her, to save her.

But He must've had better things to do that day.

Sarah hid her face, trying desperately to keep herself from being seen, but the soldier must've guessed someone was down there. Either that, or he was very clever.

"Lookee here, boys, we've got us a stowaway."

A hand clamped on her arm and dragged her out of the corner so fast she slammed her head into a beam, stunning her. He pulled her by the arm, her shoes digging into the hard-packed dirt on the cellar floor. It took her a few moments to catch her breath, and then she found the courage to fight back.

With a snarl, she kicked her attacker in the knee, then pulled out the knife while he screeched in pain. When he went for her hair, she slashed at his hand. He hissed and released her arm.

That was all the opportunity she needed.

Sarah welcomed the rage pouring through her as she jumped to a crouch, knife in hand. She was fortunate to be wearing trousers, although it was against her mother's wishes.

"You little bitch." Her attacker had dark whiskers and greasy, lank hair, and wore filthy clothes over his burgeoning belly. However, the one feature that struck her was his eyes. They were blue like the sky in winter and completely empty, as though he were dead inside. She tightened her grip on the knife and focused on him, truly afraid yet unwilling to let that fear rule her actions.

When he lunged for her, Sarah knew she wasn't fighting for her innocence anymore. She was fighting for her life.

Chapter One

September 1875, Appleton, Virginia

Sarah Spalding stood with her back to the room as the conversation went on behind her. At the bay window, she stared out into the blackness of the night, looking for an answer, yet it wasn't forthcoming. Her friends were arguing about whether or not she should close the boardinghouse while she was gone. As if she wasn't going to come back, a fact they couldn't yet know.

After ten minutes of listening to the bickering, she turned around. They all stopped and watched as she lit a cigarette, then took a puff.

"Well, aren't you going to say anything?" Vickie, her oldest friend and voice of her conscience, stood by the fireplace with a glass of whiskey in her hand.

Sarah looked around at her friends and tried to memorize their faces. Vickie was a curvy, vivacious blonde with a big laugh and a bigger heart. Red and Doreen were the original boarders and considered Sarah their older sister and good friend. The three women meant more to her than any family she'd ever been fortunate or unfortunate to call her own. Their loyalty was unwavering and consistent.

Lorenzo was the all-around guard at the boardinghouse, an Italian immigrant she'd found when he was a thirteen-year-old orphan eating scraps in an alley. At twenty, he was a handsome man. Unfortunately he'd decided Sarah was the woman for him, although she was too old for him. He'd had a constant melancholy expression on his face since she'd announced her intention to travel to Colorado to be reunited with her brother.

Micah.

She hadn't seen her brother in so long, more than ten years. Not since she'd stitched up the wound in his face and he'd disappeared from her life. Micah had been a battered soldier with more ghosts in his eyes than she could count. His actions that day had added a few more.

Now it seemed he'd settled in the wilds of Colorado and was getting married in less than a month's time. His intended bride, Elizabeth, had wired her with an invitation to the wedding, as a surprise for Micah. Now all Sarah had to do was figure out how to say good-bye to her friends and get on the train in the morning.

Neither one would be easy.

"What do you want me to say? It takes weeks to get to Colorado. Then I'm sure I'll want to stay and visit with my brother. I have no idea when I'll be back." Sarah must've lied convincingly enough because they all looked like they believed her.

What she hadn't told them was she had no intention of coming back, ever. Sarah's Boardinghouse was closing for good. It had been her anchor in a sea of tumult and uncertainty for many years, but the time had come for it to close. Coward that she was, she couldn't tell her friends that she planned on staying in Colorado, away from the blood-soaked ground of Virginia, away from the nightmares that kept her from a full night's sleep in more than ten years.

Sarah pressed a fist against her stomach. She couldn't remember a time when her stomach hadn't been tied in knots. Time and circumstances hadn't changed much, not enough to untie the Gordian knot she carried like a babe within her. It had become a part of her to the point where if she woke up one morning and it was gone, she would feel a loss.

"I told you girls you can live here, but the rest of the women have to go. This is no longer a boardinghouse."

Red snickered, one titian curl bouncing against her alabaster cheek.

Sarah scowled at her, cutting off the young woman's mirth. "Just because I let you do whatever business you want in your bed doesn't make me anything but a boardinghouse owner. I've never taken a cent from any of you except rent money."

"What about me?" Lorenzo's deep voice had the lilt of his Italian upbringing, muted but still there.

"I'm sure the girls will need someone to keep up the house if they decide to stay. You can sleep in your room in the carriage house, as always." Sarah couldn't turn him out. She couldn't turn any of her friends out. This decision was hers to make, but she wanted to make their suffering as brief as possible. "Look, all of you, the only thing that changes are the women who come and go from here. You can live in this house as long as you like. Considering I don't know when I'll be back, it's just closing the door for anyone else but you. Lorenzo will still be here to protect you."

Vickie came over and tried to throw her arm around Sarah's shoulder, but there was an eight-inch difference in height and Vickie ended up just putting her hand on Sarah's arm instead.

"You're too damn tall, Sarah," she grumbled as she pushed her heavy blond curls back. "We're not worried about the boardinghouse. The rest of them girls can go to hell and find themselves another bed to lie in. We're worried about *you*."

Sarah couldn't have been more surprised. "Me? Why are you worried about me?" She fingered the knife in her sleeve, its worn grip comforting. "I can take care of myself."

"You hired that bitch Mavis Ledbetter to be your companion, instead of asking one of us to go." Vickie ticked off on her fingers as she added, "You're closing the boardinghouse. You've packed everything you own, including those old books of your daddy's. And you've been moping around here for a week since you got that goddamn telegram."

Sarah swallowed, realizing they knew she wasn't coming back. "What are you saying, Vic?"

"She's saying we know you're leaving for good." Doreen, the youngest of the crew at twenty-two, had the looks of a doll with tight brown curls, a curvaceous little figure, and brown eyes with the longest lashes known to man.

"What makes you say that?"

"You brought life back into us. You *saved* us and you think we're going to let you leave without being honest?" Red stood, her gaze hopeful. "Will you let us come with you?"

Sarah hadn't expected it and the question hit her with the force of a horse kick. They wanted to go with her? She was trying to close a chapter in her life that needed closing, yet the most treasured pages were trying to slip into her pocket for her new journey. Impossible.

"First of all, none of you have money to buy a train ticket all the way to Colorado. Second, there's no reason for any of you to change your lives for me. I love you all, but the answer is no." Sarah prided herself on being able to tell the hard truths, even if her stupid heart prevented her from doing so on occasion.

Of all of them, Vickie looked the most hurt. She pulled her hand away from Sarah's arm and stepped back. Her lips were pressed together so tightly, they were white. "You're leaving us behind on purpose."

Sarah shook her head. "No, I'm leaving me behind."

"What the hell does that mean?" Vickie picked up her glass from the table behind the sofa and slung back the rest of the amber liquid like a seasoned drinker.

"I don't know if I can explain it." Sarah shook her head again. "Just know that I'm not leaving any of you behind. You'll always be part of who I am. But I want to start again— can you understand that?"

Deep in Vickie's gaze, Sarah saw the truth. She understood, but that didn't mean her friend was any less hurt.

"If it was anyone but family, I might have to stop you from going." Vickie's voice had become huskier. "You're breaking my heart, Sarah." She held up one hand and walked from the room, her head held high.

The other two girls followed, leaving Sarah alone with Lorenzo. The naked longing in his gaze made her throat close up. He was such a *boy* regardless of his age. Lorenzo hadn't been exposed to the very worst life could offer, but Sarah had cut her teeth on it.

"I will go with you, to protect you." He offered a tremulous smile.

Sarah shook her head. "I'm sorry, but the answer is still no. The girls need you, and will need you more when I'm not here. Take care of them, please."

He nodded, then left the room with one last mournful look. Sarah swallowed the curse that threatened to appear as she realized it would be her last evening at the boardinghouse. She was going to start over again, a clean slate in a new place where no one knew her or her past. Perhaps the opportunities there would be more plentiful than in a state still recovering from the ravages of war.

Sarah might have prayed for good fortune on her journey and destination, but she'd long since given up on the practice. She made her own luck and her own way in life.

The road to Colorado waited for her.

In the soft lamplight of her room, Sarah packed the last of her things into her traveling bag. It wasn't much, truth be told. She had lived simply for so long that possessions had become few and far between. The only indulgence was her father's books. She'd hidden them from the Yankees and the bastards after the war who thought the house was theirs for the taking.

One of her fondest and faintest memories was of him reading to her. He had a knack for becoming the characters as he read, keeping young Sarah enthralled. Yet he died right as the war began, leaving her and her mother to fend for themselves in a cruel, hostile world. The books reminded her of a different time, a different life.

As she packed, a wave of melancholy washed over her. Sarah was leaving behind the house she grew up in, learned in, survived in and became a cynical nearly thirty-year-old woman in.

It was past time to move on, and she knew it.

"All packed up?"

Vickie's voice didn't surprise Sarah. She turned to her friend and managed a small smile.

"More than you know." She sat and patted the bed.

Sarah could tell Vickie was still hurt about her leaving, but there was nothing Sarah could or would change. Done was done and the time had come for her to leave.

"Do you remember when I caught you stealing?" Sarah could picture Vickie eleven years earlier, a little sprite with barely a curve on her thirteen-year-old body.

"I wasn't stealing." Vickie cleared her throat. "I was hungry, so I was only taking food to fill my belly." She looked as though she almost believed it.

Sarah burst out laughing the same time Vickie did. The friends shared a moment of mirth before the mood reverted back to one of sad endings.

"Of all the people in my life, I will miss you the most." It wasn't easy for Sarah to be emotional, even for her best friend. "You and I, we survived together. There isn't a person in the world I am closer to than you. The good thing is, you are a survivor and life goes on. Perhaps with me leaving you can find your own path instead of trailing along by my side getting caught up in my battles."

Full of too many emotions and in need of surcease from all

the drama, Sarah squeezed Vickie's hand. "Now let's get these bags downstairs and have a drink."

Vickie looked at Sarah with so much sadness and even a hint of betrayal in her blue eyes. "I can't imagine living here without you, Sarah."

Sarah waved her hand in dismissal. "You are the toughest person I know. Don't get all sappy on me now. The sun will rise and you *will* still be alive and kicking." She wasn't about to accept her friend's emotional well-being into her keeping.

"I know you don't like to talk about feelings and such, but I have to say this and then I'll stop, I promise." Vickie took a deep breath, the fabric of her blue dress straining against her ample endowments. "You saved my life twice. First when I was a child, hungry, scared, and confused. Then when I was on the edge of leaving life altogether. For that, I will always be grateful. Aside from that, you are my best friend, the one person I can tell my secrets to, and you were going to walk out of my life without saying good-bye. That hurt, a lot, and while I understand it, it's going to take me time to forgive it."

Vickie knew exactly what to say to make Sarah regret her actions, as she damn sure did right then. The opportunity to start fresh had presented itself, and Sarah had jumped at the chance, regardless of anyone or anything else. Hurting Vickie had not been part of her thought process, but apparently she'd done more than hurt her—she'd damaged their friendship.

Sarah cleared the lump that had taken up residence in her throat. "I'm sorry, Vic."

Vickie nodded, her blond curls bouncing gently with the movement. "I know you are, but you are still leaving, aren't you?"

"Yes. There's nothing in the world going to keep me in Virginia. I need to clean my own slate and write the story I was meant to live." Sarah picked up her traveling case and the small bag containing the books. "I didn't mean to hurt you, but my mind's made up. You coming for that drink or not?"

Uncomfortable with the conversation, Sarah waited while emotions flitted across Vickie's face. She finally rose and took the small bag from Sarah's hand. "I wouldn't miss it for the world."

For the first time in many, many years, Sarah felt the sting of tears. She blinked them away and blew out the lamp.

In the wee hours of the night, Sarah returned to her room, the whiskey washing through her veins like an old friend. She hadn't intended on having more than one drink, but once they'd gotten started, it was difficult to stop.

She'd miss Vickie, and telling her dear friend that had been too difficult to do. Instead she'd kept drinking until her vision had started to blur. Sarah had managed to say good night and give Vickie a very brief hug, and then she'd stumbled off to her room.

What was wrong with her? She just couldn't seem to allow anyone to know she had a heart. A cold bitch is what everyone saw.

Sarah slid off her clothes and climbed into bed nude only to realize she wasn't alone. A body lay next to her, a hot, hard body. She should've been afraid, but it wasn't the first time Lorenzo had snuck into her room.

"*Cara mia*, I'm sorry, I just had to try one more time." His accent deepened as he skimmed his hand up her leg.

She stopped him before he reached anything important. "I've told you before, I don't have sex with my employees. Go back to your own bed."

"Ah, but I don't work for you anymore."

Sarah could almost hear him smile in the darkness. Dammit, he was right, of course. She'd given her business interest to her friends, signing away the house and business she'd held on to for so long.

"Doesn't matter. Lorenzo, I'm not changing my mind about leaving. I don't think it's a good idea for us to do this." No matter what words were falling out of her mouth, her body was responding to his. Lorenzo's calloused, strong hands kneaded her legs and feet, working their way up to her now-throbbing pussy.

She didn't want to be aroused by her friend, but in the inky blackness of the night, in her half-drunk state, her brain finally started working.

"Get out."

"I can feel you heating to my touch. Mmmm, I can even smell you." He tried to pull her closer.

Sarah knew she needed to kick Lorenzo out of her bed for both their sakes.

"Lorenzo, please get out. I will not ruin our friendship by letting you in my bed. Now get out *now*." Her voice caught, but it stopped his wandering hands.

"But I love you, Sarah. Please." His pleading made her heart ache for him, but she couldn't—she wouldn't—do this with him.

"I love you as a friend, Lorenzo. Nothing more." Sarah rolled out of bed to her feet. She reached for her chemise. "Now if you don't leave, I'll shoot you in the ass."

He managed a chuckle, albeit a strangled, painful one. "There will never be another woman like you."

Sarah started shaking and it took a huge amount of effort to stand there and be strong. "There are better women than me."

Lorenzo slid out of bed with a heavy sigh. He stood and made a big show of pulling his pants on. By the time he was done, Sarah's courage had reasserted itself. He was trying to manipulate her and it annoyed the hell out of her.

"Start acting like a man, Lorenzo. I'm too old, too jaded and there is absolutely no future for you and me." She opened the door and welcomed the cool air from the hallway. Her body was still half aroused and along with her anger had chased away any thought of sleep.

He shuffled toward the door and stopped to take her hand. When his lips touched her skin, she sighed. Lorenzo was a good man; he deserved a good woman.

"Good-bye, Lorenzo."

He nodded and left her alone. As Sarah watched him walk down the hallway, she let go of the last tie holding her to Virginia.

Her new life was about to begin.

Chapter Two

"You're running away."

Whitman Kendrick stared at his mother. "Mother, I'm not running. I'm choosing to start my life over again somewhere else."

She turned away and walked toward the window. Her silver bun shone in the lamplight as her tiny form blocked the moonlight. The small house had been her home the last two years since he'd brought her to Maryland. She'd refused until the farm was repossessed by the bank. Then she'd had no choice but to accept her son's help, which she called charity.

Bonnie Kendrick was a proud woman, too proud sometimes for her own good. She'd passed on that overabundance of pride to Whit, much as he wanted to deny it.

"You're running plain and simple. Don't tell me any different." She shook her head. "I thought you were stronger than that, more like your father."

After an hour of listening to her, he was past annoyed and on his way to angry. Whitman gritted his teeth. "Don't bring him into this."

"Why not?" She pointed one finger at him. "Whether or not you want to remember him, he was your father."

When Whit was twelve years old, his father had died from a mule kick on their farm in New York. The death of Bradford Kendrick had had a profound effect on his young son's life, which flipped upside down.

His relationship with his mother had turned into a twisted parody of what it had been. They'd spent the last twenty years or so trying to find a way to talk to each other. This was just another example of failing to find a way.

"I said don't bring him into this, Mother."

"You used to call me Mama. Do you remember that? Before those people turned you into a cold snob." Bonnie didn't believe in mincing words.

Whitman bit back an angry retort. His mother knew exactly how to get his back up, and she seemed to enjoy doing it. "I grew out of a lot of things, including childish nicknames for you."

"Why Kansas City?" She sat down heavily in the chair she'd had since he could remember. It was the one piece of furniture along with her bed they'd taken from the farm. The green chair was as hideous as vomit, but she clung to it as if it held the ghost of her dead husband.

"I'm traveling to Kansas City and then San Francisco." He'd explained it a hundred times already. As he ran his hand through his hair, she stared hard at him.

"Whit, you're leaving me." Her voice broke on the last word.

So did Whitman's anger. He knelt in front of her and took her small hands in his. "I'm not leaving you. I'm finally starting my own life. Can you understand that? I need to find my place in the world. All I know is it's not in an army barracks, it's not on a farm in New York, and it's not in the boardroom at Kendrick Industries."

She shook her head. "I don't believe that."

Whit made one last effort to make her understand. "It's true. I can't be happy here, no matter what. I'm not disappearing; I'm moving to someplace new. Maybe one day you'll want to move there too."

She looked as if he'd told her to forget she had ever loved Bradford Kendrick. "Never."

"Then that's your decision. This is mine. I'm going to California, by way of Kansas City."

He stood and started walking out of the room before she spoke again.

"Who's in Kansas City?"

Whitman paused, his hand on the door. "My future."

On the train platform, Sarah spent her time sitting on the bench and watching other people. There was quite a variety, from well-dressed older women to raggedy children begging for coins. As the sun rose on the horizon, the train at last pulled into the station. The urge to run to the train before it stopped moving nearly overwhelmed her.

Sarah had spent the last ten years learning how to control her impulses, even if that control slipped now and again. She was proud of the fact she allowed a woman and her children to get on the train ahead of her. What she really wanted to do was push everyone out of the way and get the hell out of Virginia as fast as she could.

However, Sarah hadn't been able to run for so long, she doubted she could even manage a fast hobble. As she waited to walk up the steps, her heart did a funny flip as freedom came within reach. She sucked in a breath through her teeth, gritting them against the loss of control that threatened.

"One, two, three. One, two, three," she counted slowly under her breath until the woman and her children were safely on the train.

When her right foot hit the first step, a man appeared from her left who apparently had abandoned all semblance of good manners. The bowler hat–wearing fool tried to push past her, without regard for the fact she was a woman, and a cripple, for all intents and purposes. Yet Sarah had learned a few tricks and the fool never knew what hit him.

She whipped her cane around to smack him in the shin with a resounding crack, then hooked it around behind his knee and yanked. The obnoxious fool landed on his pin-striped, well-padded ass while Sarah made her way onto the train, a smirk in place of the grimace she normally wore.

"If you're fixin' to sleep you'd best change your mind."

Sarah opened one eye to see Mavis Ledbetter grinning at her. She nearly regretted the impulse to pay the woman to be her companion to Colorado. God help both of them if the woman didn't let her sleep off a hangover.

"Why is that, Miss Ledbetter?" Sarah's voice was rusty from exhaustion and too many drinks of whiskey.

"There's another passenger comin' and he's a big 'un." Mavis pointed one bony finger toward the front of the car. She cackled.

"There's plenty of room beside you." Sarah felt sleep tugging at her and she didn't want to resist.

"Oh no, he cain't sit there. It wouldn't be right." Mavis fussed with her traveling bag, perched on the seat beside her. The four-seat compartment would be their temporary home from Virginia to Kansas City. Sarah had settled in comfortably while they waited for the train to leave the station.

Now it appeared a stranger would join them, disrupting Sarah's much needed nap.

"Why wouldn't it be right to sit near you, but it's okay to sit by me?" Sarah pushed up her bunched-up coat after it slipped from beneath her head.

"Well, I'm a respectable spinster and you're, well, there ain't nobody in town that didn't know about you and your gentlemen callers at the boardinghouse, Miss Spalding." Mavis clearly had no idea how to be diplomatic when she spoke. "I mean, we all done what we had to during the war, but you kept it up for ten years. Likely ain't a man in twelve counties that don't know you and your business."

Sarah closed her eyes and willed away the curse that threatened to appear as a result of the old woman's accusations. "I am a businesswoman, Miss Ledbetter, not a whore."

"Six of one and half a dozen of the other." Mavis shrugged. "I ain't judging you, just saying the good Lord didn't see fit to give me a man, so I'm as pure as I was the day I entered the world."

Sarah clenched her fists together and counted to ten.

"Good morning, ladies." The stranger's voice was deep enough to make Sarah's bones vibrate.

She pretended to be asleep so she wouldn't have to respond. After Mavis's speech about how unpure Sarah was, well, she had no desire to even see a man much less talk to one.

"Mornin', sir." Mavis sounded as sweet as honey, which made Sarah want to snort. She held it back through force of will, but it was a near thing.

"I believe I have a seat in this compartment."

The first thing she noticed was the accent. He was a Yankee through and through, a kind of flat nasal tone permeating every syllable. Now she was glad she hadn't spoken to him. Just hearing a Yankee speak made her break out in a cold sweat.

One thing Sarah couldn't stand to be around almost as much as carpetbaggers was Yankees.

She could almost feel him looking her over, judging the clothing she wore with its scalloped edges, the fashionable hat covering her eyes, and the fancy shoes on her feet. Sarah didn't care much for what he thought. She liked the way she looked, so he could go to hell if he didn't like it.

"You can sit next to Miss Spalding. She don't mind." Mavis was ever so helpful. Sarah wanted to kick her bony ass off the train.

The man sat down. A whiff of bay rum, man, and something else wafted past Sarah's nose. Good smells she had to force herself to ignore. She still didn't open her eyes, unwilling to give in to the curiosity to see just how big the man was or perhaps how handsome he was. Men weren't high on her list of priorities anyway—most of them were dumber than stumps. Especially one from the wrong half of the country.

As the train finally pulled out of the station, Sarah settled back in the wooden seat and forced herself to keep her hands still. She needed to think of a way to ignore the Yankee who'd settled in her compartment.

Whitman Kendrick didn't know what to make of the woman beside him. She was tall, a bit thin, with outlandish clothes, and she was taking up more than half the seat. Whit wasn't a small man, so half was barely enough to keep him from falling on his ass.

However, being a gentleman, Whit couldn't wake her up simply for his own comfort. He'd have to wait until she woke to politely ask her to move over.

"My name is Miss Mavis Ledbetter." The older woman had steel gray hair, a sugary sweet smile, and the most god-awful dull brown outfit. "And you are?"

"Whitman Kendrick." He managed a small smile before he looked away, hoping she'd get the hint he wasn't in the mood to talk.

"I detect an accent, Mr. Kendrick, that's not from around these parts." Obviously Miss Ledbetter wasn't going to be the quiet companion he wanted. He could at least say the sleeping woman was.

"No, ma'am. I'm not from Virginia originally." Whitman wanted to get a book out of his traveling bag. Perhaps if he started reading, she'd stop talking.

"I can't quite put my finger on it. Where are you from exactly?" Miss Ledbetter smiled, a wide, toothy grin that didn't make her any more attractive, unfortunately.

The woman beside him suddenly spoke from beneath her hat. "For pity's sake, Mavis. He's a Yankee. It doesn't matter where he's from. Now if you could both keep it down, I'm trying to get some sleep." She flipped her hat back and frowned at him.

Whitman's hard-to-rile anger stirred like a hibernating bear. The silver-eyed she-devil had thick brown, wavy hair shot with reds and golds. Currently her narrow gaze was sharply focused on him.

"Excuse me." He used his captain voice, sure to make most men snap to attention within a second. "I hadn't realized I needed to get permission to speak in a compartment I paid for."

The woman sat up abruptly, nearly knocking him on his ass. She had some power behind her regardless of her thin frame. He grabbed hold of the back of the bench and pulled himself back up, knocking his hip into hers.

"Sarah Spalding, mind your manners. I was just having a polite conversation with Mr. Kendrick. You've no call to take the man to task for simply conversing with me." It appeared Miss Ledbetter would be an ally.

Sarah Spalding.

Her name even hissed like a cat, right along with her mouth. Whit took control of his runaway anger and swallowed it like a bitter pill. He couldn't let this Southern belle ruin his ride to freedom. No sir.

"Mavis, you are my employee, not my conscience. All I wanted was to get some sleep." Sarah did sound tired if not particularly polite.

"Mrs. Spalding—"

"That's *Miss*," she corrected.

Somehow Whit wasn't surprised she hadn't snagged herself a husband. She wasn't exactly friendly.

"Miss Spalding, I am a passenger on this train, same as you. I plan on treating you with courtesy. I expect the same from you."

She snorted, surprising the hell out of him. "You leave me alone and I'll do the same. That's all I can promise."

His blood zinged through his body, and it was because of a woman who apparently didn't want him in the compartment. Ironic that the one person to make him feel alive in ten years was the last person he should tangle with. Miss Sarah Spalding was obviously not interested in him and unpredictable. He'd do best to ignore her and focus on the heaven that awaited him.

Whitman Kendrick was on his way to get married.

Sarah wanted to shout at the big Yankee, but truth was, he'd been polite. She could've shown him the same, but she'd been half awake and still feeling guilty about leaving her friends behind. It embarrassed her to lose control since she'd fought so hard to get her emotions reined in. One word out of the man's mouth and she'd almost become the raving teenager who'd turned as wild as the fields around their house.

Those two years were blurry and unpleasant. Sarah did her best to forget all she had had to do to survive. This man, Whitman Kendrick, turned on all her survival instincts. She was hard-pressed not to be completely rude to him. However, she would keep control of herself if it killed her.

Chapter Three

The first stop on the two thousand–mile train ride was only two hours from where they began. Mr. Kendrick had fallen asleep, snoring almost louder than the sound of the damn train. She took great pleasure in watching him jerk awake when the train stopped. After all, he'd disturbed her slumber.

He turned to look at her and she was surprised to see he had the most lovely green eyes, nearly the shade of the rich grass that grew along the bank of the river behind the Spalding Plantation house. Or had, anyway. His chocolate brown hair was cut short in a nice cut that accentuated his strong jaw.

Dang, the man was attractive.

Whitman looked confused as he met her gaze. The moment seemed to stretch on as they stared at each other. Of course, the fool had to open his mouth and ruin her good mood.

"Melissa?"

Sarah almost reached for the cane to conk him when Mavis tutted at her.

"He's obviously not quite awake yet." Mavis nodded her steel gray–topped head. "Mr. Kendrick, this is Sarah, not Melissa."

"I think he's already aware of that, Mavis." Sarah settled back into her corner and watched the play of emotions on the man's face.

He had a shadow of whiskers already, and it wasn't even noon. Obviously he had to shave twice a day or risk giving whoever Melissa was the whisker burn of her life. Not that she cared who the woman was, but Jesus, he didn't have to call her by that name. It annoyed her more than she wanted to admit.

"Melissa is my intended bride. I'm to meet her in Kansas City." Whitman ran a hand down his face, the whiskers scraping against his skin. "I was dreaming about her."

Sarah raised one brow. "I'll bet you were."

"Now you just stop it. You hired me to come along on this trip but I won't put up with your shenanigans. You're not an unruly girl anymore. You're a spinster and, as such, have a duty to behave properly." Mavis peered out the window as if she hadn't just ripped into Sarah without mercy. "Oh look, another passenger is getting on the train."

Sarah swallowed the anger, and the hurt, from the older woman's comments. It was disconcerting to have her shortcomings paraded in front of a stranger, a Yankee at that. The most exciting day of her life was turning into a miserable pile of pig shit in front of her eyes.

With a sigh, she glanced out the window at the town they'd stopped in. It was a small depot with an almost deserted platform. The only person standing there was an older man with a bowler hat and a crooked polka-dot bow tie.

The porter went out and helped him as he walked ever so slowly to the train steps. With Sarah's luck, the man would probably have a ticket for their compartment too.

Oh boy. Such joy.

"It's all right, you know."

Whitman's voice was right next to her ear, nearly a whisper. Sarah almost started, but years of teaching herself to be as still as death allowed her to control her reaction. She turned to find herself six inches from that green gaze and the longest eyelashes she'd ever seen on a man.

Whitman had a crook in his nose. No doubt it had been broken. There was a scar bisecting his right eyebrow and he'd obviously nicked himself shaving, because there was a small cut on his chin. He was definitely all man, and damn he smelled good.

Sarah pulled hard on the reins of her shocking arousal. No way in hell she should be sexually interested in Whitman Kendrick. For one thing, he was from the North, and for another, he was getting married. She'd do best to keep her appetite for big men in check.

"What's all right?" She frowned at him.

"Miss Ledbetter was pretty rude right there. I wouldn't pay her any mind." He smiled and Sarah's breath caught. Whitman was not just handsome, he was devastatingly beautiful.

Oh, hell.

Whitman saw confusion race across her gaze and wondered what she was thinking. He had been trying to be polite to her and she acted as if he'd stood on his head and sang "Yankee Doodle Dandy."

Miss Sarah Spalding was already confusing the hell out of him. He'd do best to keep to himself for however long she was going to be on the train.

After the older man finally made it on the train and settled next to Miss Ledbetter, it gave Whit the opportunity to open a book and avoid conversation.

As Mr. Abernathy settled in, the introductions were made and then Whit surreptitiously pulled a book from his traveling bag. He didn't care what book, as long as he had something to read. Strangely enough, Sarah seemed to eye his book with interest.

The day passed, if not quickly, at least the sunset arrived without any more drama. Whit was grateful for the reprieve. The trip out to meet and marry his future wife already had him on edge. Most folks would've thought him crazy to marry someone he'd never met, but it was the very reason he finally decided to give up his bachelor status.

The women in his life had been few and far between. With no charm or finesse to speak of, Whit decided a mail-order bride was his best choice.

In two weeks he'd be married and free to start the rest of his life on a newly purchased farm. He just had to get through the trip out there.

When the train stopped for the evening, everyone gathered his or her belongings to disembark until the morning. Miss Ledbetter never stopped talking as she picked up her traveling case and left arm in arm with her new boon companion Mr. Abernathy.

As Whit put his book in his bag, he glanced at Sarah. She pulled one bag from beneath the seat and put it up across from her. When she looked around, she cursed under her breath. He wondered exactly what the relationship was between the two women. Obviously Miss Ledbetter wasn't concerned about Sarah.

"Thanks, Mavis," she muttered. After noticing Whit watching her, she frowned fiercely. "Something I can help you with, Mr. Kendrick?"

"Can I help you get to the hotel?" The words were out of his mouth before he even thought about what he was doing.

Surprise flashed across her face. "No, thank you."

She certainly didn't mince words. Reminded him a bit of his mother, strangely enough.

Whit watched her struggle with the second bag under the seat, which was apparently much heavier than the first. No matter what she said, he wasn't going to allow a woman to step on his chivalrous duty.

He took the bag from her and stood waiting while she glared at him.

"That's my property, Mr. Kendrick."

"I realize that. However, I am a gentleman, so just accept

my help." He wondered how she'd even gotten the bag out from under the seat; it weighed at least twenty pounds. "What's in here anyway?"

"My belongings. Now please give it back." She reached for the bag, but he stepped backward toward the door.

"You'll just have to follow me to the hotel to get it back." With that he turned and stepped off the train. He hoped like hell he wasn't pushing her far enough to call the law. Jesus, he just wanted to help the prickly woman.

Whit waited two full minutes before he peeked back in through the window. His stomach fell to his knees when he saw Sarah struggling to stand with a cane in her hand.

A *cane*.

He'd had no idea she was crippled. No wonder she had a companion traveling with her, one who didn't apparently care enough about her, unfortunately. Whit knew Sarah wouldn't accept charity and certainly not pity. That was a proud, stubborn woman right there. He decided to try a different method.

He poked his head in the open door. "Hurry up, would you? What's in here, rocks?"

She had finally gotten the other bag on her arm and was straightening up. Her face was flushed, and her eyes, oh those silver eyes, flashed at him like fire. He felt an unexpected jolt of awareness zip through him.

Whit shouldn't be surprised but he was. He shouldn't even be remotely attracted to her, yet apparently he was, judging by his body's reaction.

Damn.

"No, they're books, if you must know. If you damage them, you'll be paying for them." She'd obviously been used to giving orders and being in charge. It definitely didn't sit well with Whit, but hell, she was just a stranger on a train.

It didn't matter a bit.

*　　*　　*

Sarah was embarrassed—something that didn't happen often. Mr. Kendrick had caught her at her worst struggling with her damaged leg and the damn cane. No matter how long or hard she fought against it, Sarah needed help with tasks others took for granted. Such as carrying her own luggage.

She should've thanked him, but the words got stuck in her throat. Nothing about this trip was easy, starting with relying on others, strangers or acquaintances, to assist her. At home, one of the girls or Lorenzo would've helped without asking. A painful reminder that Sarah was no longer among friends.

The first thing she should do is fire Mavis. The woman was not only self-righteous, she was incompetent as a companion. She'd left Sarah alone to struggle with the bags. However, the thought of not having even a remotely familiar person to help her made Sarah break out in a cold sweat. She'd have to rely on people like Whitman Kendrick, who was currently tapping his foot as he waited by the door.

At least he hadn't treated her like a cripple.

"I'm hungry, Miss Spalding. If we don't get to the hotel dining room, we might miss out on the evening meal." He checked the watch in his vest pocket before shooting her an impatient glance.

For some odd reason, his behavior pleased her. It gave her something to focus on other than the knot in her stomach or the ache in her leg.

"I'm working on it, Kendrick." She walked excruciatingly slowly at first until the stiffness in her right leg started to work itself out. It was always worst when she had been sitting too long. One thing she definitely hadn't looked forward to while traveling across the country by train.

By the time they made it off the train, Whit had taken her other bag and her arm. Sarah really ought to protest or at least thank him, but she kept quiet and just accepted his assistance. He didn't seem to mind, and after all, she hadn't asked him.

"I assume you're continuing on the train tomorrow?" Whit's voice broke the silence.

"Yes. All the way to Denver." She tried to ignore the clipped Yankee tone, but it was damn hard. His speech was different from that of the man in her nightmares, but it was close enough to make her uncomfortable.

"Then I'll meet you at your door at six and we can walk to the train together." He opened the door to the rather shabby hotel and gestured for her to enter.

"I do have my own plans you know. Perhaps I was going to ask someone at the hotel to help me." She actually appreciated the offer to walk her to the train. Who knew where Mavis would be, and the porters wouldn't carry her bags to or from the hotel.

Whit raised one brow. "Considering you're probably going to fire Miss Ledbetter, I know I would probably do the same. However, since I'm going to Kansas City, I can be your new traveling companion."

Sarah opened her mouth to protest but closed it almost as fast. He was right and she knew it. Most men would've either taken pity on her or treated her as if she was a nuisance. Whit treated her as if she was just another person, albeit one who needed help.

"Fine, but don't think you're entitled to any special rewards from me. We're just two strangers on a train, nothing more." She made her way into the hotel and to the desk, feeling the burn of his gaze on her back. Perhaps he'd change his mind. Sarah would just have to find a way alone, as she always had.

After she checked in, Sarah walked to the steps and looked all the way up. She hated stairs, the main reason she'd turned the sitting room into her bedroom back home. Nothing showed her inability to function as a normal woman more than a set of stairs. No help for it, she'd just have to do what she needed to do.

Sarah made it to the first step before the key was plucked

from her hand. She glanced at Whitman, who was currently grabbing the bag from her.

"Stay here. I'll be right back."

Before she could protest, he was bounding up the steps two at a time with both of her bags and his own. This gave Sarah an unobstructed view of his behind. With a start, she realized it was a very nice, well-shaped and muscular behind. The view was spectacular and she watched until he was out of sight.

Sarah didn't want to be physically attracted to Whitman. She'd chosen her bed companions very carefully. A dalliance with a Yankee was simply out of the question, particularly when she knew she'd be in the train compartment with him until they reached Kansas City.

No, Sarah would just have to squelch any impulses and maintain control. That was her way, after all.

The dining room was nearly bursting at the seams. There was only one unoccupied table by the time Sarah and Whitman arrived to eat. Unfortunately, it was in a corner and made for two.

"Told you to hurry," Whitman grumbled under his breath.

Sarah couldn't stop a very unladylike snort, again. "Next time I'll run up the stairs and you stand at the bottom then."

He didn't respond, but she saw the corner of his mouth twitch, as if he was holding in a laugh. Perhaps the serious Yankee did have a sense of humor after all.

When they sat down, Sarah realized it was the first time they were face-to-face. On the train and even walking to the hotel, they'd been beside each other. Facing Whitman was an entirely different experience.

He wasn't classically handsome, but damn, he was exactly the kind of man Sarah was attracted to. His face was angular, the late-day whiskers only added to his appeal, his nose was slightly crooked, and a few scars were scattered here and there as if he'd been wounded by small pieces of something.

But it was his eyes that captured her attention. Deep, green, and framed by those long eyelashes, Whitman had the sexiest gaze she'd ever seen. Fortunately or unfortunately, she felt a tug of sensual awareness just looking at the tousled chocolate locks above those eyes.

Hell and crackers.

He frowned. "Why are you scowling at me?"

"I'm not scowling." She fiddled with the fork and knife on the table while hoping the missing waitress would appear to save her from the awkward situation.

Damn Mavis Ledbetter. The woman was over by the window with that same gentleman, completely ignoring the fact she'd been paid to take care of Sarah. Whit had been right—she was going to fire Mavis and leave her in whatever town this was.

"She looks to be a spinster." Whit followed Sarah's gaze. "Looks as if she hasn't given up the quest for a husband, though."

"She spent so much time declaring she was a spinster, she kept most men away from her." Sarah frowned at Mavis. "Nobody in town wanted anything to do with her because of her reputation."

"You're from the same town then?"

His question was one anyone in polite company would ask, but Sarah found herself unwilling to answer any personal questions. So she decided to insult him to keep him disliking her. "You're nosy."

"You're rude."

"You're pushy."

He barked a laugh. "And you're refreshingly honest."

Sarah found herself holding back a chuckle. What was it about this annoying Yankee that set her on her head? Aside from being handsome, there wasn't anything else remarkable about him. She needed to figure out his appeal so she could combat it and keep her distance, at least as much as she could, considering they were going to be stuck in a train compartment together for fifteen hundred miles.

"Then you won't mind if I continue being honest."

He nodded. "I wouldn't expect any less."

Why in the hell did that make Sarah's heart thump like a bass drum? Back home, when she ate a meal, it was with her friends, a group where everyone chatted and relaxed. Sitting with Whit made her feel jumpy and awkward—a condition Sarah was definitely not used to.

"You make me uncomfortable," she blurted.

His eyebrows went up. "I do?"

Now that she'd gone down that path, she had to finish her thought. "I'm sure you've heard the song before, Mr. Kendrick, but Yankees aren't high on my list of favorite folks, much less one I have to rely on. It's going to take some time for me to, ah, adjust, so if you can, be patient with me."

Whit nodded. "I'll do my best."

She didn't want to demand anything from the man. After all, there was no reason for him to help her. His actions told her more than anything that he was a gentleman. "When life kicks you once, you get back up and move on. When life kicks you a dozen times, you're less willing to forgive and trust." That was as far as she planned on going with that train of thought. He seemed like a sharp guy and could likely understand why she felt uncomfortable.

"Don't worry. I won't give you any cause to kick me back. I promise." The sincerity in his gaze made her want to believe him.

Ridiculous, of course. Why should she trust a stranger? She had to rely on him to be her companion, however that would turn out. Yet expecting him to carry her bags was a far cry from trusting him with her life. Sarah could take care of herself, for the most part anyway, and she regretted the fact she couldn't do it all the time.

"Good, because I bite when I kick." She fought back a grin.

"Somehow that doesn't surprise me in the least." He smiled at the waitress as she approached the table.

The young blond thing sparkled like a new penny when she caught sight of Whitman. Sarah wanted to trip her with the cane.

"Good evening, sir. Can I fetch you something to drink? Or an order of meatloaf? It's the best in the county." The young woman smiled while her face flushed.

Sarah harrumphed at the obvious tactics the girl used. "I'd like some of that meatloaf and hot coffee."

The girl looked surprised to see Sarah sitting there.

"I'm sure Mr. Kendrick here will have the same thing." Sarah shot Whitman a challenging look, daring him to contradict her.

"Meatloaf and coffee would be lovely. Thank you, miss." He graced the girl with another smile, sending her scurrying to the kitchen.

At least the food would arrive quickly considering the girl was already enamored of Whitman.

"Are you always this honest?" Whit picked up the spoon in front of him.

"Yes, I am. Does it bother you?" Sarah was ready to show him just how forceful she could be with her words.

"Not at all." He breathed on the spoon and stuck it on the end of his nose. Sarah almost choked on her spit as she watched a grown man play at a child's trick. What the hell was he doing?

When he smiled, the force of it snatched Sarah's breath. She could do nothing but look at the grin behind the spoon and wonder if she'd stepped into a dream of her own twisted mind. He was beautiful, a Yankee, and charming as all hell.

Sarah was afraid she'd lose more than her spoon to Whitman Kendrick.

Chapter Four

Whitman was torn between being amused and fascinated by Sarah. She was unlike most people he knew, male or female. Something about her drew Whit in, made him fascinated like a moth to a flame on a summer night.

When Sarah tugged off her gloves, Whit's world turned upside down. The small finger on her left hand was missing.

His heart thumped heavily as memories of his early days in the army washed over him. The sergeant who thought he was God and the regiment who had to bow down to him. Bile coated the back of his throat as he remembered exactly where he'd seen a woman's small finger.

"That little bitch thought she could best me in a knife fight. Ha! Had a little blade tucked up her sleeve 'n' everythin'." Booker snorted a laugh. *"Ain't no woman can stand up to me."*

The big sergeant grinned his gap-toothed smile and continued eating his beans. Whitman simply stared at him.

"What did you do?"

"I taught her a lesson." He reached into his shirt and pulled out a crude necklace made of a leather strip. Dangling on the end was a tiny, desiccated finger, the nail too small to be a man's.

Whitman stared at the digit in disbelief, wondering what poor soul had previously owned it. His sergeant had likely raped, mutilated, and tortured a young woman. What was Whit to do about it? He was just a brand new corporal, a soldier with no power to stop the bullying or the pillaging.

"Did you kill her?" Whit tried to keep his voice steady, but it was hard, damn hard.

Booker shrugged. "Dunno. She tried to come after me and I cut her leg so she couldn't walk no more. Her mama might've saved her, but I doubt it. She didn't seem worried about no one but her own ass." He narrowed his gaze. "Why you askin' so many questions, Kendrick?"

"No reason. Just wonderin' how the story ended." With more self-control than he thought he possessed, Whit took a bite of his cold meal by the fire. The warm Virginia night air caressed his sweaty face as he wondered who the nameless, faceless girl was who'd had the misfortune of crossing Booker's path.

Whit should've told the captain, should've told someone, but he kept quiet. He'd been taught to follow orders, not question a superior. Who even knew if Booker was telling the truth?

No, Corporal Kendrick did nothing but listen to the crickets and try to put the image of the finger trophy out of his mind.

Until today.

Jesus Christ.

He stared at her hand long enough for her to notice. She cleared her throat.

"You know, it's not polite to stare at someone's crippled hand." She tucked it into her lap. "I hope you got a good look."

Whit felt his cheeks flush with embarrassment. He wanted—needed—to ask her if she was the unfortunate victim Booker took his sadistic pleasure with. Of course, he couldn't. God only knew what she'd do if she knew he'd been part of the regiment of soldiers whose sergeant had taken her finger, and possibly much more.

Certainly, there'd be no question of continuing their journey together. Sarah would "fire" him and then be alone, vulnerable and stubbornly independent, likely refusing any help. Whit couldn't do that no matter what. Perhaps it was cowardly that he didn't want her to know, or maybe *he* didn't want to know.

For a reason he couldn't quite explain to himself, Whit didn't want his time with Sarah to end with acrimony or so quickly. He thought the journey to Kansas City would be long and boring, but Sarah had already made it more interesting just by being herself.

Whit didn't want to lose that spark, nor did he want to lose her company. He again took the easy route and said nothing about her finger.

"Oh, uh, sorry about that. I, um, didn't mean to pry." He stumbled over his words, saved by the timely arrival of the waitress.

With a wide-eyed stare at Whitman, she put the steaming plates of meatloaf, mashed potatoes, and green beans in front of them. When she darted off, assumingly to get the coffee, Whit wasn't surprised to hear Sarah chuckle softly.

"Something funny?"

Sarah raised one brow. "No, just amused. That young thing is mighty interested in you."

As he tucked into his meatloaf, Whit realized Sarah was right. "You probably shouldn't mention it in polite company."

This time Sarah smiled. "Whoever said I was polite?"

It was Whitman's turn to swallow a chuckle. Sarah simply told everyone what was on her mind. It wasn't a skill most women had mastered or cared to exercise in many cases. It startled him to think his mother had a tendency to do the same thing.

If Sarah was the girl Booker had maimed, Whit took comfort in knowing she hadn't died, nor had she curled up into a ball of self-pity. In fact, she was the strongest woman he'd met in his life. God knew his mother was more stubborn than any iron bar. He hoped his intended bride was half as strong as Sarah. Then he'd be a lucky man for certain.

Of course, the idea his future wife could be as strong as his traveling companion had never entered his mind.

They finished dinner with a delicious slice of peach pie. Whit was surprised by how good the meal was, considering the rough-hewn floors and the size of the town and hotel. It was no big city, just a small community that depended on the money from the train passengers to survive.

"It's good." He licked a stray bit of cream from his fork. "Really good."

"I thought perhaps you were going to start gnawing on the tablecloth. Do you have a second stomach I don't know about?" Sarah shot him a teasing glance from behind her lashes.

Whit's embarrassment flared again. "I was hungry and the food was really good. I've been eating arm—" He stopped himself before he revealed the fact he'd been in the army for fifteen years, nearly a career officer. "I've never been married so I count on restaurants for good eating. This food was exceptionally good."

Sarah raised both eyebrows. "Interesting. I'm surprised to find out a man as good-looking as you hasn't been married before. You must've had to beat the women off with a stick." After her surprising comments about his looks, she looked around and spotted Mavis leaving the dining room with her new friend. "Not so fast."

She struggled to rise, but the chair had been pushed in too far for her to maneuver well. Whit wanted to help her up but knew she'd refuse him if he did. Instead he did the next best thing: he stopped Mavis from leaving.

Whit touched the older woman's shoulder, then gestured toward Sarah. "Miss Spalding would like to speak to you, Miss Ledbetter."

Although he could see the flush creeping up her face, the

older woman simply nodded and started toward Sarah. "Excuse me, I'll be right back, Mr. Abernathy."

The older man waved a hand as he shuffled toward the lobby. He obviously wasn't as enamored of her as she was of him. No doubt her grating personality was wearing thin after eight hours.

Whit looked back toward Sarah and saw her jaw tighten in anger as Mavis waved her hands in the air and shouted. As he got closer, he could hear every blessed word she spoke.

"You think because you hired me you have any right to say what I do or who I socialize with? You're nothing but a whore who ran a whorehouse for ten years. Filth under my feet. I'm glad to be rid of you, but don't think for a moment I'm giving you my train ticket." Mavis stood, her gaze full of spite and malice. "You'll regret firing me, I guarantee it."

Mavis turned toward Whit. "And now you can do your nasty business with your newest customer." She snarled at him as she passed. "Make sure you check her for diseases."

Surprise mixed with anger and fury over the way Mavis had treated Sarah. She sat there clenching the cane with whitened knuckles as she sucked in air like a bellows.

He sat down and decided the wisest course of action was to wait until she was ready to talk. Whit knew what rage felt like when it was coursing through his veins. Sarah looked as if she'd been in a prizefight and lost, but was ready for a rematch.

"I should've listened to my friend. She was right about Mavis. God, I can't believe that just happened." She met Whit's gaze, and in the depths of her silver eyes, he saw ancient pain howling in victory. In a flash it was gone, replaced by anger.

"That woman obviously is unhinged and needs to climb back under the rock she came out from." Whit wasn't saying it to make Sarah feel better. He meant it—no one deserved to be treated so badly.

"Don't patronize me." She slammed the cane into the floor. "I won't accept it."

"I'm not patronizing you. I spent all day listening to her prattle on about herself. Then as a paid companion she abandons you at the train station. To make it worse, she insulted you not once, but twice, and viciously, I might add. I am human, Sarah, and I can feel and empathize." Although he'd been burying his emotions for years, they roared back at the situation. Too many times the weak had fallen victim to the strong, or the kind to the mean. He'd become somewhat immune, or perhaps forced himself to be, until he met the hissing cat who was currently getting under his skin.

"Well, then okay. I believe you." She glanced down at her half-eaten pie. "I don't think I'm going to finish this."

He waited while she pushed her chair back and got to her feet. After a few unsteady moments, she seemed to get her balance and started walking. As before, Whit walked by her side at her speed.

When they reached the stairs, Sarah looked up and grimaced. Her lips were pinched and a sheen of perspiration coated her forehead, where wisps of her wavy hair stuck to her skin. She was exhausted yet she didn't ask for help as she started up the steps. Her right leg seemed to give her the most pain since she grunted each time she had to put her weight on it.

By the fifth step, Whit couldn't stand it anymore. He knew she'd fuss at him, but he didn't care. There was no way he'd allow her to endure any more pain that evening if he could stop it.

When he scooped her into his arms, she screeched and dropped the cane. It clattered down the stairs behind them, but Whit ignored it. He would go back for it in a few minutes.

"What the hell are you doing?" she whispered furiously. "We're not going to the bridal suite."

He chuckled at the thought. "No, that's for sure. I'm helping you. Now just shut up and let me."

"You're taking liberties, Kendrick."

"I'm helping. Nothing more." Recognizing he was lying didn't help matters much, particularly when he realized the shape of the woman in his arms was far from what he expected.

She was tall, but curvy, with round hips and plump breasts that rested just beneath his arm. Her legs seemed to be a mile long and the right one was smaller than the left. She smelled of soap and woman, and a smidge of fury.

"Well, you're still carrying me without my permission." She didn't sound upset. In fact, she sounded as breathless as he felt.

As he carried her to his room, he couldn't help but remember she'd called him handsome. Damn, they were both in trouble.

Sleep eluded Sarah. She lay in her bed silently cursing her overactive mind for not allowing her to rest. Her brain kept going over and over her evening with Whitman, minute by minute. She normally wasn't enamored of anyone, least of all one day after meeting a person, but Whitman was apparently an exception to that rule.

When she finally fell asleep, her dreams quickly took a dive into nightmares. Sarah was back in the root cellar of the house, impossible, of course, since she'd had it filled in with dirt and the door sealed shut.

Yet there she was again, in the corner with cobwebs and spiders covering her. Then she was fighting for her life, the familiar tang of fear on her tongue and cold steel in her hand. Her heart thundered as she faced her attacker for the thousandth time.

Yet something was different. She glanced around at the root cellar. The canned fruit and vegetables on the shelf, the potatoes and onions in sacks on the floor, even the broken cane chair were exactly the same.

Something, however, wasn't.

The dream Sarah circled around the greasy-haired, gap-toothed man while he tried to take her knife away. The predictable dance between them continued, as it always had, until he kicked her in the knee and she went down hard.

As they wrestled with the knife, another man appeared on the stairs. He'd been tall and blond, yet skinny. This time he was tall and dark haired with a hint of whiskers beneath the dirt on his face.

Whitman Kendrick.

Sarah woke up with a shout, the recurring nightmare fading away as she recognized her surroundings. The hotel room in the small town of Tobias, Virginia, was shabby but welcome. Her nightdress was soaked in sweat, as was her hair.

She went over the dream in her head, this time with intent. The dream had been different because Whitman had been substituted for the blond on the steps. What did that mean? Perhaps because he was a Yankee, with a distinctive voice, she'd made him part of her living nightmare.

It made sense, but it still bothered her. A lot. It had been a long time since the dream had been so vivid. She could almost feel the cobwebs still tickling her neck. She'd inserted Whitman into her past. The question was, why?

Chapter Five

Sarah eyed the cursed shoe with a sneer. Damn thing was deliberately being difficult and she was having a hell of a time getting it on her foot, much less laced. The gray light of dawn coated the room as she tried to hurry and get ready.

Whitman would be there any minute and there was no way she wanted him to see her helpless to the point of being unable to get her shoes on. Her clothes were made specifically for her, so she didn't have a problem getting those on. However, the boots were an extravagance she bought two days before the trip.

She regretted that impulse now.

When the knock at the door came, she dropped the shoe with a thunk. Damn.

"Sarah, are you ready?" Whit at least didn't sound chipper. She was not a morning person herself, and God forbid she got trapped with someone who was.

"Not quite." She bent down and picked up the shoe again. "I need five minutes."

"We don't have five minutes. You were supposed to be downstairs half an hour ago. The train leaves in fifteen minutes." He paused. "Do you need help?"

The dreaded question dropped on her pride like a rock. As Sarah wrestled with whether or not missing the train was more important than her stubbornness, Whit grew impatient.

"Look, I don't care what you need, what you're doing or anything like that, but if you make me miss the train, I . . ."

When he didn't continue, Sarah got the shoe on. *Finally.*

"What will you do?" she egged him on.

He opened the door and charged in, which made her wonder what he would've done if she was nude. The thought made her entire body clench, not what she wanted, of course, since she refused to be attracted to him.

"What are you waiting for?" He looked her up and down, noting the packed bags. "Were you hoping to challenge your walking skills this morning or my patience?"

She raised one brow. "Neither. I was hoping to actually walk in shoes this morning."

He glanced down and grimaced. Before she could stop him, he dropped to his knees and started lacing the boots.

Instead of resenting his interference, Sarah simply gazed at the top of his head, noting the still-damp waves of his chocolate hair, and the lovely clean smell from his skin. Having him at her feet was the most unique, delicious experience.

The urge to feel his hair made her fingers twitch. The fact he was lacing her shoes up sent a tingle up her legs straight to her pussy. If it had been another situation, another man, she might have followed her instincts and taken him into her bed.

Yet, it wasn't the right man or the right time. When she got to Denver, Sarah must focus on finding someone who was the right person to play with. For certain, she wouldn't have a man in her bed permanently. She'd made that decision long ago.

That didn't mean she couldn't have someone in her bed occasionally, though. She had needs and even if her body was damaged, parts of her worked perfectly.

One part was humming right then for a man she should never have in her bed.

He glanced up and met her gaze. Those green orbs were unreadable. The moment stretched on for so long, Sarah started to learn toward him. What she would do when she reached him, she had no idea.

"Let's get moving. We're going to miss the train." He rose and held out his hand. "If I'm going to be your traveling companion, you and I are going to have to set some ground rules."

Sarah's arousal ended as abruptly as it had begun. With Whit.

She accepted his help and stood. "Don't think I will simply accept your rules without argument." She hobbled toward the door, the stiffness in her legs almost excruciating that morning. Even after she'd massaged in the liniment Vickie had found for her. Damn it, she hated being crippled.

"We'll see about that." Whitman picked up her bags as they headed toward the door. "I can be just as pigheaded as you."

Of that, Sarah had no doubt. One thing was certain, their trip would never be boring.

Whitman wanted to shake Sarah. She was stubborn, maddening, and damned if he wasn't attracted to her. As she had sat there on her bed with her boots unlaced and a mulish look on her beautiful face, his world had been turned upside down.

He didn't want to be attracted to her. She obviously didn't like Yankees and wasn't shy about letting him know. Aside from that, she had a big mouth, an even bigger chip on her shoulder, and she was absolutely the wrong woman for him.

Whit was engaged, for God's sake. Melissa was waiting for him in Kansas City, ready to start their new life in San Francisco. Yet he was traveling with a woman who knocked him sideways, making him question his sanity.

What if she was the girl he'd thought about for the last twelve years? What then? He would definitely be the wrong man for her. He hadn't helped her, hadn't reported Booker, had done nothing but swallow the right thing to do, instead of doing it.

Perhaps Sarah was a test for his promise to Melissa, his promise to the future. It would be a very long two weeks if that was the case. He'd need to keep thinking about Melissa's sweet letters, and the image of what he thought she looked like.

She was a small-town girl, and the simpleness of her life attracted Whitman. He'd lived in a cauldron of complex drama that wore on his nerves. When he'd lived on the farm in New York, it had been such a happy time in his life before his father died. Melissa represented a return to that life and he wanted to so badly, he could taste it on his tongue.

Remembering where he was going and why helped tamp down the insane urge to kiss Sarah. It had come over him when he was on his knees in front of her, and it had stayed on his back as they left the hotel. Until they made it to the platform to board the train, Whit could hardly control his thoughts.

As Sarah was walking up the steps into their compartment, she fell backward into Whit.

"Son of a bitch."

The fact she cursed didn't surprise Whit in the least. The feel of her in his arms hit him like a brick wall. Her scent, the softness of her curves, even the way her height matched his. All of it made him curse to himself.

"She pushed me," Sarah snapped as Whit set her back on her feet. "That bitch pushed me."

He didn't have to ask who since he already knew. Apparently Mavis wasn't going to go quietly into that good night. She was a vengeful creature who wanted Sarah to suffer for firing her. Any normal, sane person would accept it and move on. She'd gotten a train ticket in payment, and probably cash already, so there was no need to harm Sarah.

Whit's overactive protective instincts roared to life. A soldier was sworn to protect the innocent, and even if Sarah couldn't be qualified as completely innocent, she didn't deserve to be harassed.

He helped Sarah to their compartment, then turned to look

for Mavis Ledbetter. She deserved an adjustment to her attitude and he was the man to do it, with respect, of course.

"Where do you think you're going?" Sarah's voice stopped him in his tracks. She sounded annoyed at *him*.

"To find Miss Ledbetter." He never did like bullies.

"Sit yourself back down then. I don't need you to fight my battles, Kendrick." She arranged her skirt on the seat, shaking off the dust from the walk over.

"You'll accept my help on this trip, but not my protection?" He snorted. "What kind of logic is that?"

She gave him an impatient look. "Whoever said I have to be logical?"

Whitman tried not to let his now active temper get loose yet again especially so early in the morning. The damn sun hadn't even risen yet. A commotion out in the passageway distracted him before he could give Sarah a proper retort.

"I have a ticket for this compartment and I will not allow you to stop me." Mavis's screech could be heard two states away.

A low murmur of a man's voice responded. Whitman stepped out to discover what was going on, grateful to have the opportunity to give Mavis a lesson in polite behavior.

A porter stood there shaking his head. A fuming Mavis, with her hands on her hips, tried to push past him.

"Ma'am, I told you, that ticket is for a seat in the public car up ahead, not the private compartments." He was a big man with steel gray hair and a square jaw set in stone.

Mavis stamped her foot. "That is not true. I was in there yesterday." She spotted Whitman and her gaze narrowed.

"Having trouble, Miss Ledbetter? You know what they say, what goes around comes around." Whitman folded his arms across his chest. He ignored the little voice inside reminding him there were stains on his soul, worse than pushing a crippled woman—far worse.

"It's none of your business. Porter, this man is in the same compartment as me. Ask him." She stuck a finger in the big man's chest.

"I don't have to, ma'am. I can see on your ticket where you are supposed to be. Now if you don't want to listen to me, you are welcome to disembark now." He glanced at Whitman and nodded.

"Tell him!" Mavis shouted. "Tell him I am a passenger in the private compartment."

"I am certain you are sitting where you deserve to sit." Whitman was pleased to see a flush spread across her cheeks.

"You have no right to judge me, Mr. Kendrick." She put her nose in the air. "I saw the way you were looking at that whore last night."

That was the final straw for Whitman. His temper snapped as he stalked toward her. She must've seen something in his face because she yelped, picked up her skirts, and fled.

"This isn't the end, Mr. Kendrick," she called over her shoulder.

The porter turned a questioning gaze on Whitman. "Do you know her?"

Whit grimaced. "She was a paid companion who wanted to do nothing to earn her wages."

"Looks as if someone changed her ticket." The porter almost grinned. "I don't blame that someone at all."

"Neither do I." Whitman walked back to the compartment to ask that someone what she'd done.

To his surprise, Sarah was reading, looking comfortable and calm, as if Mavis hadn't shoved her off the train five minutes earlier.

"What are you doing?" He sat down across from her.

"Reading a book. It's a binding with paper and ink formed into letters and words." Her sarcasm knew no bounds.

"What did you do to Mavis's ticket?"

"Nothing."

Whitman gritted his teeth. How could she get under his

skin so quickly? "Yesterday she had a ticket for a private compartment. Today it's a seat in the public car. Explain that."

Sarah closed the book and met his gaze. "I didn't change it. Yesterday I paid the porter extra money to allow her to be in this compartment."

He had trouble absorbing what she said. Then it dawned on him that Sarah didn't trust Mavis from the beginning. "You knew she was going to be trouble?"

"No, there are only a few people in this world I trust, and none of them are on this train. I paid Mavis to accompany me. How far was up to her. She chose to stay with me for one day." Sarah shrugged. "She still has a ticket and a week's pay."

Whitman didn't trust easily either, but he wasn't nearly as distrustful as Sarah. She assumed the woman she hired to be her companion would leave her.

"Why did you hire her in the first place?"

"I needed someone to come with me. She responded to the advertisement and I hired her." Sarah opened the book again.

Whitman tried to puzzle out her reasoning but it eluded him. "I still don't understand why you chose her."

Without looking up, Sarah spoke. "She was willing to leave Virginia."

Used to a military environment, Whitman didn't normally question orders; he carried them out. However, he found himself wanting to find out exactly what made Sarah tick. She was obviously crippled and needed assistance to travel. Yet she hired someone whom she assumed would leave her stranded.

"What would you have done if I hadn't been here to help you?"

A ghost of a smile flitted across her lips. "Believe it or not, I've been able to take care of myself for quite a while without anyone's help." This time when she looked up, her silver eyes were hard. "I always expect the worst and I'm usually not disappointed."

Her words hit him like blows. He'd said them himself to

his mother and his grandfather. Suddenly he knew why he was drawn to Sarah, why he found himself fascinated by her and desperate to know more about her.

Sarah was a kindred spirit, a person with a hardened heart who viewed the world from behind a guarded wall.

She was exactly like him.

Whitman shook off the chill that crept up his spine at the revelation. There were many reasons he should keep his distance from her, not the least of which was his promise to Melissa. Yet he knew his fascination with Miss Sarah Spalding would only grow the more time they spent together.

His journey toward a new life had just taken a hard left turn and all he could do was hold on for the ride.

Sarah felt like squirming under Whitman's gaze. He was staring at her as she attempted to read. The key word here was *attempted*—she couldn't concentrate on the words. Having him watch her was an intense experience and she had to stop herself from yelling at him to stop. The man was obviously trying to puzzle out why she'd picked Mavis as a companion.

And perhaps why she hadn't trusted the woman for a minute. Sarah knew the other woman wouldn't stay true to her promise and she didn't disappoint. Whitman might be surprised Sarah would think that far ahead, but she always did. Well, at least for the last ten years anyway.

Life seemed to enjoy kicking her in the teeth. She'd learned to avoid the blow by expecting the worst or hitting back first. What happened with Whitman was completely unexpected. She didn't have time to duck.

After she'd been nearly killed by the Yankee soldier, Sarah had clawed her way back to life. Despite her mother's pitiful care, the lack of medicine and food, she'd survived what would have been fatal for most people.

There were too many struggles since then to recount, not that she'd want to. Lean times were the standard for folks in the South following the war. For many, the war didn't end after the surrender. They were the most dangerous of all.

The very reason Sarah opened up her home as a boarding-house was for protection in numbers. Women alone were easy pickings. It was how she found Vickie so long ago, at the mercy of some ex-soldier who found raping women more pleasurable than treating them like human beings.

Sarah was as tough as nails, inside and out. Except, it seemed, when it came to one Yankee named Whitman Kendrick. He made her nervous, jittery, and aroused all at once. If she was smart, she'd find a way to get him out of her compartment.

Yet she hadn't, and somewhere deep inside, she knew she wouldn't. And that bothered her more than anything.

Whitman made her remember what it was like to be out of control, something she definitely didn't want. She was help-less to stop it.

He sat there watching her as the countryside flew past the windows. She tried to concentrate on the book but gave up when she read the same page eight times. Then she tried to take a nap, but even with her eyes closed, she could feel his gaze on her.

She reached her breaking point after an hour.

Sarah threw her arms up and gave up the battle trying to ignore him. "What is so interesting about me that you feel the urge to stare at me?"

Whitman started as if her voice had jolted him out of a trance. At first he looked surprised and his mouth dropped open. He adjusted his jacket and sat up straighter.

"I wasn't staring."

Sarah barked out a laugh. "Damn right you were staring at me. Don't bother trying to deny it."

His surprise widened at her words.

"No ladies you know let loose and cuss? Well, too damn bad, because cussing is allowed in this compartment, like it or not." She pointed at him, ignoring the slight tremor in her hand. "Are you going to stop staring at me?"

Whitman opened his mouth to answer, then, instead of speaking, started laughing. Gut-busting, knee-slapping laughing. Sarah couldn't have been more surprised if he'd stripped himself naked and run from the train.

She expected him to act like a normal person, but he didn't. Then again, she didn't either. Perhaps that's one of the reasons she was drawn to him.

"What's so funny?"

When Whitman smiled at her, Sarah could have sworn the train jumped the tracks beneath her. She trembled at the impact. It was a beautiful, wide grin that lit up his entire face, hitting her with the fact that Whit was more than handsome—he was breathtakingly gorgeous.

"You are. I've never met someone who could surprise me, confound me, and keep me on my toes. You, Sarah Spalding, are amazing."

His words washed over her like a warm waterfall on a cool day. Not many compliments had been thrown her way for a long time, certainly not from a handsome man. She tried to capture the moment, hold it as if it were a precious gem to put in her pocket and take out to admire again and again. Sarah didn't believe herself to be a ninny or a scatterbrained fool. Men told women anything they wanted, which didn't always mean the truth.

However, the sincerity in Whitman's eyes, and her own instincts, made her want to believe him.

"Do you want some breakfast?" He pointed to the basket beside him on the seat. "Since I figured you didn't have time to eat before we left the hotel, I had the waitress pack some food."

This time it was Sarah's turn to struggle for something to say. He was handsome, kind, and charming. Shit, Whitman was nearly perfect. She could fall in love with him.

Now she was more than scared—she was terrified. What she wanted to do was throw the basket and Whitman off the train. Instead, she retreated back into her shell.

"No, I'm not hungry. Thank you anyway." Her traitorous stomach took that moment to yowl like a coyote.

Whitman cocked one dark eyebrow. "All right, then, if you do get hungry, I'll set the basket next to you."

It tortured her. The basket sat there innocently enough, the smell of biscuits and possibly bacon wafting toward her. Self-control was hard to maintain under the onslaught of such culinary delights.

Yet Sarah didn't want Whitman to feel as though he was taking care of her. She would accept his help in leaving the train, and maybe getting to the hotel. But no more carrying her up the stairs and damn sure no more food.

And certainly no more kissing.

The thought trapped in her head, Sarah stopped herself before she reached for a biscuit.

Kissing?

Who'd been kissing whom? She hadn't done any touching other than to hang on while the man carried her. There had been no kissing whatsoever.

Whether or not she'd dreamed of kissing him was another story. One she refused to even crack the cover of.

With a yowling stomach and a firm will, Sarah opened her book and tried to ignore the handsome, charming, considerate *Yankee* across from her.

Whitman dreamed of Sarah. He hadn't intended to fall asleep but the lull of the train grew too much and he nodded off. It had been a rough night of thinking way too much, so it wasn't any wonder he lost the battle with wakefulness.

She was standing on a hill, without a cane, near a huge tree whose arms spread at least thirty feet wide. The grass below her feet sparkled like emeralds in the bright sunshine while the whisper of the leaves spoke to the breeze caressing them.

The day was warm, but not overly so. He wore no jacket, just a white shirt and trousers, as he walked up the hill toward her. He couldn't remember the last time he felt so content.

Sarah's hair was unbound and fluttered in the light wind. The sun made the wavy brown locks shimmer with reds and golds, like a living work of art. It was, however, her smile that captivated him.

She'd been picking the petals from a perfect white daisy as he approached her. When she spotted him, her face lit up with a smile to rival the bright sunshine.

Whitman knew the smile was for him alone and his heart slammed against his ribs. She was beautiful, like a Madonna on the hill awaiting him.

"Whitman." Her mouth moved but no sound came out. "Darling."

Darling?

He tried to speak but found his mouth didn't function. It felt heavy as if it were full of lead. The more he tried to talk the harder it became. She frowned and reached toward him, as clouds filled the sky, blocking out the sun.

The perfect day began to turn gray before his eyes. He tried to grab her hands, but no matter how hard he tried, he couldn't get close enough to touch her.

Fear coated his tongue as the breeze turned into a whipping wind, making her white dress billow behind her. Her hair tangled in the branches as she was pushed backward by the force of the wind. She again called his name soundlessly and Whitman tried one last time to reach her.

That's when the entire tree, along with Sarah, disappeared in front of his eyes. She was sucked into the mouth of a tornado, her mouth open in a silent scream.

"Sarah, no!" he shouted as he rose to his feet and reached for the wall of the train compartment.

Whitman glanced down into Sarah's very amused face. The book she was reading was forgotten as a grin crept around the corners of her mouth.

"No, what?"

He sat back down quickly, embarrassment washing over him. What the hell had happened? He'd fallen asleep and had the most vivid dream of his life.

And Sarah had been the star.

"I, uh, thought I saw a spider." The excuse felt as stupid as he did.

She nodded. "I appreciate your willingness to throw yourself in the path of the wicked spider to save me."

This time her sarcasm wasn't funny. His emotions were still swaying back and forth like a pendulum. His temper, which he'd tried to keep on a leash, let loose.

"You don't always have to be such a bitch."

Now she looked more than surprised—she looked hurt. Whitman immediately felt bad for snapping at her, but there was nothing he could do to change it. Sarah had a way of reminding him of what it meant to be a soldier. A life he intended on leaving behind in the East.

But he shouldn't have hurt her.

"Sorry." He blew out a breath and tried to calm his racing heart. With the dream of her, his emotions going from one end to the other, he could barely form a coherent thought.

She held up one hand. "I've heard much worse, been called even worse than that."

Oh, but it did, and he could see it in her eyes, no matter how fast the shutters went down over them. Sarah wasn't as tough as the persona she showed the world. It changed his view of exactly who she was, or perhaps the dream had. Either way, Sarah Spalding was not the woman he thought he'd met yesterday.

"I'm still sorry. I didn't mean to hurt you."

She scoffed, but it wasn't particularly strong. Damn, he had hurt her. "You can't hurt me, Whitman. I grew a thick skin long ago."

Whitman chose his words carefully before speaking. "Regardless of what you say, your eyes tell me something different." He took her hand, and a jolt of pure lightning jumped between them. "I'm sorry. You are not a bitch. You're a funny, honest, intelligent woman who didn't deserve to be called a name."

For that, she apparently had no response. Instead she nodded and pulled her hand away, but not before Whit saw her swallow hard. Perhaps he wasn't the only one suffering from confusing, unexpected emotions.

Sarah fished around in her bag for a new book. The one she had simply wasn't keeping her interested. She wanted to blame it on her new traveling companion, but it wasn't his fault.

She was the one lusting after him.

He leaned forward and pulled the bag out for her. "Here you go. That should make it easier."

"Thank you," she murmured, a bit grudgingly.

"You're welcome."

With a humph of impatience, she dug through the books until she found one of her favorites by Jane Austen. Much as she hated to admit it, she loved the way Austen's books made her feel.

Hopeful.

There wasn't much in Sarah's life that she could call normal or enough to give her hope for the future. Reading one of Austen's books helped her escape from that everyday rut.

"Jane Austen? She's wonderful." Whitman pointed to her book.

Sarah was more than surprised. "How do you know of Jane Austen?"

"I've read her books before, Sarah. I'm not a complete moron, you know. I do like to read." He held up the book and Sarah remembered she'd seen him reading before.

"Oh, right." Lame response to be sure, but it was the best she could do.

"Are these all your books?" He peered into her bag.

Sarah snapped it shut. "They are now."

"You don't have to talk to me, but I thought it would make the trip go easier." Whitman put up his feet on the seat next to her. "I started collecting books when I was a boy. That's when I moved to New York City. Since there wasn't much green to look at and certainly no friends to play with, I turned to books."

She stared at him, surprised by his admission.

"Now it's your turn," he prompted.

"For what?"

"To tell me about how you got started reading books. Engaging in conversation is what normal people do." He looked at her expectantly.

"They were my father's. H-he read to me when I was younger, taught me to read although it wasn't common for daughters to have the same education as sons." She shrugged. "He died and now they're mine. The end."

Whitman chuckled. "You are a hard nut to crack, Spalding."

"You have no idea, Kendrick."

He laughed again, winked at her, then opened his book.

Sarah couldn't have been more shocked than if he'd pinched her ass. He'd laughed at her sarcasm and then *winked*, for pity's sake. What did it mean?

She had no idea, so she pushed it away and tried not to think about it. The fact he loved books, and read them as an escape as well, formed a kinship between them.

Sarah didn't want it to happen, but it did. So much for keeping her distance from the Yankee.

Chapter Six

Sarah stared at her bags beneath the seat and then up at Whitman. "Would you mind carrying these?"

"Are you the same woman who got on the train this morning?" He grabbed the bags and headed for the compartment door. "Coming?" he tossed over his shoulder.

A grin threatened her annoyance with being unable to carry her own bags. Whitman had a sense of humor, unexpected and surprisingly sexy.

After their odd conversation earlier, they hadn't spoken much. Sarah finally broke down and ate some of the food he'd brought, as surreptitiously as she could, of course. Earlier, after he'd woken with a start, Whitman had looked at her as if he'd seen a ghost, his expression one of desperation and grief.

She hadn't known how to respond to it, so she'd buried her reaction deep enough where she could ignore it. Then after he'd nearly bitten her head off, dammit, he'd gotten nice again.

Sarah was confused and befuddled by Whitman Kendrick. That made her feel angry and annoyed, yet at the same time, butterflies danced in her stomach when he smiled. It was enough to make her want to trade in her compartment ticket for a seat in the crowded main car.

Yet she didn't.

Most of Sarah's relationships with men had been physical,

purely a release of bodily urges. There hadn't been a man she even considered having a conversation with since she'd last seen Micah. And he'd been practically a ghost.

To be honest with herself, she was lonely, but it was a self-imposed loneliness. Her own defenses kept every man out until Whitman came along.

He crept under the wall around her heart and knocked on the door. Perhaps it had something to do with the fact he didn't back away from her when she barked. He stood up to her, without being a total ass, and made her feel as if she'd found a worthy adversary.

However, her body was telling her he wasn't an adversary, but a partner, a *bed partner*. He'd mentioned he was engaged to be married, so there was no way he'd want to tussle the sheets with Sarah. Whitman appeared to be a gentleman—for all his rough words with her, he'd never once treated her badly.

It had been a very long time since Sarah had encountered a gentleman, certainly as long ago as before the war began. And even then, they were all Southerners.

Whitman was a Yankee.

Her mind whirled with the notion that not only was she attracted to a Northern man, but she actually liked him too. Her mother would roll over in her grave if she knew.

They walked together toward the hotel, following the trail of people as they exited the train. His arm was firm and warm beneath hers as he carried three bags with his left hand while escorting her with his right.

Her body thrummed with arousal and she half considered inviting him to her room that night. After all, they were both grown adults and Sarah was very attracted to him. More than she should be, truth be told.

She had an itch that needed scratching. Whitman was just the man for the job. That settled it in her mind. She'd invite him in after supper, and if she was lucky, they'd both be grinning in the morning. One thing she could do in bed well was sex, she didn't need two good legs to give and receive sensual pleasure.

All she needed was a willing man and a whole lot of hot, hard sex. She shivered at the thought of being with Whitman and getting to feel, taste, and nibble those muscles up close and personal.

Just the thought made her nipples pop up like little flags. He'd better say yes or she would be servicing herself.

"These biscuits taste like yesterday's leftovers." Whitman set the offending bread on the table and made a face. "Or perhaps last week's."

Sarah hadn't even taken a bite of hers. "Shame, isn't it? Biscuits are one of the best things in the world and they had to go and ruin it."

Things had been calm and polite, almost friendly since they'd left the train. Supper had been enjoyable, aside from the food. It had all been stale, tasteless, or downright inedible. He'd be eternally grateful the food at their first stop had been so delicious. If he'd tasted gravy like what was on his plate now, he'd have bought his own food at the general store and rationed it.

Sarah ate, as did he, even if the food tasted terrible. He realized both of them had been used to eating whatever food was served. A survival instinct and habit they had in common.

For some damn reason, though, he couldn't stop thinking about Sarah and his dream about her. The danger, the feelings and sensations had been so real, he couldn't shake them—a very unusual occurrence for Whit. He'd been a soldier for fifteen years, for pity's sake, and seen some of the most horrific things a human being can.

Yet the image of Sarah being hurt, even in a dream, bothered him immensely. Why that was remained a mystery. First of all, he didn't know why he dreamt of her. Secondly, the dream itself was odd. Last, the emotional effect of the dream lingered.

Whitman wanted to protect her, keep her from harm, and hell's bells, he wanted to kiss her.

It was more than kissing actually, but he didn't need to be doing any of that with Sarah Spalding. He had a fiancée and needed to stay true to her. Melissa promised herself to him, even if it was through correspondence. Whitman had his honor and it dictated he did not betray that promise.

As they walked toward the steps, Sarah's perfume wafted past his nose. It was a light scent like roses mixed with the underlying aroma of her body. All woman, and damn arousing. Whitman gritted his teeth and breathed through his mouth. If he couldn't smell her, the hard dick currently knocking at his buttons might go away.

However, it got worse when he picked her up in his arms to carry her up the stairs. She was tall enough to drape her body from his shoulder all the way down to the part of him currently acting like an idiot.

Whit started counting from one to a thousand as he walked up the steps. It didn't seem to help very much because she laughed at him, the husky chuckle echoing through his already taut body.

"What's funny?" he snapped.

Her thumb caressed the underside of his jaw. A bolt of pure lust slammed through him when she whispered near his ear. "That wasn't amusement, Kendrick. I can feel you hard against my hip."

Whitman sucked in a breath, unsure how to respond to her. He wanted to snarl and fuck her until they couldn't see straight. What he should do is tell her good night and leave her at the hotel room door.

Sarah, however, took that decision out of his hands.

When he put her on her feet, she cupped his cheeks and pulled his head down. Their breath mingled as their lips grew

THE STRANGER'S SECRETS 61

closer. Heat arced between them and Whit found himself falling into her silver gaze.

He was losing control fast. Yet he couldn't stop it, any of it, even if he tried. The moment their lips touched, a primitive howl of pleasure ripped through him.

She opened her mouth and their tongues entwined like old lovers. Rasping and winding together in a timeless dance.

They stumbled through the doorway, their mouths never losing touch. He heard the snick of the door shutting, then the key turning in the lock. Sarah was obviously skilled with her hands as she worked to close them off from the world.

Whitman allowed his eyes to adjust to the semidarkness. The light streaming through the window from the street gave the room a golden glow bright enough to see only shapes and the occasional flash of skin.

Sarah started unbuttoning his shirt and he slowly let her down to her feet to give her free access. He was rewarded with a husky chuckle.

"You like that, do you?" She kissed the skin inch by inch as the shirt opened.

Whit's dick pulsed with each touch of her lips, harder and more eager than he ever remembered being. Then she licked him from his stomach to his jaw and he almost came in his drawers.

"You can't even imagine how much." He pulled the shirt completely off and she ran her hands up and down his chest, her nails lightly scratching his nipples. Obviously Sarah was not inexperienced with a man, which was lucky for him.

As if he were under her spell, he allowed her to continue seducing him. She unbuttoned his trousers, freeing the erection hard enough to hammer nails. When her hand closed around him through his drawers, he sucked in a breath.

"God, that feels good."

"Yep, it sure does. You've been blessed by your maker, Whit." She pumped him once. "And apparently so have I for tonight."

Before he could realize what she was about, his drawers had joined his pants on the floor and she'd sat on the bed. His bare cock waited in anticipation, as did the rest of him, with his pulse pounding through him like kettle drums.

He didn't have to wait long. A light swipe of her tongue on the underside made his eyes roll back in his head. She cupped his balls and rubbed her thumb between them, sending a delicious shiver through him. Her other hand wrapped around the base of his dick and squeezed lightly.

When her mouth closed around him, Whit's knees turned to jelly and he swayed into her.

"Don't fall on me, big man." She pulled him deep into her mouth and sucked while her tongue swiped the tender skin.

Twice before Whitman had had women pleasure him with their mouths, but they didn't even remotely compare with Sarah. She started a rhythm of sucking him into her mouth as she squeezed with her hands, then releasing him while rubbing the base of his cock.

"Sarah." He gasped after a few minutes. "I won't last long if you keep that up."

She laughed softly. "Mm, well we can't have that, can we?"

After a few more strokes, she laved the head of his cock, alternately nibbling and kissing. It was the most sensual experience of his life.

"I'm going to come in your mouth."

She let him go with an audible pop. "Then the fun would be over too soon, wouldn't it?"

He couldn't quite see clearly, but he could hear her remove her clothes as his pulse pounded through his ears. If he got any harder, he might faint.

"You gonna join me on the bed, Yankee?" She let loose a husky chuckle. "I've got a few things we can do with that cock of yours."

Hearing her talk dirty made him that much more aroused. He didn't expect it would, but damned if it didn't. Whit had never been so turned on in his life.

He crawled onto the bed and came up against soft, feminine skin. Breathing in her scent, he smelled roses and the musky scent of her aroused pussy. Both were heavenly.

Whitman lay down next to her and began exploring. Her breasts were like big apples with hard, distended nipples ripe for the picking. He lowered his mouth and licked at one, earning a hiss from her.

"I like that. Do it again."

Sarah was definitely not shy.

He cupped the other breast and tweaked the nipple while his mouth continued to pleasure her. He nibbled at her and she jerked.

"Harder."

Whit smiled and bit her. She moaned in appreciation and he continued his assault. As he switched breasts, his hand meandered down her stomach until he found the springy hair between her legs.

The heat from her pussy made his dick jump against her hip. She was amazingly wet and ready. His fingers dipped into the recesses of her and discovered all the nooks and crannies.

Each time he found one she liked, he mentally made a note, then returned his fingers to caress her again. Her clit was big and extended past the hood surrounding it. He wanted to taste her, and bite her love nubbin, but it would have to wait until next time.

Instead he played with her clit, alternately fucking her with his fingers and rubbing his palm against the clit instead. She pushed against his hand.

"You've got some skills in bed." She grabbed his dick and pumped it. "Now let's see what you can do with this."

Whitman let her pull him to her, a willing participant in her commanding presence in the bed.

He rose above her, unable to see her face in the gloom, but he could see her teeth. She was either smiling or snarling. At that point, he didn't care which it was.

As he sank into her welcoming wetness slowly, she pulled at his ass.

"Hurry."

He didn't want to hurry, though. "Anticipation heightens the pleasure."

"If I am heightened any more, I might come before you are even all the way inside me."

Whit felt a chuckle bubble up and tried to imagine another woman acting like Sarah did. There was simply no comparison.

He plunged in deeply in one thrust. She gasped and tightened around him. The velvet glove of her pussy walls was like a fist, pulling him in deeper.

"Yessss," she hissed. "That's it."

Whit couldn't even form a single word. He was lost in a pleasure he hadn't experienced before. As he began to move, she moved with him. Her body pushed up as he thrust down, their rhythm matched perfectly.

It was as if they were made to be together, flesh against flesh.

Whitman leaned down and captured a nipple, pulling it into his mouth. She scratched at his back and pulled her knees up. He plunged into her so deeply, his balls touched her flesh.

"Bite it."

His teeth closed around her nipple even as his dick thrust in and out of her hungry pussy. She moaned with each bite, each glide, each suck.

Sarah was an incredibly sensual woman and she was in his arms. Whitman had never expected it.

"Faster, Whit, harder." She scratched at his back even as she clenched around his dick.

He couldn't help but move faster and harder. His balls tightened and he knew his release would be explosive, perhaps even life altering.

"God, yes, I'm coming." She arched up, pushing her breast into his mouth as the walls of her tight box pulsed around him. Her orgasm kicked his into action. He hadn't expected it to roar through him, but it did.

He thrust into her again and again. Stars exploded behind his eyes as waves of the most intense ecstasy washed through him. Whit bit her nipple as he came, earning a scream from her as she pulsed around him.

Whitman shook with the power that had just ripped through him. He rolled off her and tried to remember his name.

She tucked herself under his arm and pulled up a blanket. With a contented sigh, not unlike a cat, Sarah fell asleep on his shoulder.

Whitman, however, lay awake for quite some time, wondering just how deep he'd dug the hole he stood in.

The sunlight pricked Sarah's eyes, making her roll over to avoid the intrusion. She snuggled into the pillow and realized two things at once.

There was someone in the bed with her and they were both naked.

The night before, she'd seduced Whitman into her bed. Her plan was to scratch the itch she'd had since meeting him; however, it hadn't worked. The itch was no longer small. It was enormous and it hadn't gone away at all. As soon as she realized he was in the bed with her, snoring softly, she wanted to wake him up with her mouth on his cock.

Jesus, she was turning into the slut Mavis accused her of being. But damn, their experience the night before had been the most intense sex of her life. She wanted more, and often.

With a smile on her face, she lifted the covers and Whitman exploded off the bed as if she'd bitten him. He was delightfully naked and Sarah took in an eyeful of the big man. Not too big, but just the right size to bring her pleasure, Whitman was built to please a woman.

Right about then, Sarah was that woman.

"What's the matter, Kendrick?"

He stared at her, then ran a hand down his face. After he

looked down at his nakedness, probably noting his half-hard penis, he met her gaze. In the depths of his pretty eyes, she saw disappointment and guilt.

So Whitman didn't feel as good about their time in the sheets as she did. Not good news, but she refused to feel guilty. He was a grown man and responsible for his own actions.

"I, uh, didn't mean to do that. What we did, I mean." He started hunting for his clothes.

"I believe your drawers are over by the door." She enjoyed watching him bend and stretch to sort out their pile of clothing on the floor.

"I'm sorry, Sarah, I really am. I don't know what I was thinking." He buttoned up his trousers before picking up his shirt.

Much as she wanted to continue ogling the man's hairy chest, she wasn't cruel. He felt bad about being with her. Sarah's inner demons cackled with glee, shouting he regretted his actions because she was crippled, imperfect, not worthy.

She kicked the demons aside and focused on his regret-filled face. "Can you ever forgive me?" he said softly.

Sarah let the sheet slip, giving him a peek of her breasts. Even if the rest of her was as ugly as sin, at least her tits weren't.

"There's nothing to forgive. I enjoyed what we did, and truth is, I'd do it again in a second."

He hadn't expected her response. "You don't act like any woman I've ever met."

"Good. I never want to be part of a herd of sheep. I'd rather be the wolf."

A smile crept around the corner of his mouth as he shook his head. "You are a hell of a woman, Sarah Spalding."

"I'd curtsey but I'm naked and don't have the grace to curtsey even with my cane. Now why don't you skedaddle to your room so I can get dressed. We don't want to miss the train."

Time stood still for a moment as their gazes met. Sarah realized the brightness of the sun meant much more than day-break. It meant they'd likely missed the train.

"Son of a bitch." Whitman got down on his knees and fished around on the floor.

"What are you doing? Get out so we can get down to the station." Sarah wasn't about to show him the scars on her legs, no matter how late they were.

"I'm looking for my watch," he snarled.

"Well hurry the hell up." She tried to snag her blouse, even if it was wrinkled and wasn't too fresh.

Whitman stood up and threw her the blouse. So much for chivalry. He snapped open the case on a nice pocket watch, then cursed long and loud.

"It's nine o'clock! Jesus fucking Christ, what the hell happened? Why didn't the fucking desk clerk wake us up? Isn't that their goddamn job?" He threw his arms up in the air. "We're in a pile of shit now. Goddammit, I'm going to be late for my own fucking wedding."

Ignoring the mention of his upcoming nuptials, Sarah watched him pace, wondering how a mild-mannered Yankee had such a mouth, and a repertoire of curses jumping to his tongue rather handily. She wanted to join him.

"Well, I have someplace to be too. If you'd get your ass out of here, I'll get dressed and we can find out what the hell happened."

"What?" He glanced at her, apparently realizing she was still naked. "Oh, right, of course. I'll go get my things." Whitman headed toward the door, his bare feet slapping on the wood floor. "Be ready in five minutes."

Sarah was as annoyed as she was aroused—a common occurrence around her companion. She made her way to the edge of the bed and rose to her feet with her shirt in hand. When Whitman came back into the room abruptly, she had no time to cover herself.

His gaze immediately dropped to her abdomen, to the shiny white scars, then to her thighs. The scarred, ropy limbs bore the marks of numerous stab wounds, and the right leg had a large gap where muscle should be. It had putrefied while she'd struggled to survive the attack by the Yankee soldier, and the half-ass physician had had to cut out a chunk of her flesh in order to save her life.

Whitman swallowed hard as his face flushed bright red. "I'm, uh, sorry. I forgot to say, that is, I forgot to ask you if you'd asked to be woken at six. By the front desk, I mean." He swallowed hard and looked away.

Sarah's heart crunched so tight, it stole her breath for a moment. It had been so long since she'd allowed anyone to see her nude, especially in bright sunlight. Whitman just confirmed what she already knew about her appearance.

"Just look your fill and get it over with. I am human, contrary to popular opinion." She quickly picked up the sheet and pulled it close around her like a shield. It felt harder than a wool blanket on her tender skin.

"I'm sorry, Sarah, I don't mean to stare. I, Jesus, I just, oh hell. I'll knock next time." He turned to leave.

"Yes, I did ask the little weasel-faced man at the front desk to wake me at six." Sarah flapped her hand in dismissal. "Now please get out."

Whitman was out the door before she finished speaking. A taste of ancient pain coated her tongue as she managed to pull on her clothes. It shouldn't, wouldn't, couldn't bother her anymore.

He meant nothing to her except a traveling companion and now a bed partner. Nothing more. The Yankee would go his way to his bride somewhere in the middle of nowhere and she'd get to Colorado and finally reunite with her brother.

Everything would be better when she found Micah.

Chapter Seven

Whitman gritted his teeth so hard, he thought he heard one crack. After a hasty decision to follow his dick instead of his brain, he'd not only missed the train, but he'd taken advantage of Sarah.

Could he possibly make things worse?

Yes, apparently he could. He entered her room without permission, then stared at her like a complete idiot. Hell, he probably made her feel like a circus freak. But sweet God in heaven, she looked as if someone had used her for sharpening a knife. He couldn't count the number of scars on her belly, and then there were her legs.

Whit swallowed hard as the memory of Booker loomed in his mind. He'd made sure the girl couldn't follow him. Perhaps by damaging her legs so badly she couldn't walk.

If Sarah was that girl, Whitman could *never* let her know who he was. Someone had wreaked terrible havoc on her a long time ago, stolen her innocence and her future. God help him if she did discover Whitman was a recently discharged Yankee soldier, much less who he'd served with.

He tore off his dirty clothes and shoved them into his traveling case. Whit had packed enough to wear everything two days, but the train had left without them, so he'd have to find a laundress before arriving in Kansas City. The trunk with the rest of his clothing, including his uniform, lay in the baggage compartment of the train, chugging along toward Kentucky.

Without him.

Cursing under his breath, he quickly dressed and yanked on his boots. After a night of the most unimaginably pleasurable sex, he'd awoken to a nightmare. He'd missed the train, so he would probably miss his wedding. It was scheduled for three days after he was supposed to arrive in Kansas City.

As he stomped back toward Sarah's room, he realized he'd need to send a telegram to Melissa. The sweet, innocent woman had no idea what she was in for considering he'd been unfaithful two weeks before the marriage.

He raised his hand to knock on the door when he realized his hand shook. The combination of mental, emotional, and physical stress was taking its toll. Whit was a trained soldier, for God's sake. He needed to stop acting like a woman and put his dick back in his trousers.

Sarah opened the door, dressed, with her traveling bags on the floor beside her. He winced at her flushed, perspiration-soaked brow, knowing she had to do everything by herself without a lick of help. Another shortcoming to lay at his door that morning.

"I'm sorry I took so long. I meant to be here to help." He reached down for the bags and she whacked his arm with the cane.

"I managed." She came within inches of his balls with that lethal stick of hers. "If you plan on treating me like an invalid, let me know now. I allowed you to become my traveling companion because you didn't treat me with pity. I won't take it, not even for a second."

Sarah was furious and she had every right to be. Whit was acting differently. Hell, he didn't know which end was up anymore. And here he figured the train trip would be boring and quiet. Ha! It had turned his life upside down.

Sarah had turned it sideways.

"I'm sorry." He let loose a shaky laugh. "You're right and I have no excuse for being an ass. Let me take your bags and let's figure out what the hell happened."

She stared hard at him before nodding. "Last chance, Kendrick. I don't take kindly to pity."

Obviously Sarah's defenses were firmly in place. Whitman didn't want to make things worse by throwing pity in the mix. She was right: he needed to treat her as he would anyone else.

"Then I'll offer you none." He waited as she made her way out the door. "Are you going to hit me if I offer to carry you down the steps?"

She raised one brow. "You can carry me provided you don't grope me, because I really am sore and tired from last night. You'll need to give me time to recover."

Whitman almost dropped the bags on his feet. Who the hell thought it was a good idea for him to get involved with such a forthright, amazingly crazy woman? Especially one who joked about sex when they were in a load of trouble.

By the time they made it down the stairs, his astonishment hadn't faded. For an old soldier, being off-kilter was a new experience for him. One he didn't know how to handle.

When he set her down at the front desk, the rather large man behind the counter stared at her. Whit didn't like the way the man peered at Sarah, but there wasn't a damn thing he could do about it.

"Yes?"

His thick drawl should've given Sarah the clue this man likely didn't have an ounce of respect for her. Whitman opened his mouth to speak when Sarah began.

"What is your name, sugar?" She gave the clerk a sultry smile.

"Dwayne Adams, ma'am." The damn man nearly blushed.

"Well, Dwayne, last night I asked to be woken by six this morning and since it's now after nine, I think something went haywire." She ran her fingers along the scarred wooden desk. Whit realized both men watched the meandering digits with avid interest.

"I'm so sorry to hear, Mrs. . . ."

"Miss Spalding, with an *Ssss*." She stuck out her tongue like a snake and Whit dropped the bags.

"Be careful, Mr. Kendrick, there's valuables in there." She turned her attention back to Dwayne, the idiot. "Now I believe we missed the train, a shame because I had a private compartment. Who can I talk to about arranging transportation to catch up with the train this evening?"

Whitman realized at that moment Sarah not only was beautiful, underhanded, and bossy, she was an absolute genius.

"Why my daddy owns the hotel, Miss Spalding. I'm sure I can arrange something for you." Dwayne grinned and took her hand, holding it as a courtier would. Whitman's empty stomach gurgled.

"Thank you kindly, Mr. Adams. I surely do appreciate your assistance. I'll go have some tea to calm my nerves while you make those arrangements." She smiled again, a practiced sexy-as-hell grin that made Whit's blood heat up.

"Of course. Tell Mary I said breakfast was free for you and your . . ." The clerk looked up at Whit with an expression of pitiful hope.

"My brother, Whitman."

Whit choked on his own spit.

"Thank you, Dwayne. I'll see you in just a few minutes." With another bone-melting smile, she limped toward the restaurant.

Dwayne leaned over the counter to take a good gander at her backside, earning a growl from Whit. The man didn't need to treat her like a whore, regardless of her methods of persuasion.

"That's one fine-looking sister you got there, Mr. Spalding. She break her foot or something, that why she need the cane?" Dwayne's salacious expression made Whit want to punch him into next Tuesday.

"Something like that." Whit didn't want to compromise the assistance Sarah had obtained for them, so he shut his mouth and followed her into the dining room.

The hot September sunshine started baking Sarah like a potato in an oven. The fool Dwayne was supposed to have brought the carriage around half an hour ago. She felt like taking a bath after letting him touch her hand, but the man had the ability to get them on their way. For that, she could swallow her distaste.

"What was that all about?"

Sarah turned to look at Whit as he lounged against the building with his arms crossed and a scowl that might scare children. She wasn't in the mood to exchange words with him again.

"None of your business."

He pushed away from the wall and stalked toward her. In the three days she'd known him, Whit had never seemed threatening despite his size. However, the look in his eyes and the catlike way he approached her made her think of a panther stalking his prey. It sent a shiver up her spine.

Sarah was never one to run from a challenge. She straightened her shoulders and raised one brow. "Something you want to say to me?"

He came up close enough for her to see the flecks of brown in his green eyes. His warm breath gusted over her face when he spoke. The crazy urge to kiss him stupid raced through her.

"You practically sold yourself to that fool Dwayne. Doesn't that bother you or was Mavis right about you?"

Sarah's amusement fled in a split second. She'd been accused of being a whore for so long, the very idea he would assume it after a short acquaintance made her furious.

"How dare you."

"How dare you?" he shot back. "You got your back up when Mavis treated you like shit on her shoe, yet you just used that boy as if he were a means to an end. Don't be insulted because I accuse you of the very behavior you just demonstrated."

It was the first time she'd had someone stand up to her, truly stand up to her. Many had tried, but at the first wound from her sharp tongue, they ran.

Not Whitman.

"You are a bully." It was the best she could come up with.

"Pot calling the kettle black."

Sarah sucked in a breath and opened her mouth to let him know just how black she could get when a bright, chipper voice stopped her.

"Well, good morning you two. I hope you enjoyed your rest."

Sarah turned to find the hotel manager, a portly man in his fifties with a wide smile and a round pair of spectacles on his nose. He'd been pleasant the night before when they'd checked in. In fact, he'd been the one Sarah had asked to wake her at six. Her anger swiftly turned from the frustrating Whitman to the hotel manager.

"Mr. Howard, right?"

He nodded, his jowls jingling madly. "Yes, ma'am. I'm so glad you and your husband decided to stay here for your honeymoon."

Sarah's mouth dropped open. Husband? "What are you talking about?"

"Why Mrs. Ledbetter told me about your romantic love-at-first-sight story and about how you got married on the train yesterday." He rocked back on his heels, patting his big belly. "I must say it tugged at the heartstrings to hear of it. She told me how you decided to stay on here for a week until the next train comes through." Mr. Howard sighed like an old romantic.

Sarah steamed like a teakettle on a hot stove. That bitch Mavis stayed true to her promise. She got even for being fired, that was for sure.

"Miss Ledbetter told you all that, hm?" Whitman's voice sounded calm, but Sarah heard the fury under it. He was good at hiding his anger, unlike her.

"She lied to you, Mr. Howard. We are not married, nor did we intend on missing the train this morning." She tried to rein in her temper, but it felt as if she were fighting a runaway team of horses. Big horses.

"What?" The hotel manager's face flushed. "That pleasant woman lied to me? I-I can't believe it."

"It's true, Mr. Howard." Whitman turned his scowl on the shorter man. "In fact, my intended bride is waiting for me in Kansas City. Thanks to you and Miss Ledbetter, I will be late for my real wedding if we don't catch that train."

"But . . . I . . . that is, you looked as if you were in love. I mean, you carried her up the stairs." Mr. Howard backed away from them slowly.

Sarah tapped his leg with her cane. "I'm crippled, Mr. Howard. He carries me up the stairs every night because Mr. Kendrick is my traveling companion."

The portly hotel manager looked between the two of them and the color drained from his face. "Oh dear."

"I'd use stronger words than that," Whitman growled.

"With Dwayne's help, we're going to try to get to the train before it leaves the next stop tomorrow morning." Sarah gestured to the bags. "You can be assured we won't be back here."

Mr. Howard had the grace to look completely contrite. "Of course, of course. I will make sure the arrangements are made. If you'll excuse me."

He skittered, or rather waddled, into the hotel as fast as his little legs could carry him. The man hadn't even apologized.

Sarah contemplated throwing her cane at him.

"What an ass." Whitman took the words from her mouth.

"A double ass." She stamped her cane on the wood-planked sidewalk. "I can tell you if I ever find Mavis Ledbetter, she's going to regret what she did."

Whitman blew out a breath and ran his hand down his face. "As a gentleman, I don't contemplate hurting women. Mavis is pushing that limit."

Sarah snorted. "I don't have any qualms about hurting her."

He met her gaze. "You really know how to pick a companion, don't you?"

"Apparently. Look what happened after Mavis." She smiled at him until she saw a twitch in the corner of his mouth. "Now let's go catch a train."

Whitman felt as if an army of ants had landed on his body and set up camp. As they trundled along in what appeared to be a retired stagecoach, he sat beside Sarah and fidgeted.

The night before had seemed surreal, a dream with more emotion and sensation than he ever imagined possible. Whitman wasn't a virgin by any means, but his liaisons with women had been few and well chosen. He'd always maintained control of everything.

Until Sarah.

Until he'd met the woman who defied any explanation or expectation. He could almost hear his grandfather's eyebrows slam down in disapproval if he ever met Sarah. The old man was born a snob, and it only got worse as he got older. Whit had never been so out of control in his life, even when he ended up under the old man's care at the tender age of twelve.

That had been the most emotionally intense experience of his life.

Until Sarah.

What the hell was he going to do? He couldn't miss his own wedding, but traveling with her for the next week and a half might be his downfall. What if Sarah ended up pregnant? What if Melissa found out he'd been unfaithful? What if Whitman found himself permanently stuck with Sarah?

"If you grind your teeth any harder, you'll never be able to eat steak again," Sarah commented from beside him.

He huffed and stared out at the passing landscape. "I have a right to grind my teeth in peace."

It sounded ridiculous even to his own ears, but he wasn't going to take it back. Sarah made him trip over his own tongue, for pity's sake.

"I'm angry too, Kendrick. This isn't how I intended on traveling across the country." She hung on to the strap as they hit a bump big enough to make him almost bite his tongue off. "Jesus Christ, is he aiming for those holes?"

Whitman realized he himself was uncomfortable, so she was probably in agony. Her body wasn't in good physical condition. No doubt the bumps felt like punches to her.

"Do you want my coat?" He started to take it off to give her to sit on.

"No, thanks, I'm not cold."

"Well, I didn't offer it to you for warmth. I'm being a gentleman again. I thought maybe you might want another cushion."

She glanced down at the seat. "Another cushion? I didn't think I even had one. This thing probably lost all comfort twenty years ago."

"Exactly why I offered you my coat." Whit held it out to her.

"I'd rather have your lap," she challenged.

"Excuse me?" Whitman's blood rushed through his veins at the very suggestion. What the hell was that all about?

"You heard me." She raised both brows. "It's a long ride, so I thought maybe we could make it, ah, smoother."

Whitman almost choked on his words as they tumbled out of his mouth. "I don't think that's a good idea."

Sarah pursed her lips. "I understand. Now that you've had the whole cow, the teats aren't quite as good, right?"

"That's not what I meant. Why do you always turn everything into an insult?"

"Because that's usually what happens anyway. I strike first before I get hurt." She almost bared her teeth then. "You think you're too good for a crippled whore?"

Whitman's temper bubbled nearly to the top. Sarah had the innate ability to make everything into an argument. For some stupid reason, she reminded him of his own behavior as an angry ten-year-old boy in a new house of strangers.

"You are an angry woman, Sarah Spalding."

"You have no idea how angry I can get."

What Whit didn't expect was for her to nearly launch herself at him. Her lips collided with his and then he forgot why he was angry.

The sensations of the night he spent in her bed came back at him like a tornado, with just as much force. He wrapped his arms around her and pulled her against him. Her round breasts rubbed against his chest, the hardened nipples leaving goose bumps in their wake.

Their tongues coiled around each other, angry and full of passion. The argument had brought back everything he loved about being intimate with her. How could anger lead to sex? It should lead to them going their own separate ways.

Yet it hadn't. Not even close.

She yanked up her skirts and straddled his lap. He could feel the heat from her pussy already, and so did his dick. It jumped to life, hard as an oak tree in seconds.

"What are we doing?" he gasped into her mouth.

"I don't know but I don't want to stop." Sarah yanked on his hair on the back of his head. "If you do, I'll have to shoot you."

Whitman doubted she had a gun, but in any case, he didn't think he'd be able to stop what he was doing anyway.

She unbuttoned his pants and freed his dick. He groaned as her strong hand pulled at his throbbing erection. Surprisingly nimble for a woman with a cane, she positioned herself above him.

When the head of his dick touched her hot pussy through the slit in her bloomers, he gripped her hips. "Oh, God, put it in."

"Nope, not God," she gasped. "Sarah."

With that, she lowered herself onto his waiting staff and they both groaned. Sarah bit his earlobe, then moved her way down to his chest.

She clenched around him, driving him insane while she bit his nipples, then laved the tiny nubs.

"Move, woman, before you make me lose my mind."

She laughed against his skin. "Mm, but I love the way you fill me up, Yankee. You're so damn hard."

He thrust up against her and she bit him hard enough to make him groan. "Sarah."

"Hmm? I'm enjoying myself on the feast." She kissed the spot she'd bitten and he thrust up again.

The combination of her teeth and being buried deep inside him was intoxicating and more pleasurable than he imagined.

"Do it again." He surprised himself.

Bite. Thrust. Bite. Thrust. Bite. Thrust.

"I'm going to come all over you," she whispered in his ear. "Now fuck me hard."

Whitman was beyond thinking at that point. He simply obeyed.

He grabbed her hips and thrust into her hard and fast. Groans and the deliciously wet sound of their joining were the only sounds in the carriage.

He shouted her name as his orgasm spread through him. Sarah found his mouth and plunged her tongue into him even as he plunged into her. Shards of pure ecstasy spread out from the contact.

Whitman had never guessed he was the type of man to enjoy having amazing sex in a carriage with a woman. Yet he had, enough that his legs were shaking as bad as the rest of him.

He knew then his heart was sincerely in trouble. Really big trouble.

As the harsh breathing in the small carriage slowed, Sarah regained control of her senses and her bodily urges. She felt sated. Even more than that, she felt content. It was the only word she could think of to accurately describe how she felt.

Of course, her legs would probably not thank her at all considering her acrobatics in the carriage and on top of Whitman. His hair was mussed. She remembered yanking on it. The chocolate curls stuck every which way.

"You know we shouldn't have done that." He continued buttoning up his shirt, but Sarah could see little bite marks all around his nipples.

Somewhere deep inside her a primitive female creature sighed with satisfaction.

"Just because we shouldn't didn't mean we couldn't. I told you before, Kendrick, we're adults. We can make grown-up decisions."

He stopped buttoning and stared at her. "I don't believe I had a choice in that decision."

Her brows snapped together. "That is a big fat lie and you know it. I'm a crippled, skinny woman and you're a big, strapping man. Are you telling me you couldn't pluck me off you if you really wanted to?"

"That's not what I said."

"But that's what you meant. You meant that I forced you, which isn't true."

To his credit, he didn't continue that line of thought. He obviously knew he was only lying to himself. Sarah would never believe it, not even for a second.

He had enjoyed what they'd done immensely, judging by the whisker burn on her neck and breasts, which were currently pulsing. There's no way his body could lie even if his mouth did.

"I don't remember the last time I felt so tired." He blew out a breath and sank down lower on the seat.

Sarah laid out on the seat across from him, using one of her bags as a pillow. Her legs were already beginning to stiffen, but she didn't care—at that moment, anyway. She'd care quite a bit later when she fully recovered.

"Where did you grow up, Whit?"

Startled, he simply stared at her until she repeated the question.

"It's not a secret is it? You didn't pop out of an egg fully grown, did you? Or maybe it was a pumpkin?"

"I was just surprised you asked is all. You don't seem like the type that, uh . . ."

"Type that what?"

"Type that's interested in getting to know someone."

"Well, you're right, I'm not, but we're stuck in this carriage for God knows how long. And we certainly can't repeat what we did for at least several hours, so I thought I'd be polite and ask you about your childhood. To pass the time."

"You've got a chip on your shoulder bigger than the entire state of Texas, you know that?" He frowned at her.

Sarah narrowed her gaze. "That's obvious. Most people notice it right away. But thank you for pointing it out. I had forgotten."

A small grin played around his mouth. "You've got a lot of sass, woman."

"And you've got a nice set of balls. We're even. Now, where did you grow up?"

A rusty chuckle sounded in his chest. Sarah wondered for just a moment or two what it would feel like to have her ear pressed against that chest when he laughed. The warm skin, the crinkly hairs, the safety of being in his arms.

It was a fairy tale, a dream. The type she never allowed herself to have. Somehow it had wormed its way into her thoughts after meeting Whitman Kendrick.

"My parents owned a farm in New York. We raised corn, a little tobacco."

"Did you have chickens and pigs too?"

"You don't need to look down on me because I'm the son of a farmer."

She flapped her hand. "That's not what I was doing. I basically grew up on a big farm with the fancy name of plantation. But it was a farm, a cotton farm. We had chickens and pigs."

Whit held her gaze for a few moments before nodding. "We had a couple of chickens, but no pigs. My mother couldn't abide them. Said they were the dirtiest creatures on the planet. Of course, she'd play with the dog who ate his own, ah, leavings."

This time it was Sarah's turn to chuckle. "It's all about perception, isn't it?"

"That it is."

"So why did you leave the farm and how did you end up in that natty-looking suit on a train headed to Kansas?" She tried to find a comfortable spot.

"I left home because my father died when I was a boy. I've only been back once." He cleared his throat. "My mother, unfortunately, refused to leave until she couldn't keep up with the payments."

She could tell by his body language and his tone, there were raw emotions attached not only to the farm but also to his mother. Of course, Sarah couldn't cast stones. Her mother was the epitome of what not to do as a parent.

"So where else did you live?"

"New York City, in a brownstone on Seventy-fourth Street."

Sarah tried to picture what a brownstone was but gave up. She had no idea. "Interesting. I don't think I would have guessed you were a farmer, but I wouldn't have guessed city folk either. Did your kin take you in? Is that why you didn't live on the farm anymore?"

"Something like that." He speared her with an intense green gaze. "You grew up on a plantation. Tell me about you. Tit for tat."

Sarah shook her head at him. "You're avoiding the question, Kendrick."

"So are you, Spalding."

She couldn't deny that—it was the truth. "Yes, I grew up on

a cotton plantation in Appleton, Virginia. I was the younger of two children. My older brother, Micah, and I were very close as children."

"And your parents?"

Since she started the conversation it wasn't as if she could claim that he was being nosy or pushy. However, she didn't want to answer the question either.

"My father was killed early on in the war. My brother fought and survived. He's living in Colorado, getting married actually." She pictured Micah as she had last seen him, his face bloody with the stitches she had sewn together with her clumsy, shaking hands, and his haunted silver gaze that mirrored her own. "I'm looking forward to seeing him."

"It's a long journey. You must love him." Whit's eyelids grew droopy.

"He's all I have." Sarah was startled to hear the admission, and even more startled to realize she meant it. She'd left behind everything she had become accustomed to for Micah. She didn't know if what she felt for her friends was love, or just fierce loyalty.

Sarah didn't know if she could love enough for a real relationship. That, of course, was part of her deepest fear.

"What about your mother? You haven't mentioned her." Whit let loose a jaw-cracking yawn.

Sarah yawned too. "That's another story for another day."

"No fair."

"Sometimes life's not fair and there's nothing we can do to change it." Sarah closed her eyes and the rocking motion of the carriage became soothing instead of annoying.

"You are a very secretive woman, Sarah." Whit sounded a thousand miles away. She heard him shift on the seat and grunt as he punched the cushion. "And this carriage is mighty uncomfortable."

"Baby." She shifted her traveling case until she found the perfect spot.

"Obnoxious hag."

Sarah let loose the chuckle that threatened slide from her throat. "You know, I think I like you, Kendrick."

He grunted a response, but she didn't hear it. This time her eyes slid shut completely. Sleep crept over her like a thief in the night, snatching away her thoughts and leaving her to slide into the blackness of unconsciousness.

Whitman woke from another dream about Sarah to her sleepy voice calling his name.

"Whit, wake up."

He forced his eyes open to find the dying afternoon sun making the interior of the carriage glow pink. Sarah leaned up on her elbow, her hair tousled and clear pain written on her face.

"What's wrong?"

"My legs hurt." She sucked in a breath. "I need you to distract me."

Whitman rubbed his eyes, the grit telling him he barely had gotten any sleep. "How do you want me to distract you?"

"Tell me a story. Any story. Please." Her tone was almost pleading, something he would never have expected from her.

He peered at her across the deepening light. "Sarah, how bad does it hurt?"

"Bad enough that I want to listen to you tell a story." Her chuckle was more like a sob.

Whit stepped across the carriage and picked her up. As he sat with her snuggled on his lap, her sigh gusted across his neck.

"Who'd have thought a big ox like you would be comfortable?"

He held her close, absurdly pleased to feel her heart beating next to his. "After my pa died and I went to New York, I was like an apple in a room full of oranges. You see, he had left behind a rich family to marry my mother, a common maid.

The almighty Kendricks had disowned him, left him to live in squalor without a dime."

"Snooty bastards."

Whit chuckled. "That they were. I was twelve years old, scared to pieces, and the first person I met was my grandmother. She was cold and stiff, never had a hug or kiss for me. They wouldn't even allow me to see my mother. And she wouldn't leave the farm. It was all she had left of my father."

"You missed her."

Whit wanted to say no, but it would be a lie. He chose instead to ignore it. "My grandfather was a self-righteous old man who wanted to make me into what he'd wanted his own son to be. They sent me to a private school." He closed his eyes against the memory. "I did my best to get kicked out."

She laughed against his chest. "So you were a bad boy, hmm?"

"Something like that. I should've stayed in the private school because they sent me someplace worse." The military academy had turned him from a farm boy into an unfeeling soldier. "I escaped from their control at eighteen. My grandfather wanted me to sit on the board at Kendrick Industries, but I refused. I left to make my own way in the world."

She touched his cheek. "You were lonely."

Whitman had no idea how she knew that, but it was more than true. He had spent too many years denying his family, his mother, his heritage, hell, even his responsibility to them. The army had become his family. Then, at the age of thirty-three, he realized his life was empty. There was nothing for him but an empty room and an empty heart.

He looked for a wife to fill that hole in his life and found Melissa through a newspaper advertisement. Little did he know the careful life he'd constructed would become nothing more than feathers in the wind.

The wind's name was Sarah.

*   *   *

The next time Sarah woke it was full dark. The carriage lumbered on, like a horse-drawn boat on the river Styx.

Whitman held her gently. She was still surprised how comfortable he was for being a big, muscular man. "You awake?"

She sighed, careful not to move too much. "Unfortunately."

He chuckled. "It's a hell of a lot less comfortable than the train, and that's not saying much, is it?"

"At least the food's good."

Her sense of humor had survived, which was good.

"How about you tell me a story?" He shifted lower in the seat until she was nearly lying on top of him.

"What?"

"I told you a story, now it's your turn."

"I don't have any stories." She didn't want to relive much of her life, especially with Whitman.

"That's not fair, Sarah. You owe me a story." He sounded almost as stubborn as she was. "The one person I haven't heard about is your mother."

Sarah's stomach dropped. The one person he wanted to hear about was the person who almost destroyed her.

"I can't."

He stroked her hair, the warmth from his touch both foreign and welcome. Whitman had a way of putting her at ease, a talent no one had used successfully on Sarah Spalding.

"Please."

She sighed and snuggled closer. To be certain, she couldn't look him in the eye. "She was a true Southern belle, a woman who prided herself on how she, her house, her husband, and her children looked. Vain is a kind word; selfish would be accurate. She probably never would have become a mother if it hadn't been for the servants who took care of us."

The faces of the women and men who helped raise her flashed through her mind, all gone now, leaving the selfish Spaldings behind. Sarah hadn't blamed them—she would have left too if she could have.

"There were just two of you? You and Micah?" he prompted.

"Yes, Micah was planned, of course. Every man wants an heir, but I was a mistake." The word left a bad taste in her mouth, now so many years after hearing it.

"I don't think so."

She sucked in a whiff of his scent, and it calmed her. "After the war began and my father died, she began to change for the worse. By the time it ended, she had done unspeakable things to survive, including selling her body and nearly killing Micah."

That bloody day would be forever in Sarah's nightmares. The screaming, the accusations, the former friend of Micah's who dared to buy their mother's flesh for an hour. Micah had survived, with some poor stitching by Sarah to close the saber wound in his face.

"I can't talk about what happened, but we all survived somehow. My mother, however, never forgave me for helping Micah. In her mind, he was dead, and since I'd helped him, I was worse than dead. I was a viper in her house, and treated as such."

Then there was the attack on Sarah, and the way her mother simply gave her over to the soldiers who invaded the house. There was no way in hell she was ready to tell Whit that story. Just thinking about it made her hand itch where the little finger had been cut off.

"Toward the end, after the war was over, I think she lost her mind completely. She thought life was exactly the way it had been, with the parties and the beautiful people. But we were dirty, hungry, and scrambling to survive." Sarah closed her eyes against the prick of tears. She would *not* cry for her mother again. Ever.

"What happened to her?"

Sarah shook her head against the image of her mother's death. "My mother took the coward's way out and hung herself from the banister in the great hall. After I buried her, I opened my house to women who were orphaned or widowed by the war."

Whitman continued to stroke her hair, absorbing the painful

memories. Amazingly enough, Sarah actually felt better after telling him about her mother. Vivian Spalding had been a horrible person, one who had shaped her children's lives into the misshapen messes they were.

"I'm sorry, Sarah."

The sincerity in Whitman's voice nearly sent her self-control packing. Sarah, however, held on with both hands.

"Nothing for you to be sorry for. Say thank you that I told you a story." She could always be counted on for her sharp tongue.

He kissed her forehead, ruining the sarcasm, and making Sarah's heart thump once, hard. "Thank you for telling me your story."

Right then and there, Sarah knew it was too late. She was already half in love with the big Yankee.

Lord help both of them.

Chapter Eight

By the time they pulled into the small Kentucky town in the inky darkness, Sarah had never felt so tired. That was saying a lot since she'd worked for the many calluses on her hands. Yet the fighting, the sex, and the emotion of being with Whitman drained her energy down to nothing.

She'd given up the fight and slept against him the last two hours. He'd woken her when he'd seen the lights of the town in the distance. Sarah had no idea what time it was, but since it was still dark, they hadn't missed the train.

"We should go straight to the train station." His voice was as rusty as she felt. "I think it's about an hour from dawn and we don't want to miss the train again."

Sarah grunted in response. Apparently it was the best she could do because when she tried to sit up, she fell back against him. Her muscles screamed in agony and the memory of straddling Whit while he plunged inside her whipped through her brain.

"What's wrong?"

She let out a big sigh. "I think I might have hurt myself." The admission cost her dearly; he had no idea how much. But considering she couldn't even sit up, she had to tell him of her weakness.

"Well then, you probably shouldn't have jumped on my lap before." He at least hadn't stooped to pity again.

Sarah managed a chuckle. "I had to work out some anger and you were convenient."

He sucked a breath through his teeth. "Are you saying you used me?"

"Of course I did. Just as you did me. That's what adults do, Whit." She tried to ignore his fantastic scent and the delicious memory of how his skin tasted on her tongue.

"Funny, I hadn't considered you an adult," he responded. "You act more like a spoiled child, the way you push me away."

"I only do what I must to survive." That summed up quite a bit about Sarah Spalding.

"Well, I don't believe you for a minute, you know. You did not use me in this carriage. There was a hell of a lot more going on there."

Sarah wanted to continue arguing with him, but the carriage finally stopped and she nearly fell off the seat. Whitman picked her up and held her close to his chest. The steady thrum of his heart echoed through her, made her feel safe, an unusual feeling, to be sure.

"Be nice and I won't drop you on your head." He stepped out through the door and groaned when his feet hit the ground. The bags swayed against her leg. She had no idea how he managed to carry all of it. "I think I may have a few aches and pains myself."

Sarah bit at his neck. "Mm, you taste good." Her arousal was ill timed and downright stupid, but she couldn't seem to stop it.

"Jesus, woman." He shifted her weight, and pain shot through her legs and up her spine.

Sarah gasped for air as she tried to control the urge to cry. It had been too long since she'd allowed a tear to fall from her eye. There was no way in hell she'd do it in front of Whitman.

"God, I'm sorry, Sarah. My arms are sore and I needed to move you just a bit." He walked so slowly she thought he might have stopped.

"I'm not a piece of china, just a crippled woman who's been fooling around too much." She could hear the pain as it took hold of her. Too bad Vickie wasn't around to rub the liniment into Sarah's leg. She'd been the medic in the group and had discovered horse liniment worked wonders on Sarah's emaciated muscles.

She was headed toward a full day of lying in bed in agony and there was nothing she could do to stop it. Sometimes Sarah wished she could find the soldier who'd done his best to saw off her legs. She would never allow the knife to leave her hand again.

"Don't lie to me, Sarah. I think after being with you so much, I can tell when you're not being entirely honest. Believe me, I've had my ears blistered enough." He slowly ascended the steps to the platform. Each movement felt like someone was poking her with a burning stick.

She opened her eyes wide enough to see Whitman's face as he carried her into the train depot. Shock rippled through her to recognize worry and concern. This man, this upright Yankee, whom she'd treated as if he were a stable hand, was worried about *her*.

Sarah hadn't expected it and it hit her with the force of a blow. As she tried to suck in a breath, she twisted and the pain screamed through her with razor-sharp teeth.

Just before she blacked out, she swore tears had leaked from her eyes. Impossible, of course, because Sarah never cried anymore.

She had run out of tears.

Whitman wondered if he'd stumbled into his own personal version of hell. Not only was he tired, grumpy, and sore as hell, but now Sarah had just passed out in his arms, after screaming and crying in pain.

He frantically searched for someone to help him, but the depot was deserted. Thankfully there were benches, albeit wooden ones, he could lay Sarah down on. The tough, no-

nonsense Southern belle had surprised the pants off him when she broke down.

Honestly, he wouldn't have believed it unless he'd been there to see it. And he had. Unfortunately.

Her skin was pale as milk, allowing hidden freckles to pop out on her nose and cheekbones like cinnamon treasures. Her lashes seemed absurdly long against the whitened cheeks. The good news was, she was breathing.

The bad news was, her face was wet with tears, and whatever they'd done, or hadn't done, in the ancient carriage had reduced her to her current state. If Whitman had just listened to his head and not his dick, none of it would have happened.

Sarah was a strong-willed woman and might have pushed him to get her way, but Whitman had a brain, a rather large dose of common sense, and free will. He should've chosen the higher road, but he'd instead chosen the path of the flesh.

And oh what amazing flesh it was.

Whitman nearly slapped himself for his train of thought. Jesus please us, what was he thinking? She was unconscious, for God's sake. He had no right to even remember what her flesh felt like beneath his hands, much less crave it when she lay prone on a wooden train depot bench.

No doubt his grandmother or his mother would gladly slap him silly for it.

Without any water or supplies to help her, Whit felt helpless to do anything. However, he could do a few things. There was a gas lantern with matches near the door. After lighting it, he made a pillow from his jacket and tucked it under her head and sat on the floor beside her holding her hand.

Over the next ten minutes, he thought about all the reasons he should never touch her again, and then she began to stir. He leaned over and gently patted her cheek.

"Sarah?"

He picked up her hand again. So much for not touching her—he couldn't even leave her alone for ten minutes.

"Sarah?"

Her eyelids fluttered and those silver orbs locked in on Whitman. He smiled right before her right hook caught him in the jaw.

Whit fell backward in pain and shock, landing on his ass on the dusty wooden floor. His face throbbed at the sheer force behind her punch while he tried to figure out if all his teeth were still in place.

"Don't touch me." Her deadly tone sent a skitter across Whit's skin. He hadn't heard such a murderous tone since the war. The idea it came from a woman was astonishing to him.

"Sarah, it's me, Whitman." He gingerly touched his jaw. "You didn't have to hit me."

She tried to sit up and howled in pain. "God fucking dammit!"

Whit got to his feet and dusted his trousers off. "If you promise not to punch me again, I'll help you to a sitting position."

Sarah's cloudy expression began to focus and she looked around her, then at him. "Whit, I hit you? Where the hell are we?"

"Yes, you hit me. And I'll have you know your punch nearly knocked out a few teeth. Woman, you have a hell of a right hook." He sat down near her feet. "You are in the train depot at whatever town we're in, in Kentucky."

"How did I get here?" Perspiration broke out across her brow as she struggled to move.

Whitman had to sit on his hands to keep from helping her, from touching her. "I carried you, as I have each night since we left Virginia. Unfortunately, this time the ride in the ancient carriage caused you undue harm and you fainted."

She stopped moving and scowled at him. "I don't faint."

"Yes, you did, regardless of whether or not you believe it." He peered at her eyes. "Do you remember me now?"

Sarah frowned. "Sorry, Whit. It was the Yankee accent that threw me. Don't pay me no never mind on that punch. You understand I was protecting myself." Her drawl grew deep as she struggled to get control of her obviously pain-filled body. "I didn't mean no harm."

"You didn't hurt me." *Liar.* "I understand you were confused and just waking from a faint."

"I don't faint. If you don't quit saying that I'm going to punch you again."

He managed a small grin. "You'll have to catch me first."

This time he saw a glimpse of amusement in her gaze. "Bastard. You know without my cane, I can't catch anyone." She glanced around. "I need my liniment. Where're my bags?"

"Oh hell." Whitman ran outside and across the platform, praying the bags were where he dropped them. He'd been in such a hurry to get help for Sarah, he hadn't even thought of their bags.

Fortunately, they lay in the semidarkness where he'd dropped them. It was a good thing dawn was just hinting at the horizon or everything they had would likely have been gone already. Folks in most of these small towns didn't look a gift horse in the mouth if someone decided to leave a pile of goods to pilfer.

He scooped everything up, including Sarah's cane, and carried it toward the depot. The cane began to slip through his sweaty hands, and when it slid toward the ground, he took hold of the crook.

Only to discover he held a very lethal-looking blade in his hand instead.

Apparently Sarah had a cane made with a weapon in the top. Very clever, and very much like her. A whole lot of force encased in a sleek exterior.

Whitman shook his head and put the cane back together and headed back toward the depot. The first thing he noticed when he walked in was Sarah staring at her hands; the second was that she looked as if she'd been poleaxed.

"Why is my face wet?"

She looked so confused, Whitman couldn't tell her the truth, so he lied. Again.

"You were sweating, sorry to say. For a woman, you definitely can perspire with the best of them." He set the bags down and waited for the smart-ass response.

He didn't have to wait long.

"How kind of you to notice. Now bring me the damn bag so I can get my liniment out. Took you long enough, by the way." She sounded as pushy as she always was, but beneath it, low and deep in her voice, he heard the agony. She was probably trying to distract him and herself.

Sarah was stronger than he estimated, which was saying a lot. Her pain threshold was obviously very high and she'd reached the limit. The crying was so out of character she couldn't understand why her face was wet.

What else had the war taken from her?

Whitman forced himself to stop thinking about Sarah and how she'd been scarred inside and out. Whatever liniment she wanted was obviously what she needed. He shouldn't be selfishly mooning over Sarah's problems. Although deep down, he secretly wished there was a way he could take her pain away.

Permanently.

When he brought the bags to her, she waved away the heavy blue one. "Not that one. It's got books in it. I need liniment, not prose. Open the green one."

Whitman kept his patience while he obeyed her terse commands and opened her bag for her. She rummaged around until she found a tin, then held it up.

"Thank you, Vic."

He had the awful thought of finding out who exactly Vic was and where he was. What the hell was wrong with him?

"I need to put some of this on my legs, so you're going to have to either turn your back or get the hell out." She set the tin on her belly and again tried to sit up.

"You're joking with me, right?" He scowled. "Do you honestly think I'd leave you to do that yourself?"

"Excuse me?"

"Climb off your high horse, Sarah. We're in this together

and if you don't like me helping you, that's too damn bad, because there's nothing you can do about it."

He wasn't normally so pushy and bossy with women. However, he'd had plenty of practice with the men under him in the army. Sarah made it easy to remember how to be a captain and give orders.

Whitman snatched the liniment off her belly and tucked it in his pocket. While she sputtered at him, he pulled up her skirts to her hips.

"You're on dangerous ground, Kendrick."

She hissed in a breath and her eyes grew wet with unshed tears of pain.

"Sit still, Sarah. I'm not trying to hurt you, believe it or not." He gentled his touch. "Let me help you."

She swallowed hard, then blew out two breaths before she nodded almost imperceptibly.

"Fine, get on with it."

Whit was nearly gleeful with the small victory, for a moment at least, until he realized he'd have to take off her bloomers.

"Shit."

"Careful, your foul language is going to singe my virgin ears." She hadn't lost her dry sense of humor at least.

"I need to lift up your behind so I can pull these down." Unbelievably, he felt his cheeks heat with embarrassment.

Sarah laughed. "Oh my God, don't make me laugh like that. It hurts. You-you can't possibly be sh-shy now, Kendrick."

He made a face at her and put his hands on her bloomers. "Get ready, Spalding."

As gently as he could, he held her up with one hand while the other attempted to pull down her bloomers enough to access her thighs. His breath got choppy and uneven as he shook with the strain of trying to keep her as steady as possible.

"I'm sorry, Sarah."

She bared her teeth. "Just get it done."

This time Whitman ignored the tempting triangle between her legs in favor of giving her relief from the agony currently gripping her.

He was surprised actually. Whitman didn't spend his time considering other people's comfort, or at least that of women he had sex with two days after meeting them anyway. Sarah should be back in the last town waiting on the train, not before him at his mercy half dressed.

Yet there he was smearing greasy stuff on his hands and preparing to touch her again. Melissa would hopefully be understanding of his motives. Very understanding.

When he looked at the tin, he stopped and sniffed. "Horse liniment?"

"I thought the same thing the first time I saw it, but it works and nothing else the stupid doctors gave me did." She glanced at his hands. "Your hands are much bigger, so hopefully stronger. Don't be afraid to rub it in."

He put his hands on her right thigh and again wondered how he'd gotten into such an odd situation. The smell of the liniment was odd, something he couldn't quite identify. He hoped it actually wasn't made of horse.

"It smells horrible."

She managed a small snort. "You should smell it after two days."

Whit didn't want to think about that. He ignored the stench and focused on her legs. At first he didn't see the scars, only the pain they caused.

However, as he started moving his hands, she huffed impatiently. "I told you not to be gentle. You've got to unknot the muscles and you can't do that touching me like my grandmother. You've got big hands, nice calloused strong ones. Use them."

That's when he really looked at what he was touching. The creamy skin of her thighs seemed incongruous next to the scars marring the beautiful skin. The shiny whiteness of the shallow ones, next to the deep color of the thicker marks.

He'd seen the scars in the hotel room, but he hadn't really looked, because he'd felt embarrassed and sorry for her. Of course, the pity could never be revealed or she'd bite his head clean off.

Whit put his hands on the right leg, the one with the missing chunk of muscle, and started massaging in the liniment. He was surprised to find her leg as hard as a piece of wood. Apparently her muscles had either atrophied or gotten to the point where they stiffened completely without regular massaging.

The hardness softened slightly as he worked. He really did have to use his strength. After a few minutes he developed a rhythm moving up one side then down the other. Sarah's fists began to unclench and Whit felt a smidge of pride.

She was a hard woman to please and if massaging stinky horse liniment into her knotted muscles was the answer, he was more than glad. He was, for a brief moment, satisfied.

Whitman almost gasped at the realization. It had been twenty years—more than that—since he'd felt satisfied with anything in his life. And he felt it for an abrasive, scarred woman with a tongue that could cut glass?

He felt a chuckle threaten at the absurdity of the situation. Yet he continued to massage her pain away. She sighed as he added more of the liniment to his hands and then moved to the other leg.

"Dare I ask if I'm doing it right?"

She sighed. "Yes, actually you are. I've only had one other person do it and your hands are much stronger."

Well, that was good news. Apparently Vic was not much of a man.

"Is it helping?" His nose began to burn from the combination of sweat, heat, and the liniment.

"Yep, it is. It's been a very long time since my legs have felt relaxed enough not to make my ass as tight as a tick."

A chuckle erupted out of Whitman; he couldn't help it. At that moment, the door opened and a tall thin man in a blue cap stepped in. His mouth dropped open at the sight of a half-naked woman with a kneeling man massaging her legs on the bench.

Sarah howled with laughter and smacked Whitman on the shoulder. "You think he's gonna let us on the train?"

Whitman did the only thing he could think of. He laughed with her.

Chapter Nine

After Whitman explained in his very Yankee, formal voice why they were in the depot, and why Sarah was half naked, the confused depot clerk finally hesitantly nodded. He said the train was leaving on time and disappeared behind the ticket window.

Sarah should have been embarrassed by everything—the pain, the fainting, and the depot fiasco—but she wasn't. The truth was, she was grateful to Whitman for helping her. The pain had been unbearable, and she'd no doubt have lost her mind if he hadn't been brave enough to do what he did.

She didn't think he'd pull her bloomers down or touch her hideous legs. Not to mention the liniment. Vickie had known it had healing abilities for humans. Too bad it smelled like horses.

Whitman had performed through all of it as if he'd been her companion for years. Most folks would've cringed at all of it. Perhaps it was because they'd been intimate twice already, but she knew that wasn't the entire reason.

There was a connection between them, a deep connection she didn't understand. Yet it comforted her, oddly enough. Very few things gave her comfort anymore.

However, a virtual stranger, a lover, a Yankee did.

She sat on the bench and watched him pace in front of the

window as he looked out at the platform. In ten minutes they'd be allowed to board the train. God help anyone who tried to take their compartment. Sarah would use her cane if she had to.

Her stomach rumbled and she wondered if they should get food before boarding. However, she didn't want to take a chance on missing the train again. It sat there like a big iron monster, as if it hadn't caused them a twenty-hour wild ride from Virginia to Kentucky to catch it.

Whitman stopped pacing and stared out the window. Sarah's instincts stood at attention as she waited to see what he'd seen. Then the one person in the world she wanted to find appeared fifteen feet from him.

Mavis Ledbetter.

The fury hit her so hard, Sarah didn't remember getting to her feet or hobbling out the door as fast as she could. She found herself passing Whitman and almost running after the old bitch who'd left them to rot. Mavis knew where Sarah was headed and how important it was to get to Colorado and see her brother.

Yet the older woman had allowed petty stupidity and a taste for revenge to get in the way of common decency. Sarah intended on making her eat her decision. Bite by spiteful bite.

A strong arm clamped around her midsection, pushing out her breath and stopping her cold. She tried to suck in air, but Whitman's hold was too tight. When she tried to kick him, he squeezed harder, and she saw spots in front of her eyes.

"Let go of the lady." Whitman's voice came from somewhere to her right.

If he hadn't grabbed her, who did?

"It's my job to protect the citizens of this town. I reckon I can spot trouble when I see it." The stranger's voice was raspy and smelled like yesterday's onions.

Sarah was desperate for air, so she tried clawing at his arm. Within moments, she would lose consciousness or maybe even her life. Suddenly the thought of slapping Mavis held no consequence. When death winked at her again, Sarah's survival instincts took over with a battle cry.

"If you don't let her go, you and I are going to have a problem." Whit sounded angry, a good thing as far as she was concerned. At least someone cared if she was murdered on a train platform by an onion-smelling stranger.

Sounds echoed as if she were hearing them through glass. She knew she had only a few moments until she would black out completely. With all the strength she could muster, she kicked backward, connecting with a shin. The man loosened his hold just enough for her to suck in air. When he did, she twisted and bit a plaid-covered shoulder as hard as she could.

Sarah expected the fist, truly she did, but it still rang her head like a bell. The last thing she remembered was a bellow of rage from Whit's direction. Then her face hit the dusty sidewalk and everything went black.

Whitman's fury knew no bounds. When he saw the man holding Sarah against him, he kept his temper in check and tried to reason with the stranger. He wore a red plaid shirt and canvas trousers along with two days of whiskers and a stained, brown flat-brimmed hat.

Sarah stayed true to character and kicked and bit the man, but when the bastard punched her, Whit lost control. A trained soldier, he knew many ways to kill a man. He chose to let the moron live with a crippling kidney punch and a jab to the throat.

Sarah landed on the sidewalk with a thud. Whit glanced up to see Mavis's face drain of color, and then she ran for the train. Good thing too because it seemed her former boss had been intent on giving her a whooping. No doubt Mavis was shocked to see them, particularly considering they looked like hell. Not to mention the fistfight on the platform.

Whit picked up Sarah again and carried her back into the depot. He left the moaning and choking stranger where he lay. Served the son of a bitch right for grabbing, then punching Sarah. Whit wanted to beat the shit out of him, but Sarah's well-being came first.

She came around quickly this time, her eyes unfocused. He hoped she wasn't about to clock him again. That was truly the last thing he needed. Her cheek was already showing a bruise from where the bastard had hit her.

"Whit?"

He didn't want to recognize how glad he felt she called his name instead of punching him. It was as absurd as it was pleasing.

"I'm here. Are you all right?" He set her on her feet and she wobbled a bit.

She winced as she opened her mouth. "Ouch, dammit, somebody hit me."

Whit beat down the image of just when she got it. He might have to go back and finish what he started. "Don't worry, I hit him back."

"Good. We ought to call the sheriff on that bastard." She touched the darkening spot on her jaw.

"That's his deputy." The depot clerk's voice made Whit's heart stop for just a moment.

"That dirty, smelly bastard is a deputy sheriff?" Sarah always knew exactly what to say.

"Yes'm, it is. Walter don't take kindly to strangers, and he likes to come down here when the train stops to find folks to fine for whatever he can think up." The thin old man peered at them. "You two are a bit odd, but you seem to be good people. I'd make a run for the train if I were you. Before he wakes up and arrests you."

Whit didn't need to be told twice. He scooped up all their belongings, then Sarah. He was glad the train was boarding, and by his estimate they had at least ten minutes before it pulled out. If they were lucky the obnoxious fool of a deputy sheriff wouldn't bother them again.

They didn't need to add jail time to their growing list of interesting and crazy things that happened during their trip.

By the time they made their way to the compartment and settled themselves in, five minutes had passed. He couldn't see the platform from their seats because it was on the opposite side of the train. Whit was a grown man, a veteran with war experiences that toughened him into someone who could face any situation.

Of course, that was before he met Sarah Spalding.

"I plan on finding Mavis, you know. She had no right to do what she did." Sarah adjusted her position to bring her legs up on the seat. "She has a lot to answer for."

Whitman wasn't much for revenge, although he would like to give Mavis a piece of his mind. "What do you plan on doing?"

Sarah's silver gaze was as cold as ice. "Making her pay for what she did. An eye for an eye and all that."

"Do you think that's necessary?" He peered through the window trying to see the platform. Another five minutes and the train would leave.

"Yes, I do." She smacked his arm. "What are you doing? You're as nervous as all get-out."

"I am not nervous. The deputy sheriff could be looking for us right now. Do you want to spend the night or possibly longer in his jail?" There was no way Whit would again risk missing his own wedding.

"But you're not nervous?" She snorted. "Whit, if I poked you right now, you'd probably screech like a cat."

He frowned at her. "I just want to be on my way, to leave behind everything about this town, and that damn carriage. I don't plan on suffering like that again."

Sarah kept quiet from then on, her silence unusual for a woman who always made sure she was heard. Until the train began to lumber from the station, Whit couldn't relax. He couldn't. As an ex-soldier, he respected the law and the men who upheld it.

He kept wondering what he would have done differently if he'd known the man was a deputy sheriff. Sarah had been in trouble, and he had promised to help and protect her. And he couldn't abide men who took advantage of or hurt women.

The foolish deputy sheriff was doing both. Could Whit have solved the problem without knocking the man on his ass?

Whit glanced over at Sarah. She had folded her arms and was currently staring out the window, her expression unreadable.

"I guess we won't be going to jail today." He tried to summon up a smile, but he felt so completely out of control, he just couldn't manage one.

Sarah didn't respond to his statement.

"Sarah?"

She flicked her gaze to his and he felt it like a slap. Whitman opened his mouth to ask her what was wrong but recognized that when she was angry, it was best to let her break her own silence.

As the train picked up speed, he started to doze off. It had been a very long night, or was that an entire day? Waking up in Sarah's bed had been a hundred years ago, but in reality, it had only been two days.

In those two days, Whit had gone from being amused and interested in Sarah to being fascinated and a bit obsessed. Why hadn't he met her before he asked Melissa to marry him?

Simple. Sarah was a Southern woman who didn't like Yankees, most particularly soldiers. And he was both. The knowledge of what Booker did, and the possibility it had been Sarah, burned in his gut. There was no future between him and Sarah.

Then why did he wonder if there was?

Sarah refused to be hurt. There was no way Whit's casual remarks about their journey in the carriage would bother her. Not in the least.

For one, he was a Yankee and her scars both inside and out attested to her near hatred for what he stood for. Thank God he wasn't a soldier, though. At least he had that in his favor.

Whitman was also engaged to be married. This thing between them, whatever it was, was no more than a man sowing his oats before settling down. Sarah had been the one to initiate the sex between them, although he had been a willing participant.

Aside from all that, Sarah was impervious to petty emotional wounds. There was no point in getting upset over the little things in life—too many big things to overcome.

However, there she sat like a five-year-old with her scowl and her lip practically pooched out over what he'd said about the carriage ride. It hadn't been important to her, after all, and should not bother her in the least.

All the logic in the world wasn't going to change the fact they had shared not only their bodies, but their thoughts. Jesus, she'd told him about her mother, for pity's sake. Not many even knew one iota about that infamous bitch.

Yet she'd told Whitman.

As Sarah tried to puzzle out her reaction to the big Yankee, he snored across from her. Obviously their antics on the way over, and the amazingly odd run-in with the deputy sheriff, had worn him out. She wanted to attribute it to their fantastic fuck but knew it wasn't entirely true.

Sarah had done so many things wrong in her life, she didn't know how to do much of anything. If she was honest with herself, she wanted to do more than be a traveling companion and part-time lover to Whitman Kendrick.

The very thought made her shake, literally, on the seat. Her heart raced at the idea of putting her neck out on the chopping block. Whit could pick up an ax and lop her head off, leaving her bleeding in the dirt.

Or he might open his arms to her.

Sarah needed to talk to someone. Her first choice was

Vickie, but she was four days behind the train running the boardinghouse. No one knew as many of Sarah's secrets as Vickie, and she'd stayed a true friend through everything.

There was the possibility of sending her a wire, but what would Sarah say? *I've fallen in love with a Yankee and I don't know what to do. STOP. Help me. STOP.*

Sarah sucked in a breath at the word *love*. It hadn't entered her mind before that moment, but she knew it had lurked deep down in the tiny little chamber of her heart she'd locked away so long ago.

The first problem was his fiancée. The second was the fact he was a Yankee and she came from the right side of that particular fence. Two very large, seemingly insurmountable obstacles.

One thing was for certain: she had to decide right quick what she wanted. The chance at love, perhaps even a man at her side for good, or continuing her lonely existence as a spinster with an occasional lover.

Sometimes life just wasn't fair.

Of course, that was a lesson Sarah knew all too well. Her legs ached but the excruciating pain had vanished under Whitman's care. Vickie had been strong but had nowhere near the strength of his hands.

Through the haze of the pain, which had been strong enough to make her want to vomit, she'd focused on his voice and the sensation of having him touch her. He'd touched her before, of course, but it had been either sexual or a casual thing.

It was silly to even think it, but there was magic in that experience. Sarah wasn't one to ascribe to any notions of witches, ghoulies, or that kind of nonsense. However, every other occasion she'd come to that point in the pain cycle, where it was unbearable, it had taken a week before she could walk again.

This time, after Whit's touch, not only had Sarah walked

immediately, but she had nearly run out onto the platform after Mavis. The memory of that moment sent a shiver down her spine.

How the hell had she managed to do that? It didn't make a lick of sense. Of course, magic never made sense, did it?

Chapter Ten

The day was filled with awkward silences, stilted conversations, and unsaid truths. Sarah didn't know which end was up and being around Whitman was confusing her. She didn't like that one bit so she pulled out her bitch cloak and put it on.

By the time they pulled into the station, she was ready to get back some control of the situation. When he picked up her bags and held out her hand, she let her claws show.

"Helping the cripple again, are you?" She struggled to her feet, the stiffness in her legs making it more difficult.

"Of course I am. Who else is going to?" Whitman, being the gentleman he was, took hold of her elbow to steady her. She hissed at him.

"I'm not completely helpless, you oaf." She shook off his touch.

"I realize that, as does my back, which bears the mark of your sharp nails."

Sarah didn't know who was more surprised by the slap. She stared at the red imprint on his cheek as his jaw tightened.

She could actually see the wall slide down in place over his eyes. Her heart hiccupped at the sight, but she knew it was necessary for her sanity and his upcoming marriage.

"My apologies, Miss Spalding." His formal tone told her

all she needed to know. "I didn't realize assisting you was a hanging offense."

Sarah knew he could throw out barbs just as well as she could, and they stung just as much. "You're more than welcome to find another cripple to help."

Although she knew she shouldn't, Sarah picked up her bags with her left hand and attempted to walk to the door. The weight of the books nearly sent her careening into the compartment wall. She tried to right herself, but the more she struggled the harder it became to simply stand upright. She probably looked like a turtle unable to right itself.

Whitman didn't ask for permission to help her or wait for her to request any help. He simply snatched the bags out of her hand and scooped her up into his right arm. She couldn't get a breath in beneath his strong hold, but before she could even muster the words, he'd deposited her on the platform.

His green eyes were like glass, hard and cold. Sarah had done that to their partnership and although she regretted the loss of the ease between them, she wasn't about to change it.

She couldn't.

"There they are, right there." The portly conductor who'd been rude to Sarah on more than one occasion waddled up with another man in tow. "These two are the ones you're looking for."

When Sarah saw the star on the other man's chest, her stomach cramped up and the image of the lawman lying on the platform that morning flew through her mind.

Well, shit.

She met Whitman's gaze and in an instant knew he already had the same idea she did.

"What's happening, sir?" Whit used his stuffiest Yankee tone.

The sheriff, a middle-aged man with silver at his temples, peered at them from beneath his flat-brimmed hat. "It appears a man and a woman beat the tar out of the deputy sheriff back in Belleville."

"Where?" Whit raised one dark brow.

"The last train stop. Got a wire this morning that a big man and a tall woman left the sheriff with a few broken ribs, busted-up jaw, and two black eyes." He pointed at Whitman. "You're a big man and she's a tall woman. Sounds like it was you two. She's also sporting a big bruise on her cheek."

Sarah wanted to curse the idiot, but she held her tongue and let Whitman do what he intended. She was enjoying the show.

"Ridiculous and preposterous. Sir, I am Whitman Oliver Kendrick the third from New York City. This lovely lady is my wife, Sarah. We are on our way to Denver to her brother's wedding. In no way were we responsible for any assault on an officer of the law." He put a protective arm around Sarah's shoulders.

She tried to ignore the fact the weight and warmth of his touch were extremely comfortable.

"You sure do talk fancy." The sheriff peered at him. Sarah could tell by the man's expression he didn't believe Whit's story. She also noted the stiffening of the man's spine at the Yankee accent.

Time for Sarah to step in.

"Sheriff, can you tell us what happened back yonder?" She made her drawl as Southern sounding as she could. "We might have seen somethin' that could help y'all."

The sheriff's suspicion turned to surprise. "You're not from New York City, Mrs. Kendrick."

Mrs. Kendrick.

The name sent a shiver of longing through her. She pushed it aside and focused on saving their asses.

"No, I'm surely not. I'm Virginia born and bred." She held out her hand. "Sarah S-Spalding Kendrick." Stumbling over the name, she covered up her mistake with a wide grin. "Pleased to make your acquaintance."

"Sam Miller." He shook her hand lightly, the rough calluses attesting to the man's hard work. Any other time, she might have actually liked the man enough to spend some time with him. But not today.

"How did you get that mark on your face, ma'am?"

"I'm not particularly graceful, Sheriff. I'm afraid I tripped gettin' on the train this morning." She tried to look as sweet as possible. "Can you tell us what happened in Belleville?"

"A woman was causing a ruckus on the platform, threatening another woman. The deputy sheriff—his name's Walter Tipton—tried to stop her. That's when the man beat him. That's all I know." He peered at Sarah. "Tell me why you're not that woman?"

Sarah swallowed. "I'm not. What did you say she was doin'?"

Sam seemed to think on his response before speaking. "From the wire I got from the depot clerk, she ran screaming toward another woman. Mebbe with a knife."

This time, Sarah's laugh was genuine. "Sheriff, that was definitely not me." She held up the cane. "I've been crippled for over ten years. I couldn't run if my life depended on it."

He eyed the cane, then turned to the conductor. "You didn't say anything about her being crippled."

"I-I didn't know. She was sitting the whole time and they looked like the folks you was looking for." He swallowed hard as his face flushed in the evening light.

"If the woman was running, then it was obviously not Mrs. Kendrick." He tipped his hat to her. "I apologize for bothering you."

She saw the invitation in his gaze and chose to ignore it. One man in her bed was more than enough.

"No need to apologize. I surely hope you find them." She looked up at a stony-faced Whitman. "Let's get to the hotel, Whit."

With a tight nod at the sheriff, Whit took her arm and started walking down the platform. Sarah felt the sheriff's eyes on her. The man was definitely not as stupid as Whitman probably thought he was.

They'd do well to keep out of sight until the train left in the morning.

Whitman didn't have any right to be jealous, but dammit to hell, he was. The way she fluttered her lashes at the idiot sheriff made him want to tear the man's arms off. Then beat him with them. Of course, he didn't. It was bad enough he'd already beaten the hell out of one lawman; he didn't need to do it again.

What was wrong with him? It didn't matter if Sarah flirted with or had sex with a man of her choosing. He had no claim on her and no right to judge her choices. After all, he'd cheated on his fiancée.

He walked stiffly beside her as they made their way to the hotel. The idiot conductor was behind them, still red faced and suspicious. The way Sarah had taken hold of the situation told Whit she knew exactly how to be charming. It was a different side of her, one he hadn't seen before.

Apparently she reserved the too honest, sharp-tongued version of herself for him. Did that make him special or unlucky? He didn't know and, at that point, couldn't even try to figure it out.

Whitman was angry and flustered, two emotions he wasn't used to letting loose. Control was an integral part of his life for the last fifteen years. He was uncomfortable with losing that iron grip on control. Sarah had snatched it away from him.

By the time they reached the hotel, he had calmed down a little, but not enough. Whitman needed to get away from Sarah for a few hours. She confused him, kept him spinning in circles. He'd never met a woman who had the power she wielded with a master's touch.

The hotel was a bit nicer than the last one. At least there was a larger restaurant and a well-appointed lobby. It made Whitman breathe a little easier because it was familiar. Since he'd lived in New York as a young man, and in military headquarters in Washington as an adult, clean, orderly buildings were what he was used to. Strangely enough, it was almost comforting.

Sarah glanced around the lobby, her gaze narrowing. "Keep an eye out for Mavis. She's got a lot to answer for."

Whit was startled to realize he'd forgotten about the older woman and what she'd done. She had started a sequence of events that led Whit and Sarah to miss the train, Sarah to be beaten, and the two of them to be almost arrested and jailed.

Not to mention the emotional and mental strain of the last two days.

He should never forget what Mavis had done, because it tested him. Honestly it tested his fortitude, his cunning, and his intelligence. Even with taking short naps on the train, he was simply exhausted. He hadn't really slept since their first stop on the train west.

As they checked in, he was pleased there was a first-floor room available for Sarah. He couldn't touch her anymore that day. The overload was dragging him into a dark hole he needed to climb out of.

"Do you need help going to your room?" His voice was hoarse with exhaustion and emotion.

Sarah cocked one brow. "Let's have supper first. Then we can go to our room."

He stared at her, not recognizing what she said. "What are you talking about?"

"Married couples share hotel rooms, Mr. Kendrick." Her dry sarcasm felt like a slow scrape.

The idea he had to spend the night in the hotel room with Sarah hadn't occurred to him. However, with the sheriff watching them, the conductor literally five feet from them, and the threat of arrest hanging over them, they had to keep up appearances as a married couple.

He swallowed the lump in his throat. What was he supposed to do? Whitman was completely out of his element and he damn sure needed to get his footing back.

"Of course, Mrs. Kendrick. I need to stretch my legs and take a walk." He took the key from her hand. "I'll just put our bags in the room."

Sarah tugged at his arm. "We need to talk."

Whitman couldn't imagine sitting down and trying to talk about what had happened. He could barely think about it. "I don't care."

Before she could say another word he walked off toward the room, away from the woman who haunted him, day and night. He knew he was actually running from Sarah, but he didn't want to admit it even to himself.

Sarah stared at Whitman's back as he disappeared from view. She wanted to throw something at him, shout insults, or maybe whack him with her cane. Yet she let him walk away without a word leaving her mouth.

When they'd stood on the platform facing the sheriff, she thought for certain they would be in jail in minutes. However, together they became stronger than standing alone. His intelligence and her Southern charm mixed together to create something wonderful.

It was the first time she could remember working as a team with a man. Her brother, Micah, had loved her, but he was a childhood playmate. She didn't know him as an adult, hadn't seen him in so long. Thinking about getting to know him was a bit intimidating but she was looking forward to it.

Whitman, however, was a different situation. Thrown in together on a train had been an accident, a twist of fate. It hadn't been her choice to meet him, get tangled up with him, and fall half in love with him.

Whitman was just a man, a Yankee, and his dismissal shouldn't hurt. She'd be lying to herself if she didn't admit that it had hurt. Much more than it should for a man she'd known only five days.

"Mrs. Kendrick?"

The hotel clerk's voice startled her out of the moping place she'd stepped into. "Yes?"

"Your husband left his bag." The freckle-faced man pointed to the small travel bag on the counter.

"I'll take it." The bag was surprisingly light when she picked it up. The leather handle felt warm in her hand as she hobbled toward the restaurant.

She knew she shouldn't look inside it but the urge to do so grew with each step she took toward a table. With a quick glance to be sure Mavis wasn't around, she sat down gratefully and put the bag on the chair beside her.

It was as if Whitman were there in spirit daring her to open the bag.

"What can I get for you, ma'am?"

The waitress startled her out of the new obsession with Whit's bag.

"Coffee, maybe some chicken and biscuits if you've got any." Sarah wasn't hungry but knew she needed to eat. It had been more than a day since she'd had a decent meal.

"We surely do have some fried chicken. The biscuits are from this morning but they are still tasty." The silver-haired woman glanced at the bag. "Your husband joining you?"

Sarah had a moment where she envisioned what it might be like if Whitman was her husband. She smashed it like a bug on a glass.

"No, he's getting some air this evening." And good riddance for the night too.

"Likely down at the Purple Posy. Most of the men coming in on the train end up down there." The woman's face reflected a sadness Sarah knew too well.

"He can do as he pleases. It's not my business." Sarah, of course, didn't want to contemplate what Whitman might do at a place called the Purple Posy.

The waitress humphed. "Your choice. I'll be right back with the vittles."

After the woman walked away, Sarah turned her attention

back to the bag. It stared at her daring her to be the naughty girl she could be.

Sarah reached for the toggle holding the bag closed.

Whitman entered the saloon looking for a release. He needed to break the shroud of frustration and confusion around him. Sarah had turned him on his head, much to his consternation.

The bushy-haired bartender took one look at him and grimaced. "Woman trouble?"

"Is there any other kind that drives men to drink?" Whit sat down and knocked on the scarred wooden bar. "Set me up with some whiskey, and not the cheap rotgut. I want the good stuff."

"You show me coin to pay for it and you can have anything you want." The man put an empty glass on the counter and waited.

Whit pulled out a gold eagle and flipped it to the bartender. "Keep the whiskey pouring and you and I will get along fine."

"You got it." The bartender pulled a bottle of Kentucky whiskey from beneath the bar and splashed the amber liquid into the glass.

Whit ignored the fact his hand shook when he picked it up. He needed a drink, damn it to hell, and he needed to forget about Sarah Spalding.

The moon was high in the sky when Whitman made it back to the hotel. The lobby looked different in the light cast by the gas lamps on the counter. He saluted the freckle-faced clerk and stumbled down the hallway toward his room.

Their room.

The room he was supposed to share with his supposed wife.

The most difficult night of his journey, to be sure. Even riding in the damn carriage for twenty hours straight didn't compare to knowing he was going to sleep in the room with Sarah.

He regretted his choice to take the train from Virginia. He should have left a week earlier so he wouldn't have met Sarah. Life wouldn't be rolling in the mud getting messier by the second.

After trying the door and realizing it was locked, he knocked. Loudly.

How dare she lock him out.

The door flew open and Sarah stood there in the same clothes she'd been wearing earlier with a scowl on her face. "What the hell are you doing?"

"Entering our room, dear wife." He slurred so badly, even he had trouble understanding what he said.

"You're drunk, hmm? Purple Posy, right?" She made a disgusted sound. "Get in here before you embarrass me and yourself even more."

Whitman half expected her to light into him for drinking, but instead she was worried about waking the neighbors. That thought made him laugh.

"You forgot your traveling bag." She pointed to the small case on the chair. "The desk clerk gave it to me."

A chill raced through him at the thought Sarah had possession of the bag. In it were all his important papers and belongings, including his army discharge papers and his commendations at the bottom of the bag.

"Did you look inside?" He stumbled toward the chair. "Did you?"

She pursed her lips. "What if I said yes?"

He swung around and nearly fell on his head when the room spun from the action. "What?"

"You left it behind, so obviously you didn't care about me finding it." She shrugged. "I'm as curious as the next person, so yes, I did look inside."

Whit's heart dropped to his feet. "You went through my private things?" He started shaking at the thought she'd discovered he'd been in the Union Army.

"I started reading the letters from your intended bride,

Melissa, but then I threw them back in and closed it." She folded her arms. "It was so boring it was putting me to sleep."

Whitman's relief that she didn't find his secret flooded him. God only knew what she would have done. Then she opened her mouth again.

"How dare you marry someone you've never met," Sarah snapped. "What the hell were you thinking?"

"I was thinking I wanted to get married. Melissa is a kind, gentle person. We met through correspondence, and, well, one thing led to another." He didn't want to tell Sarah that he was having doubts. "I made a promise to her, to start a new life in San Francisco. We're compatible and both of us want to settle down and be a family."

"Ha! Compatible, what about the spark? Have you read those letters? She's as exciting as a washrag." Sarah scrunched up her face and started speaking in a high tone. "Today I picked the beans in the garden. They were green and snapped nicely as I got them ready for supper. Today the cow got out of her pasture. For God's sake, the woman couldn't be more boring if she tried."

Whit felt the urge to defend the woman he intended to marry. "Melissa is a wonderful person, a kind and caring woman who took care of her dying mother instead of marrying ten years earlier. She's thirty, single, and perfect for me. I couldn't ask for a better wife."

"You aren't even looking for a better wife. You're settling for what's safe. I think that's your motto in life: Whitman Kendrick takes the safe road. You're throwing away everything to marry someone you've never met with the promise life will be normal. Let me tell you something, life is never normal." Sarah threw up her arms.

"How dare you judge me. It sounded to me as if you had a whorehouse back in Virginia. Not exactly an upstanding citizen, were you?" Whitman was letting all the demons out, riding on the fumes of the whiskey polluting his veins.

"You don't know anything about me. I ran a boarding-house for women who'd been thrown away. Mothers, daughters, sisters—all of them lost their usefulness to some bastard who tossed them out like rotted meat." Her hair glowed with the halo of light behind her, as much as her face, lit with the passion he'd seen only when she'd been in his arms. Sarah truly believed what she had been doing was the right thing. "I gave them a home and a family, such as it was. What they chose to do with their time was their choice, not mine. Exactly how it should be."

"So, in other words, they turned themselves into whores."

He expected the slap, and the pain pulled him back from the precipice of falling completely in love with the incredible woman in front of him. He'd never met someone who was giving and unselfish, yet hid behind a persona of sarcasm and insults.

"Say it one more time and I'll hit you with the cane right in the balls." She picked it up from its perch beside the bed. "Those women were survivors of things you can't possibly imagine. They deserve respect, dammit, and I won't let anyone dishonor them."

Whitman nodded, ashamed of what he'd assumed about her and the women she took in. Sarah had a kind heart, albeit a guarded one.

"You're right and I'm sorry. I was angry you'd gone through my personal things, for which you owe me an apology." He swayed as he pointed to the bag. "I would never do that to you."

"Not necessarily true, but you're right about the apology. I'm sorry I touched your stupid bag and read the innocuous, boring letters of a woman you're going to have under you for the next fifty years." She looked disgusted. "You're a coward."

He clenched and unclenched his hands, fury ripping through him. Sarah was the only person he knew aside from his grandfather who knew exactly what to do to make him so angry he couldn't see straight.

"I am *not* a coward." His voice sounded rusty and raw. "You have no right to judge me."

That seemed to be the right thing to say, or perhaps the wrong thing. She opened her mouth, then closed it and sat down on the bed heavily.

"You're right. I shouldn't judge you any more than you should judge me." She flapped her hand at the chair in the corner. "You can sleep there tonight or on the floor. Whatever you decide to do. I'm done talking."

Whit was surprised to see she meant it. The unflappable Sarah Spalding turned her back on him and climbed into bed. As he stood there fuming, angry and drunk, she rolled over and sighed.

Chapter Eleven

If Sarah had thought things couldn't be more awkward, she was wrong. Whitman wasn't even speaking to her, actually wasn't speaking to anyone. He was pale and shaky when they went to breakfast in the morning.

No doubt he had a hell of a hangover. Sarah wasn't cruel enough to stomp her feet or bang the door open, but she also wasn't going to be sympathetic. He'd made the decision to pickle his brain and he had to live with the consequences.

As she dug into fresh eggs and bacon, he sipped coffee while he kept his gaze averted. Sarah wasn't sure if he was angry at her or himself, so she didn't start any conversation.

When the sheriff walked up to the table, she almost wished she had.

"Good morning, Mr. and Mrs. Kendrick." He gave them a tight smile. "I trust the hotel met your needs."

Sarah swallowed the bite in her mouth with a bit of effort. She didn't trust the friendly greeting for a second. "Good morning to you, Sheriff. The hotel was just fine. What can we do for you?"

She reached under the table and took hold of her cane, hoping they didn't have to knock another lawman unconscious before boarding the train that morning. Especially considering she found this particular man attractive.

"Well, it appears a woman was murdered last night and

several passengers say you had words with her." Sam peered at her from beneath the brim of his hat. "Do you know Mavis Ledbetter?"

Two things occurred to Sarah at once. First, someone had set her up to take the blame for Mavis's death. Second, she'd more than likely dragged Whitman into the murder and he'd never make it to Kansas City and his waiting bride.

Damn it all to hell.

"Yes, I do. We started on the train ride from the same small town in Virginia." Sarah took a fortifying sip of coffee, knowing every word out of her mouth was being weighed carefully by the sheriff. "Is she the woman who was murdered?"

He rocked back on his heels. "Why yes, she was. The interesting thing is, another passenger told me she was the woman threatened back in Belleville by that couple I never did find."

Sarah met Whitman's gaze and saw his panic mirror her own. She needed to keep a cool head to keep the hounds off their heels.

"Obviously someone had a bone to pick with Mavis, then. I'm afraid I don't know anything about it." It was difficult to keep her voice steady when her heart was thundering like a herd of horses.

"Yes, that's what it appears to be. Apparently someone beat her to death with something, like a large stick or possibly a cane." He smiled at her. "May I see your cane please, Mrs. Kendrick?"

Cane? Oh, now that definitely wasn't good. Whoever it was definitely knew what they were doing if they wanted to blame Sarah.

"You can't possibly think I had anything to do with Mavis's death, can you, Sheriff Miller?" She pulled the cane out from beneath the table. "I can't say I was friendly with her, but I would never cause her harm."

At least she could be honest about that. Sarah might let her mouth run away sometimes, but she would never have hurt Mavis beyond a slap. Or two. She at least deserved something for what she'd done. However, the older woman didn't deserve to be beaten to death.

"I don't believe much of anything right now, Mrs. Kendrick. I am investigating this murder to the best of my ability." Another carefully controlled smile. Sam examined the cane as if it were a delicate piece of glass.

Sarah could feel Whitman's anger emanating in waves across the table. It practically singed the hair off her head. He had no reason to be angry with her—she hadn't harmed Mavis.

"Is there some reason why you suspect my wife of this crime?" Whitman apparently found his voice.

"Well, there're plenty of reasons to question her. You both fit the description of the couple in Belleville who beat the deputy sheriff. Mrs. Kendrick here knew the deceased and maybe had a quarrel with her. Not to mention the cane your wife has with her at all times." Sheriff Miller lost all semblance of a smile when he handed the cane back to Sarah.

"I didn't kill Mavis." Sarah was pleased she was able to disguise the anger building inside her.

"That remains to be seen." The sheriff looked back over his shoulder. "Deputy Barnes will take you to the jail for questioning. Mr. Kendrick can come along too. I hear he did some hell-raising of his own at the Purple Posy."

Sarah pointed to her breakfast. "Do you mind if I finish my meal first? I was quite famished this morning." She needed time to think, to puzzle out what could have possibly happened.

"No doubt." The sheriff pulled out a chair from the table beside them and sat down. "By all means finish your breakfast, Mrs. Kendrick. Fortunately or not, Miss Ledbetter isn't going anywhere and neither are you."

Whit could barely swallow the dry spit in his mouth. What the hell had happened? He'd left Sarah alone in the hotel for a few hours and she'd murdered Mavis? Was that even possible?

He was still partially drunk, for God's sake, and could barely even swallow black coffee. His brain certainly wasn't functioning well enough to figure out what was going on.

Sheriff Miller was a wolf in sheep's clothing, a fact that hadn't escaped Whit last night. The man might look like a stupid cracker, but he was far from it.

Sarah sat there and shoveled in her food as if she hadn't a care in the world. If Whit hadn't seen the fright in her eyes minutes before, he might have believed she was carefree.

Whatever happened they were both in it together, like it or not. The woman had been in their compartment, had had words with his supposed wife, and now she was dead. They were in big trouble.

"You surely do have an appetite, for a woman, Mrs. Kendrick," the sheriff commented as he sipped his own coffee brought by a beady-eyed waitress. "I like that about you."

Sarah shrugged. "I don't think it's necessary to pretend not to eat. Women have done terrible things to themselves in the name of vanity. I refuse to follow those particular habits."

Whit knew that firsthand. Two of his cousins actually had had ribs removed to keep their waists tiny. He agreed with Sarah, although he shouldn't be surprised to hear her opinion. She was a strong-willed female, to be sure.

He had come to know Sarah intimately in more ways than one. She could never have murdered Mavis.

"It was one of the first things that caught my attention about Sarah." Whit let a mouthful of hot coffee slide down his throat, thankfully easing the dryness. "She's an advocate for women, not a killer of them."

The sheriff's brows rose. "That so? Hmm, I never met an advocate for women before. Not sure I know what it is either."

"It means Miss-Mrs. Kendrick helps women in need," Whitman said through a tight jaw. "Not hurts them."

"Ah, I see. She surely didn't help Miss Ledbetter, now did she?"

Sarah choked on something, probably egg. Whit handed her a glass of water from the table. Her face flushed as she coughed louder and louder. She really looked like she was choking. When she pressed her face into the napkin, her left eye peeked out at him and winked.

At first Whitman didn't know what to do. What the hell was she doing? Then it dawned on him she was stalling for time. No time like the present to dive into the pool of lies a bit deeper.

"My wife is choking, Sheriff. Do you have a doctor in town?" Whit stood and started rubbing her back.

"That's mighty convenient."

"Look, Sheriff Miller," Whit snarled. "I refuse to allow my wife to choke to death because the lawman in town accuses her of murder and some other nefarious deeds. If you refuse to help her, I will have every attorney from the firm of Robards and Newman down here from New York in a matter of days. Then we'll see what kind of medical assistance she can get and whether or not you'll still have a job."

He didn't know where the anger had come from, but he was pleased to see the sheriff pull back a step or two. There might have even been concern for Sarah on his face.

"We have a good doctor a few doors down. If you'll carry her, I'll take you there." The man was obviously unsure of whether or not Sarah was pretending. He also was smart enough to recognize a real threat.

Too bad for him Whitman was lying through his teeth. Robards and Newman were his grandfather's attorneys, and since the old man hadn't spoken to him in years, there was a slim chance he'd get help from them.

There was no reason to think about his tangled family tragedies. He didn't need anything else to stress about.

He scooped up a wheezing Sarah and followed the sheriff and deputy out of the restaurant. The train passengers watched and whispered as they passed. No doubt there'd be fodder for gossip for the rest of the train ride.

In the back of the crowd, a bow tie caught his attention. Whitman stopped short and tried to see through the crowd. The old man Mavis had become chummy with. What was his name? He knew it was vitally important to remember.

"Sheriff! Hold on there."

Sarah pinched under his arm but he ignored her.

"What is it, Mr. Kendrick? I thought your wife needed medical attention."

"She does, but I want to be certain that every passenger on that train is questioned in this matter, and that we are not singled out as suspects." He knew it was vitally important to keep the attention on all the passengers and not just them.

"What? You can't possibly expect me to keep all these people from their journey." Miller eyeballed the crowd of at least fifty people.

"Oh, I expect it. As a matter of fact, I insist. If Mavis was murdered by a fellow passenger, then it could be any one of these people." Whitman felt a measure of satisfaction as the logic of his argument sank into his opponent's expression.

"Damn."

Sarah coughed harder.

"Deputy, stay here with all these folks. Get a manifest from the conductor and start dividing them into groups for questioning. I've got to take the Kendricks down to Doc's before she expires from fake coughing." The sheriff slammed his hat on his head as they exited the hotel.

Whitman had bought some time and, hopefully, the sheriff would be smart enough to find the real killer. If not, he and Sarah would have to.

The doctor's office was sandwiched between the post office and the mortician. Sarah didn't know if that was a comment on his status in the town or whether it was the only building available. She was hoping it was the latter.

Her choking and coughing fit had been the right move, she was sure of it. The sheriff couldn't well let her expire right there in front of him if indeed he had any evidence she was a murderer.

Justice liked to hear the neck crack at the end of the noose, after all.

Whitman's entire body was strung tighter than a guitar string. Instead of the warm, supple chest and arms she was used to, he was stiff and unbending. If she poked him with a stick, it might just break off.

Of course, pretending to choke made it hard to breathe. She started to get light-headed and clung on to his jacket.

"Don't push your luck, Mrs. Kendrick," Whit said.

"I wouldn't dream of it."

The sheriff pounded on the whitewashed door until a be-spectacled young man no older than Sarah's boots appeared. "What's happening?"

"Got a train passenger choking on her food, Ben. Can you take a look at her?" The sheriff pushed past the boy before he could answer. "The quicker the better."

The young man pushed up his glasses and peered at them. "Who are they?"

"Boy, get your ass in here," Miller bellowed from inside the house. "I've got things to be done and I can't be waiting on you."

Why had Sarah ever though Sam Miller was handsome? He was a bully, that was for certain. She wiped the hair from her forehead and tried to get a good look at Ben as Whit carried her into the house.

He nearly knocked her unconscious as he banged her head into the doorway. She yelped in pain and dug her nails into his arm. To anyone watching them, they likely appeared as a normal couple.

However, that certainly wasn't the case.

"What happened to her?" Ben squeaked from behind them.

"I told ya, she was choking on her eggs." A few bangs sounded from a room to the right.

From what Sarah saw of the house it was cluttered with

journals, books, and an odd assortment of knickknacks on shelves, tables, and chairs. Apparently Ben was a bit of a collector.

"Follow the noise. The examining room is on the right." Ben loped along behind them.

Whit managed to get her through the door without knocking her head off her shoulders at least. The bastard pinched her behind as he set her on the table. Obviously having seen better days, the thing creaked under her weight.

She had to restrain herself from smacking her "husband." He was pushing her beyond where she'd accept his behavior, fake marriage or not.

"Ben, this here's Mr. and Mrs. Kendrick. Fix her." Miller crossed his arms and filled the doorway with his bulk.

"This is the doctor?" Whit sounded as incredulous as Sarah felt. "He's barely old enough to blow his own nose."

"I assure you, Mr. Kendrick, I'm almost thirty and have been a physician for more than eight years." Ben pushed up his glasses again. "I'm more than capable of treating your wife."

"Fine, but know that I'll be watching your every move." Whit parked himself against the opposite wall, allowing him to glower at the sheriff and Sarah at the same time.

The young man leaned toward Sarah and sniffed. "What happened?"

Sarah let loose one more cough. "I don't know. I was eating eggs and then I started to choke." She swiped at her eyes, more for effect, but she'd really made them tear up with all the damn coughing.

"Hmm, does your chest hurt at all?" He pulled a stethoscope from his pocket, then picked off a piece of lint from the earpiece.

Sarah wanted to run in the other direction.

"A little, I suppose." She closed her eyes, rather than see the eccentric doctor press the cold end of the stethoscope to her chest. Damn good thing she still had clothes on.

"Are you sure he's a doctor?" Whit grumbled.

"He is, although he's been known to see the four-legged kind too. Out here in Kentucky we make do with what we have." Miller turned his razor-sharp gaze at Sarah. "And we don't take it for granted or throw it out with the pig slop."

She had no idea what level of hell they'd stumbled into, but it obviously involved a hard-ass sheriff and a mad horse doctor. There was only one thing she could do.

Faint.

Whit watched Sarah's eyes roll back in her head and wondered if she was pretending to swoon or if she really was fainting. It didn't matter, of course, because her intent was to stall for time, and it worked.

"She's fainted, Sam." Ben's face drained of color. "She's still breathing, though."

"I'm sure her husband is pleased to hear that." Miller stepped into the room. "Now any other person I'd think she was putting on a show, but seeing as how she's a good, upstanding Southerner, I'm going to give her the benefit of the doubt."

Whit stepped up next to Sarah and took her hand. "You're too kind."

Miller pointed at Whit. "That kind of shit is going to land your ass in jail."

"Sam! You shouldn't cuss in front of a lady." Ben was a bevy of surprises. Whit wouldn't have suspected the man of being a gentleman.

"She's unconscious or faking being unconscious, so it don't matter either way." Strangely enough, the sheriff's logic made sense. "Now as for you, Mr. Kendrick, I don't take murder lightly. If you or your wife was involved in the death of that poor lady, I will find out. That I can promise you."

The sheriff stomped toward the door. "Don't let them leave the building, Ben. I'll be back."

Ben sputtered at Miller's retreating back, then eyeballed

Whit. "I don't know what he thinks I could do to stop you if you did want to leave."

Although the young doctor could definitely be described as odd, Whit decided he liked him. "I don't plan on leaving Sarah here alone. And we didn't murder Miss Ledbetter."

Ben pushed up his glasses. "I'm glad to hear that. I had to examine the body and it wasn't something I care to repeat anytime soon." He visibly shuddered.

Ah, that was good news. The first opportunity for solid information from someone other than the judgmental sheriff.

"Can you tell me what you found when you examined her?" Whit pulled up a stool next to Sarah and sat down, hoping she was listening in her not really unconscious state.

The young doctor hung the stethoscope around his neck and looked up as if he was searching for information in his brain. "She'd been dead a while. My estimate was about nine hours."

"Where was the body found?" Whit wished he had pen and paper to write all of this down. Perhaps he was lucky enough that Sarah had a good memory to fill in the places he might forget.

"Behind the hotel, near the kitchen entrance. Alexander— that's the hotel manager—keeps the slop buckets back there, empty crates and the like. Miss Ledbetter was lying between two crates on her stomach." Ben shook his head. "Darn shame what folks will do to one another."

"Isn't that the truth." Whit knew firsthand just how low a human being would sink to take advantage of another. It was just one of the many reasons he left New York.

"Yes, it surely is." He glanced at Sarah. "Do you want a cold compress for her forehead?"

Whit put his hand on her damp skin. "No, she'll be okay. She'll come around in a little while." Of course, she'd pick the exact moment to wake up soon so as not to overhear any of their conversation. Damn clever woman.

"So how was Miss Ledbetter killed? The sheriff didn't tell us exactly what happened."

"Well, as I told you she was found behind the hotel in the alley. There was a great deal of blood." Ben swallowed and shook his head. "More than I've seen in one place before. Quite messy." He paused and looked at a spot in the distance, his blue eyes magnified by the thick glasses.

"Doctor?" Whit wanted to give him a shake but refrained. He didn't need to make any more enemies in town.

"What? Oh yes, Miss Ledbetter. She had been beaten severely about the head until she was nearly unrecognizable. I can't imagine who would be angry enough to do such a thing." Ben's expression told Whit he truly had never seen the evil men could do against each other.

Lucky boy.

"Could you determine what was used to beat her?" Whit knew Sarah was listening very carefully.

"I believe it was an inch-wide stick, perhaps a cane or a spindle, but I can't be certain." Ben glanced at Sarah. "She should be regaining consciousness soon."

Whitman almost snorted. Little did the naïve young doctor know exactly what Sarah had been doing the last fifteen minutes.

"Yes, she will be just fine. I think the idea that Miss Ledbetter had been killed along with the notion that she was a suspect was just too much for her." Whit could choke on his own theatrics, but Ben appeared to believe every word he said.

Definitely naïve.

"Could you get a glass of water? She'll be thirsty from the coughing."

"Of course. I'll be right back." Ben skittered out of the room on his thin legs and disappeared down the hallway.

"He's a nice boy," Sarah whispered.

"You are a terrible person." Whit crossed his arms and stared down at her.

Her silver eyes popped open and he felt the impact of her gaze. They had become inextricably linked, like it or not.

"At least I'm a better actor than you. What was that all about? Ben must truly be a complete fool to believe you." She smiled. "I did an amazing job. Even had Miller believing me."

Damnit, it was true, but he wasn't about to give her the satisfaction of agreeing with her.

"Forget all that. What about Mavis? Tell me you didn't kill her."

For just a fleeting second, he saw pain in her gaze. "You can't possibly have just asked me that question. Why the hell would I have killed her?"

"I had to ask, Sarah. I'm guilty by association here, and I wanted to be sure." He felt bad for broaching the subject, but he had to. Survival drove people to distrust everyone, even when their minds told them different.

"Nicely done, Kendrick. I might be a loudmouthed bitch with a sharp tongue, but I do not murder old ladies in alleys," she snapped.

It brought him back to their first day on the train, when she discovered he was from the North. She'd been unfriendly and uncommunicative while Miss Ledbetter had talked and talked until Whit thought he'd have to gag her.

Then she'd focused on the old man with the bow tie.

"Abernathy!"

"Excuse me?" Sarah sat up and straightened her blouse.

"The old man Mavis had latched on to that first day. His name was Abernathy." The more Whit thought about it, the more convinced he was that he was on to something.

"Shuffling old man with the bowler hat and the awful bow tie, right? I do remember him." Sarah grabbed his arm. "What are you thinking?"

"I'm thinking we have a suspect."

Chapter Twelve

Sheriff Miller frowned hard enough to make his eyebrows form a brown V. "Who in the world is Abernathy?"

"He's a man Miss Ledbetter met on the first day of the train trip. I've told you that already." Sarah tried to remember she was supposed to be recovering from a fit of the vapors. Yet all she wanted to do was throw the chicken dinner at the stubborn cuss.

"And he's an older man in a bow tie? I don't remember any passenger who looked like that." He took a bite of his ham sandwich and maintained his hard-ass stare.

"He boarded the train in Virginia and had a compartment ticket. At least I think he did. Mavis pulled him into ours and I didn't even think to check." She glanced at Whitman. "Did you see his ticket?"

Whit set his chicken leg down and wiped his mouth on a napkin. "I don't think I saw it, but I remember the conductor taking it. You know, the chubby one who was determined to blame us for every crime committed in town."

"Now watch your tongue, Kendrick. Alfred Bannon has been an employee of the railroad for at least ten years." Miller waved his sandwich as he admonished them.

Sarah gripped her cane and counted to five. "I'm happy for him. Now can we get back to the subject?"

"What subject would that be? Wild accusations?" The sheriff quirked one eyebrow at her. "You surely are an attractive woman when you're angry, Mrs. Kendrick."

She still had trouble getting used to being called Mrs. anything, much less Kendrick. Whit was a Yankee, for pity's sake, and a hardheaded, big-mouthed bully. Never mind she was half in love with him and one hundred percent in lust with him.

The big oaf had the audacity to wink at her. "She's not too shabby. I think I'll keep her."

Miller chuckled. "Lucky for you then. I expect more than one fella in this town would find a way to court her. Tall women make good breeders."

This time Sarah couldn't stop the cane. It came out from under the table and smacked the son of a bitch in the shin. He yelped and dropped the sandwich, ham flying every which way. Whit started choking or laughing, she wasn't sure which.

"Jesus, woman, what the hell are you doing?"

"Oh, Sheriff, I'm so sorry. I was just shifting positions and there must've been some grease on the floor. It slipped out of my hand. Are you all right?" She fluttered her lashes and leaned forward, giving him a bird's-eye view of her still-unbuttoned blouse. Those four buttons had bought her a lot of leverage in her lifetime.

"I'm glad it was an accident. I'd hate to have to arrest you for assault too." He spoke directly to her tits.

"Do you need a cool cloth? I'm sure Whitman would be happy to get one for you." She smiled at her "husband" and he smirked. It was amazing that two people who had known each other less than a week could communicate with only their eyes.

It sent a shiver of pure fear through her.

Sarah was all for self-preservation. She couldn't stop her instincts. They had saved her more than once. Her long-unused heart was battling with her oft-used senses.

No doubt it would be a bloody battle.

"I don't think I need one." Miller rubbed his shin. "That cane of yours surely is a weapon."

This time Whitman's gaze was as sharp as a knife. "Sarah didn't kill Mavis."

"Were you with her all night, Mr. Kendrick? Can you swear to her whereabouts?" Miller wiped his mouth on his sleeve, earning a frown from Sarah.

She couldn't abide people without table manners. Even if they were eating weevily hardtack, she always expected a sense of decorum at the table.

"Be careful how you answer that question, because I have a few folks who can place you at the Purple Posy." Miller stuck one finger in his mouth to pick at food stuck in his teeth.

Sarah wanted to smack him again.

"Obviously I can't swear to her whereabouts. You already know where I was for part of the evening." Whit met Sarah's gaze. "But I know she didn't kill Mavis."

Sarah could hardly believe what she was hearing. All her life she'd struggled to find someone whom she could put her trust in, who would have faith in her. And he turned out to be a stranger on a train.

"Thank you, Whit." Her voice was husky with unused emotion. "I think you mean that."

"I do."

"Touching, but none of that means a rat's piss in a court of law." Miller touched the brim of his hat in Sarah's direction. "Pardon my language, Mrs. Kendrick."

Sarah could see in his gaze he wasn't really apologizing. The sheriff seemed to think Sarah wasn't who she said she was. A dangerous thing, to be certain.

"Of course. I understand how men feel the need to cuss sometimes."

Dammit.

"Tell me if there is anyone who can verify where you were last night." Miller speared her with a piercing gaze.

Sarah, however, wasn't easily intimidated.

"I was alone in my room after I finished supper. I'm sure many folks saw me make my way down the hallway, including the desk clerk. After that, I read and went to bed." She didn't blink or back down from the lawman's stare.

He had no hard evidence to connect her to Mavis's death. Since he'd already kept the train in town an extra day, throwing off the entire schedule, he'd have to let them go in the morning.

Sarah was sure the railroad company was giving him a bit of leeway due to the murder, but there was no way it was going to give him two days. He couldn't keep dozens of people in custody for more than a day.

"I'd like to believe you, Mrs. Kendrick, but the evidence leads me to you." Miller stood up and looked between them, hands on his hips. "You are not cleared of this crime. The deputy from Belleville will be here by morning. If he says you two aren't the couple who beat him, then you can be on your way. If he says you are, then you'd best get used to my little town, because you're going to be looking at it for a good long time."

The sheriff tipped his hat as he left. Sarah wondered if the train trip was testing her brain, body, and heart. Because it was certainly doing a damn good job of it.

She met Whitman's gaze. "We've got less than eighteen hours to prove we're innocent."

"No, we've got less than eighteen hours to find a killer." He stood, grimacing. "Let's go hunting."

Whitman led Sarah to their room after asking for paper and pen from the desk clerk. They needed to sit down and record all they knew about Mavis and her death, particularly what they remembered about Abernathy.

"What are we going to do about the deputy from Belleville?" She touched the healing bruise on her cheek. "That bastard deserved what he did, but he's going to sink us like a lead weight. I don't plan on going to jail for a murder I didn't commit."

Whit snorted. "Let's concentrate on what we can do instead of what we have no control over."

"That's not helpful."

"I didn't say it was supposed to be. Now shut up and let's get busy." Whit opened the door and gestured for her to go in.

"It's a good thing I don't hate you," Sarah grumped as she walked in.

"Good for whom? I'm on the receiving end of that sharp tongue, you know."

Sunshine streamed in through the window, reflecting off the crystals dangling from the light on the dresser. Sarah turned to give Whit another cut from her sharp tongue, but the words deserted her.

He looked so tired, so worried, it made her want to comfort him.

What the hell was that all about?

Sarah didn't know what to do with the softer emotions, so she turned to what she did know. A physical release.

Whitman simply watched her as she hobbled over to him. Sarah was tall enough to reach his lips without standing on her toes, a good thing for a crippled woman.

His lips were unresponsive and a bit cool. She didn't let that stop her, though. They both needed to relax, to find a sense of peace, at least for a few minutes.

"Whit, let me in," she whispered against his neck.

"We can't do this, Sarah." He sounded pained and just a bit breathless.

"Why not? We're married, right?" She chuckled. "For all they know we're taking a nap."

He might be saying no, but his body was saying yes. She cupped his balls, noting the hard cock pressed against the buttons on his trousers. Whit couldn't deny there was something between them in the bedroom, or hotel room, as the case may be.

"It's not right." Whitman's voice had sunk to a hoarse whisper.

"It's perfect."

Any worries or concerns he might have had before they walked into the room flew away like dandelion fluff on a summer breeze. Now was her time with Whitman and she intended to capitalize on it.

After divesting him of his shirt, she unbuttoned her own and removed it in one swift movement. The cool air of the room contrasted with the heat of her skin, sending shivers down her body. His green eyes were nearly completely black as they dilated, drinking in the sight of her bare breasts.

"God, Sarah," he whispered as he reached out to cup them. As his calloused thumbs swept back and forth across her nipples, her knees grew weak and her drawers grew wetter.

"Whit, I . . ."

When his mouth closed over one nipple, Sarah lost all ability to even think. She just let herself feel. The roughness of his tongue, the scrape of his whiskers, and the jolt of his teeth on her sensitive skin heightened her senses. With fascination, she watched him lave and suckle her. His tongue was hot and wet and felt incredible. She wanted more.

Yes, this is what she needed.

His strong arms swept her up and he kissed her deeply as he walked toward the bed in the center of the room. He set her on the edge, his gaze hungry. She couldn't stop looking at his chest. It was covered with the same raven hair that spilled down his shoulders, wide with bronzed skin stretched over muscle and sinew. Scars dotted here and there on that beautiful skin. She reached out and traced them with her finger.

When she glanced into his eyes, she saw the acceptance in their depths.

She pulled off her skirt and drawers and lay down on the bed, her heart thumping like a drum in her chest. Let it never be said that Sarah was afraid to take what she wanted. Whitman shucked his pants faster than she could follow, and finally, finally, he was naked against her. Chest to chest, leg to leg, lips to lips.

His hands traveled up and down her body, touching and teasing, driving her to distraction. His cock was hard against her hip, teasing her with its hardness. His hand landed between her legs and began to caress her nubbin of pleasure until she was even wetter than before.

"Whitman."

She hadn't realized she'd said the name out loud until his mouth, mere centimeters from hers, tilted into a small smile before he kissed her. Slow, sweet kisses that nearly drowned her in their sensuality. Her nipples peaked against his chest, while a pulse thrummed through her. She wanted, needed, to touch him.

His tongue swept across her lips, hot and wet, wanting. She accepted the invitation and soon their mouths fused as one. And oh, holy shit, he was *hard*—granite hard—against her. Not just his chest and his arms, but his cock too. He slowly rotated against her belly, pushing his erection against her softness, just enough to heighten her arousal to near desperation.

"Now, Whit." She was surprised to hear her voice actually working, but damn it all, she needed him. Whit slowly climbed onto her and parted her legs. His body was warm, not hot. She felt every hair and callus on his body rub against her and she arched into him.

Inch by inch, he entered. They fit together like a key in a lock. *Snick.*

Stroke by stroke, he drove her insane, making her pant and beg for more. By the time he was settled deep inside, Sarah knew nothing would ever feel this perfect.

She rose to her peak too quickly, her body pulsing with the heat of a thousand suns. As the waves of ecstasy washed over her, she scratched at his back, holding in the word that threatened to escape in a shout.

The word would be Whitman.

* * *

Whitman pulled on his clothes and wondered how the hell he kept falling into bed with Sarah. She was beautiful, but he was engaged. Yet there he was again, his body weak, his dick wrung dry, and his conscience beating on him.

The afternoon sun had dropped, bathing the room in heat. He walked over to the basin, in need of a quick lukewarm wash.

Sarah lay on the bed watching him. Her silver gaze was almost as sharp as her tongue.

"Why are you watching me?" He poured the water in the pitcher and picked up the washrag.

"You're a fine specimen of a man, Kendrick. I'm admiring the view." Her playful tone annoyed him.

"We're not in a situation where we can be lounging around in bed fucking." The words rushed out of his mouth so fast he couldn't snatch them back.

"Ouch." She shifted to a sitting position, the sheets covering her bare breasts. He could still see the whisker burn on her neck.

Did he have no self-respect?

"You're throwing some daggers there, Yankee." She ran a hand through her hair. "There were two of us in this bed."

"I realize that." He lowered his voice, recognizing a loss of control yet again. "Let's try to focus on finding Mavis's killer instead of on how many different ways we can break my marriage vows before I speak them."

"So that's what this is about? Little Melissa?" She scoffed. "Her letters are so boring, anything you bring to your marriage bed will be like fireworks to the poor girl."

"That's it!" He swung around, rage spilling through his veins. "This isn't funny, Sarah. We could go to jail and you're taking potshots at my fiancée. I'm so tired of the sarcastic shit that spills from your mouth. Maybe I ought to just ride out of town and leave you to face what you've done."

She stood, the sheet falling from her shoulders. Her body

shook with what he could only assume was rage. "I was right about you."

He picked up his shirt and punched his arms through the sleeves. "I don't even care to hear what you were right about."

She limped toward him, looking like a warrior queen on the rampage. For just a moment, Whit remembered why he respected her and liked her. Then it was gone, swallowed by his self-pity and anger.

"Too bad, because you're going to hear about it anyway. You're a pompous, self-righteous prig who looks down his nose at the world. You think you're better than me because you won the war. Let me tell you, Yankee, you're not."

Sarah reached up to slap him but he stopped her arm.

"Don't you dare hit me."

"Don't you dare belittle me."

"Look who's talking." He shook her arm. "You think you know everything about me, but you don't."

"Same here."

Whitman knew she was right, but he was so tired of arguing, all he wanted to do was escape. Again.

As he headed for the door, her cane hooked around his leg, stopping him. "Let me go."

"Oh, no you don't. You're not running anymore, Kendrick. We are in this together, like it or not." She pulled him back an inch or two. "We're partners, whether or not we exercise the right to romp around in the sheets together. You're stuck with me and I'm stuck with you."

Whit felt so completely out of control, his body vibrated with an onslaught of emotion.

"You can be angry with me all you want, but don't blame this entire mess on me." Her voice got huskier as she spoke. "I did nothing to Mavis other than fire her. We need each other."

Much as he wanted to deny it, it was true.

"Fine, so let's figure out what happened so we can get the hell out of this town and out of each other's lives."

Sarah paused for a few moments before responding. "Agreed."

They had gone round and round the same circle since they'd met. Fighting, fucking, fighting, fucking. He realized part of the reason they fought so much was because they were so much alike. The other part of the reason was the undeniable attraction they felt for each other.

Neither the attraction nor their similarity was encouraging to him. He didn't want to like her or need her.

He refused to examine why.

Chapter Thirteen

"I'm sorry, I don't remember him." The freckled desk clerk shook his head. "I'm sorry, Miz Kendrick, I really am."

Sarah forced a small smile. "It's okay, Patrick. I'll just keep searching."

It seemed to be the same story no matter whom they spoke to. Nobody remembered the older man Mavis had cuddled up with on the train. Of course, once Mavis had left the compartment, Sarah had seen the other woman only a couple of times.

Abernathy could have slipped away after murdering Mavis. But he was an old man, wasn't he? He couldn't slip away too fast.

Sarah wanted to scream in frustration. The last four hours had gotten them nothing but dead ends and lost time.

Whitman had left to talk to the other passengers, leaving Sarah to stay at the hotel and do the same. However, she'd done nothing but get empty stares and blank looks.

Dammit to hell.

The conductor from the train stood near the door, watching her. Sarah decided to turn on the charm and find out what she could about the ten-year railroad man.

She walked over, emphasizing her limp, with a bright smile on her face. Fortunately, he didn't run, so she didn't have to trip him with her cane.

"Alfred Bannon, right?" She held out her hand. "Sarah Kendrick. It's nice to finally introduce myself. Will you join me for some coffee?"

He looked like a rat caught in a trap. She smiled wider.

"Well, uh, I'm not sure. I am to meet someone for dinner." He pulled a watch from the pocket in his vest, the chain glittering in the lamplight of the hotel lobby.

"Oh, it's at least an hour before dinner. Please join me." She took his arm, pleased to note the slight shaking beneath the chubby exterior.

"Mrs. Kendrick, I don't know if I should. The sheriff says you killed that woman."

Sarah feigned shock. "That's a horrible thing to say, Mr. Bannon. I am a good Southern woman with an impeccable reputation. I never thought you'd disparage me."

Oh, she was about knee-deep in the horseshit she shoveled at the man.

Bannon's jowls shook as his eyes widened. "Mrs. Kendrick, I would never do such a thing."

"But you just did. I was trying to be friendly-like and speak to you so you can see I'm not the evil woman you think me to be." She dabbed at her eyes with her sleeve. "I understand your reluctance. I won't bother you again."

Sarah extricated herself from his arm and did her best to walk away with her back straight in hurt resignation.

Of course, she was waiting for him to call her back. She didn't have to wait long.

"Mrs. Kendrick, please wait."

Apparently their suspicious train conductor had a conscience after all. Sarah hid her smile as she turned back.

Whitman was supposed to be speaking to the other passengers to find out who else had seen Mr. Abernathy. It seemed that the older man was their favorite subject; however, it also seemed the man had disappeared into thin air.

They were getting nowhere, and after hours of finding nothing, Whitman needed to relieve some of his stress. Back at the barracks—hell, even back in New York—he would've boxed. Nothing like a good fight to chase out the demons who were biting at his ass.

There were no boxing matches or a gym. And no place to find a good fight in this small Kentucky town except a saloon full of men who were armed. Probably not the best choice, considering he didn't know which one of them might pull a weapon on him.

He decided to run. Although he wanted to run from town, instead he just did circles around it in the fading afternoon sun. They were running out of time fast.

The only witness to his mad running were the animals inhabiting the brush around him. The more he ran, the more his blood pumped through him and the more his mistakes over the last week became bigger and bigger in his mind.

When he realized that Sarah was the woman Booker had likely crippled, he should have left the train right then and there. Whit couldn't help her. God, he couldn't even help himself.

He'd spent the last twenty-one years fighting a ghost, trying to be better than his father, make wiser choices, be a better person, a stronger person. After all, his father had left his family to marry a woman, like a coward, instead of facing down his own father.

He should have insisted on his family accepting the woman he loved. Instead he chose to become a pauper and live on a farm, scraping by. Whitman didn't want to make the same choice, ever.

In his third circle around the town, he felt a scream building somewhere near his feet. It traveled up through his knees, his legs, up to his stomach, which tightened as if he'd been punched. Then through his heart, which ached, and up to his throat until it exploded out of him.

It was a primal shout of fear, anger, self-pity, and yes, even love. He hadn't meant it to happen, certainly didn't want it, but somehow he'd fallen in love with Sarah Spalding.

When his lungs burned, his muscles screamed, and the sweat soaked his body and clothing, Whitman finally slowed down to a walk. He found a small creek outside town and splashed his face with the cool water.

By the time he reached the main street, he'd regained control, or at least enough to function. He'd been fighting what he already knew, but he realized he could never confess his love for Sarah or even take that step, or entertain the thought of making her his own.

He couldn't because that would mean he'd have to tell her who he really was, what he was, what he had been.

A Yankee soldier.

Whit was the enemy of all she held dear in her life. Even worse, he was the man who'd done nothing to save a young woman from the brutal hands of Sergeant Booker.

As he passed the Purple Posy, a young swarthy man stepped away from the building and walked toward him, hands in his pockets. He couldn't be older than twenty-one, a puppy in a world of dogs. Fresh faced and nary a scar on him, probably either inside or out.

The man fell into step beside Whit. "You are Mr. Kendrick?"

There was a hint of an accent in his voice, probably Italian.

Living in the Washington, D.C., area the last ten years since the war ended, Whit had occasion to run into people from all areas of the world.

"Who's asking?" No matter how young the other man was, Whit didn't trust him.

"No one, but I hear that you and your wife, well, are in trouble. I want to help."

Whit stopped in his tracks and turned to look at the young man. "You want to help us? Exactly why would you do that? You don't know me and I sure as hell don't know you."

"I know you did not hurt Miss Ledbetter, and your wife, her name is Sarah, no?"

Whitman scowled. "You're not being serious, are you? Were you on the train?"

"Your wife, please, her name is Sarah? She is your wife?"

As Whit looked into the young man's brown eyes, he saw the same demon he himself had been running from outside of town. He didn't know who the boy was, might never know who he was, but he felt a strange kinship with him.

"You know Sarah?"

The other man couldn't hide the recognition in his gaze. "Maybe, I might. Is she tall, with long hair kissed by the sunset, and silver eyes?"

Oh, for certain. The stranger had it bad for Sarah. But how? Was he a conquest who had followed her from Virginia? Whitman had been with her most of the journey, and other than the idiot desk clerk who got the carriage for them, she hadn't had an opportunity to be with another man.

At least that's what Whitman thought.

"How do you know her?" He took a fistful of the stranger's shirt. "Who the hell are you?"

"Please, who I am is not important. I just want to help you. I want to help Sarah." He tried to remove Whit's fist, but years of army training were on the older man's side.

"Then you're going to tell me who the hell you are, how you know Sarah, and why the hell you want to help us so badly." He shook the boy like the puppy he was.

"Okay, I'll tell you. Please let me go."

Whit set him back on his feet and stepped back. "So talk."

"My name is Lorenzo and I am Sarah's . . . friend from Appleton."

"Appleton? What the hell is that?" Whit pulled Lorenzo over to the entrance to the alley, where the sunlight streamed in as it meandered toward the horizon. Now he could get a good look at the boy's face and determine whether or not he was lying.

"A town in Virginia. It is where Sarah grew up."

Whit vaguely remembered the name of the town, and he did know she was from Virginia. At least it was a start with a kernel of truth. "Does she know you're following her?"

Although he wasn't a hundred percent sure, Whitman thought he saw Lorenzo's cheeks pinken.

"No, she does not know and I ask you not to tell her. She would be angry with me." Lorenzo put his hands together as if in prayer. "I beg you, Mr. Kendrick, don't tell her."

"Depends on how good the rest of your story is. Now talk." Whitman folded his arms and stared down at the boy with his best captain's glare.

Lorenzo began his tale. "Well, the morning Sarah left, I decided to follow her to be sure she arrived at the train safely."

Sarah sipped daintily at the tea and tried not to make a face. Lord, she hated hot tea almost as much as she hated Yankee soldiers. However, it was a close race.

What she really wanted was coffee, hot and black and strong. Her mouth almost watered with the idea. Then she took another sip of tea. He'd ordered it for her and she was being polite, way too polite.

To cover her grimace, she smiled at the conductor. "Ten years? That is a long time to work for the railroad. You must've been so young when you began."

Bannon smiled in return. "Not so young to not know what I was getting into. The railroad is a tough business, Mrs. Kendrick. There are hooligans everywhere trying to get a free ride." He shook his head.

She tutted in sympathy. "That must be very hard for you, Alfred. May I call you Alfred?"

This time he blushed, she was sure of it. "Why yes, of course you may."

"Thank you. Then please call me Sarah." She put on her most charming smile and lowered her lashes. The man preened like a rooster in a yard of hens.

"I will. Thank you, Sarah." He shoveled a biscuit in his mouth followed by a gulp of hot coffee before he even finished chewing.

Sarah's intolerance for bad table manners jumped up and down on her head screaming. She had all she could do to not admonish the man.

"Now, Alfred, I really do need your help. Sheriff Miller is determined to charge me with Miss Ledbetter's murder, but I didn't do it. You believe me, don't you?" She opened her eyes wide enough to make them sting, and right on cue, tears coated them.

"Wh-why yes, of course I believe you." His pudgy hand reached out to pat hers. "No one as genteel as a Southern belle such as yourself would ever commit such a heinous act."

Sarah dabbed at her eyes with a handkerchief. "Thank you, Alfred. Your faith in my innocence is most refreshing." She let out a dramatic sigh. "I only wish Sheriff Miller recognized my innocence as well."

"He's doing his job, I'm sure. There ain't many murders in this neck of the woods, especially of strangers from the train." Another biscuit, another gulp of coffee, another teeth-grinding minute.

"I'm sure that's completely true. This appears to be a lovely town with law-abiding citizens. I'm sure the most crimes he's had to deal with have been drunks and stray cows." She smiled again. "However, I want to be certain he investigates this crime appropriately. My husband is from New York City and he's skilled at such investigating. Do you think you could ask the sheriff to allow Whitman to assist him?"

She didn't know if half of what she said was true, but it sure sounded good.

"He's an investigator? That is something. I'm not sure I've met anyone from New York City before. Most trains depart right out of that Northern metropolis. I've been working the southern route all my career." A wistful expression came over

Alfred's face. "I've always wanted to try that northern route. It sounds glamorous."

Sarah had no idea what to make of the conductor's wish to be on the northern route of the railroad. His gaze had gone far away, leaving her to wonder what the hell he was dreaming about. Not that she really wanted to know.

"I'm sure it is. Now, may I ask one more favor of you, Alfred? I'd like to see the passenger manifest." She took a sip of tea while he digested her request. "I'm certain that man Mavis had met is the one who did her harm."

"Really? I thought perhaps you were looking for someone to blame the murder on." He slapped his hand over his mouth. "I didn't mean that."

"Of course you did, and that's all right. Everyone is entitled to their opinion, don't you think?" Her smile was growing tired, as was her patience. "Now, the passenger manifest will help me determine who that man was. I think perhaps his name wasn't even Abernathy."

Alfred's eyes widened. "You believe he traveled under a false name?"

Sarah jumped on the idea as it blossomed in her mind. "Yes, I surely do. I think the man knew exactly what he was doing. Maybe he even searches out spinsters or widows and charms them, and robs them."

"That would be a horrible thing to do." Alfred looked truly shocked.

Too bad the idea didn't even remotely shock Sarah. She'd become immune to the evils that men do.

"Absolutely despicable. Yet, the more I think of it, the more I believe I'm on the right track." Her annoyance at Alfred forgotten, Sarah focused on finding Abernathy. "He probably tried to rob Mavis, but she was as stubborn as a mule and probably refused to give her bag to him."

"Oh my."

"Yes, you're right, oh my." Sarah shook her head and

gulped down the rest of her tea. "Alfred, if you help me, you will be a hero and receive praise from the railroad for catching a killer. Maybe even get a northern route."

His face shone with pride at the notion. Sarah felt a little bad for manipulating his dreams, but hell, her life was on the line. They hung people for murder.

"Will you help me?"

He straightened his vest. "Yes, I will, Sarah. Now let's get that investigator husband of yours and get to work."

Sarah wanted to raise her fist and shout yes, but instead she gushed her gratitude. "Thank you so much, Alfred. You can't know what this means to me." She pushed her chair back. "Now let's go."

They'd ended up at the Purple Posy to talk. Whit almost grilled the boy. "You saw the man then, the one in the bow tie?" Whitman shifted the stool beneath him. "You're certain?"

Lorenzo nodded, twirling the empty sarsaparilla glass with his left hand. "Oh yes, I saw everything. He had a bowler hat, graying temples, and a brown suit with a polka-dot bow tie. He and Mavis were together almost every moment."

Whitman knew they were getting close to the truth, and for some reason, this young man had appeared to help them with that truth. Of course, according to Lorenzo, if Sarah found out he was there, she'd probably tan his hide.

That made Whit wonder exactly what their relationship was. Obviously Sarah was at least ten years older than the boy and had a great deal more experience.

Inside Whit, a green-eyed monster reared its ugly head and snarled.

Dammit to hell.

He didn't want to be jealous, not even a little bit, but apparently his heart had other ideas.

"Let's go back to the hotel. I want to talk to Sarah."

Lorenzo grabbed his arm. "No, please, Mr. Kendrick, she cannot know I'm here."

"Look, this isn't a game where you play hide-and-seek with your friends. If you want to help us—help Sarah—then you're going to have to stop this sneaking around."

Whitman stood up and looked down at the boy's desperate expression. "You tell me you are her friend, then act like one." He walked away, firmly expecting the boy to follow.

He wasn't disappointed.

Sarah walked Alfred back to her room to look for Whitman. She hoped the conductor didn't assume there was anything romantic or inappropriate about it. God knew she didn't need any more accusations leveled at her.

She opened the door and dropped her cane. Shock held her immobile as she saw two figures standing in the room. Alfred bumped into her back, nearly knocking her over.

"Sarah, what's the matter?" he asked.

She stared in disbelief at Whitman and Lorenzo. Her voice refused to work, probably because her throat had closed up.

Lorenzo squeezed his hat in his hands and kept his gaze on Sarah. The longing in his chocolate eyes was obvious to everyone around her, complicating the situation even more.

"What's going on?" She could hardly believe her eyes. What in the world was Lorenzo doing in Kentucky? In her hotel room with her supposed husband?

Her plan for proving herself innocent fell just as far as her heart. Lorenzo would expose the ruse of her marriage. There was no way Sheriff Miller or Alfred would believe a word she said.

"Who is that?" Alfred stepped around her, eyeing Lorenzo. "I remember him from the train. He was seated in the public car."

He'd been on the train? Sarah could hardly swallow that information. Lorenzo had followed her all the way from Virginia? Did he think she couldn't take care of herself? Disappointment, anger, and fear mixed together inside her gut and made her want to vomit.

"Whitman, what's happening?" She focused on his green eyes, hoping to find something to hang on to, a kernel of hope.

"This is Lorenzo Torreno. He's come to help us." He gestured to Lorenzo. "Apparently he saw the man we knew as Abernathy and he wants to help us catch the real killer."

Deep in Whitman's gaze, she saw what she needed. He told her without words that he knew who Lorenzo was, and why he was there. Yet his neck was in jeopardy too, and the young man's assistance could clear both of them of a murder charge.

She wondered if Whit knew Lorenzo was in love with her.

"That's wonderful, young man." Alfred relieved her of the duty of actually speaking for a moment or two. "Your help is greatly appreciated. Sar—that is, Mrs. Kendrick and I came up with a theory."

Whitman's eyebrows shot up. "Did you now? I can't wait to hear it."

With Sarah's heart thumping, her gut churning, and her mouth as dry as the cotton she grew up with, they sat down and spoke of everything they'd seen.

They were a strange group of four, but she fervently hoped they'd be able to solve Mavis's murder, come hell or high water.

Chapter Fourteen

Alfred, true to his word, brought the passenger manifest to their room. Whitman couldn't quite accept the fact the portly conductor was helping them out of the goodness of his heart. There had to be a gain for him.

Whit sure as hell hoped it wasn't a night in Sarah's bed, or he might have to knock the man into next week.

When did he get so emotionally out of control? He could hardly focus on what they were saying as he sat between the young man who loved her and the fat man who wanted her.

Whit was the man who had her, but couldn't keep her.

Sarah and her bevy of men.

He almost snorted at the thought. She didn't realize how much being in the room with all of them nearly drove him to run again. Sarah leaned in close at the page he was currently reading.

"I don't see an Abernathy. You were right, Lorenzo. He didn't travel under his own name." She stopped and sniffed, then narrowed her gaze at Whitman. "What is that smell?"

The sweat from his late afternoon run through the lonely countryside had obviously dried on him, leaving behind an odor she didn't take kindly to.

"I was getting rid of some anger," he offered lamely.

"Doing what?" She apparently wasn't going to give up.

"Running. I ran around until I almost passed out. I'm

going crazy here, Sarah. We're fighting for our lives." He didn't mean to snap at her, but it came out that way anyway. "I'm sorry."

Whitman stood up and ran his hand through his hair, his fingers tangling in the remnants of his crazy run. "If you'll all give me five minutes, I'll wash up and change."

His hand landed on the first button of his shirt and her gaze locked in on the movement. A pulse thumped between them and Whit knew she felt every second of the arousal as much as he did. They were connected.

"Why don't we go to the dining room and use one of the tables?" Alfred was surprisingly helpful. "That way we can give Mr. Kendrick some privacy."

The conductor and Lorenzo gathered up the manifest and walked out the hotel room door. Sarah, as she always did, rose slowly until she gained her balance.

Her silver gaze collided with Whit's as she limped toward him. "You are a helluva good-looking man, Kendrick." She pulled him down by his hair for a fierce, soul-stealing kiss.

Her tongue danced and tangled with his, pulling him into the whirlpool of sensuality he had tried to escape. His arms closed around her, bringing her flush against his aching staff. She yanked at his hair, again, as she pushed her hard nipples into his chest.

Whit saw a movement at the door. Recognizing a full-size shadow, he realized it was Lorenzo.

He broke the kiss and pressed his forehead against hers. "We've got company," he whispered.

"Lorenzo?" Her voice told him she already knew the answer.

"I think so." He steadied her on her feet, then kissed her softly. "You'd better go before we start something we can't finish."

In her gaze, he saw something he didn't want to see and wasn't ready to accept. Instead of acknowledging the emotions, he turned away.

"I'll be there in five minutes."

The silence between them was as awkward as it had been the first day on the train, only a week earlier, but it felt like a lifetime ago.

"Fine. We'll be waiting." She shuffled out, closing the door softly behind her.

Whit heard the murmur of voices and knew Lorenzo had been waiting for her. Perhaps in another lifetime, Whit would be the right person to marry Sarah in reality and she would be Mrs. Kendrick.

For now, the marriage was as much of a lie as his denial of how he truly felt about Sarah Spalding.

Sarah allowed Lorenzo to walk her to the dining room, her mind and body whirling with a thousand different emotions. She'd seen the truth in Whitman's face and he'd pushed her away.

Another rejection.

Another reason to never trust a Yankee.

Sarah wasn't a woman to allow her heart to open to anyone, much less a Northerner like Whitman. Yet she had, almost against her will. And when she had finally allowed him to see how she felt, he had turned away from her.

She almost choked on the tears that threatened. Sarah simply didn't cry, especially over a man.

Lorenzo squeezed her arm. "You love him, Sarah?"

She shook her head, even as her heart screamed yes. "There's no future there, Lorenzo. He's a Yankee. Couldn't you tell? Besides, he's got a fiancée waiting in Kansas City."

"For true? Oh, that is wonderful." Lorenzo's demeanor changed from sad resignation to hopeful jubilation. "You did not marry him then?"

Sarah considered her answer before speaking. "Oh, I married him. He's my husband just as sure as the sun will rise tomorrow."

What she didn't say was the marriage wasn't legal. It was

one of raw emotion, sensuality, and souls. Whit might not want to acknowledge it, but they were joined as one.

"And the fiancée? What of her?" Lorenzo's jubilance had melted back to melancholy. He was such a dramatic person.

"I don't know, Lorenzo, and honestly, I don't want to talk about it. Let's just get this investigation over with so the train can leave tomorrow morning with us on it." She walked the rest of the way to the dining room without speaking.

Lorenzo, smart man that he was, stopped talking too.

It gave Sarah a chance to slow her racing heart and put the steel back in her spine.

Alfred waited for them at one of the larger tables with the manifest spread out in front of him. There were ten pages in all, with approximately ten to twelve passengers on each page. Since there were multiple stops along the way, passengers came and went each day.

Their task was to find the man who boarded in Virginia alone and stayed on the train. A needle in a proverbial haystack, but Sarah was determined to find him.

"I've ordered some coffee." Alfred glanced up at them. "I wasn't sure if you needed tea as well, Sarah."

"No, coffee will be fine." She couldn't stomach another cup of tea, no matter what Alfred thought of her.

"Oh, that's lovely. I like a woman who drinks a man's drink." He smiled at her.

She wanted to punch him.

"Let's get started then." Lorenzo saved her from committing an act of violence.

She sometimes wondered if she'd ever be normal enough not to want to hurt people. Honestly, she doubted it, but it was a good goal to try to attain.

Whitman arrived a few minutes later, the scent of his freshly scrubbed skin like ambrosia. Sarah attempted not to smell him, just as she tried to avoid remembering just how delicious that skin tasted.

"How are we doing?" he asked as he sat down.

"We're making a list of male passengers who boarded the train in Virginia and continued on the train through Kentucky." Alfred had a paper and pen to his right. "We can then interview them one at a time. They should all be in this hotel."

"Sounds good, but how do we know if they are traveling alone or with someone?" Whitman picked up a page and started reading.

"We don't until we talk to them. That will give us the opportunity to not only get a good look at them, but figure out if they are alone or not." Sarah didn't meet his gaze, simply because she couldn't.

Whitman was too dangerous for her heart.

They worked through the rest of the afternoon until the dinner hour. By the time folks began arriving for dinner, they had a list of twenty-four men after eliminating Lorenzo and Whitman. None of them was named Abernathy, but they'd come to the conclusion he had given them a false name.

"Now what do we do?" Lorenzo looked as determined as any young man with love in his heart.

"We find them by splitting up into two teams. We can cover more ground that way." For a moment there, Whitman sounded like a soldier giving an order to his troops.

Sarah speared him with a gaze. "You want to try that again? This time without the pompous order?"

He looked away. "Sorry about that. Old habits die hard. Why don't Lorenzo and I start in the dining room, and you and Mr. Bannon can speak to the desk clerk. Does that sound good?"

Sarah nodded tightly. "Sounds just fine to me." She rose and held out her arm. "Alfred?"

The portly conductor scrambled to his feet and gathered the passenger manifest with one of the copies of the list of potential suspects, then handed the other copy to Whit. "I am ready, Sarah. Let's catch us a killer."

As she walked off on the man's arm, she felt two pairs of eyes burning into her back. The boy who wanted to make her his and the man who didn't want her.

In her own way, she loved them both.

Whitman ground his teeth together at Sarah's dismissal. She was obviously angry with him, and rightly so. He'd treated her as if she were no longer welcome in his arms.

Nothing could be further from the truth, but it was the necessity of survival. For both of them.

Lorenzo gazed at her retreating back like the puppy he was, the love and longing so poignant, Whit had to turn away. He couldn't handle anyone else's emotional issues since he could barely handle his own.

"Let's start talking to people." He stalked toward the first table with the list in his hand. They had to find Abernathy, or whoever killed Mavis, so he could escape.

His sanity depended on it.

The evening progressed slowly, although by the time Whitman had spoken to every man in the dining room, he'd eliminated ten names from the list. That was a good start.

He and Lorenzo walked out to the lobby, but Sarah and the conductor weren't at the hotel's front desk. The freckle-faced clerk was gone, and in his place was a white-haired old man with wire-rimmed glasses.

"Excuse me, have you seen Mr. Bannon and Mrs. Kendrick?"

The old man looked up at him. "You Mr. Kendrick?"

"I am." Whit wondered why the other man felt it necessary to ignore common courtesy.

"I'm Gunderson, owner of the hotel. I sent Patrick back to my office with your wife and Mr. Bannon. The hotel register is back there." He curled his lip. "I doubt you're going to find someone to blame your crimes on, though. My guests are not murderers."

Whit's hands clenched into fists, but before he could think

about teaching the man a lesson, Lorenzo lunged for Gunderson. Whit grabbed the boy's collar, stopping him short.

"No need to waste your energy on Gunderson, Lorenzo. He'd no doubt have you arrested if you lay a finger on him." Whit was surprised how strong Lorenzo was. Love must've turned him into a raging bull, a feeling Whit knew all too well. "Will you tell me where your office is?"

Gunderson looked between them, his lips compressed tightly. "In the back, behind the desk. But I don't think all four of you need to be in there. My grandson can help but I refuse to allow him to face four of you at once."

Whitman had to restrain himself this time. What was it about people in this town? Why was everyone so suspicious of strangers?

"Fine then, we'll wait here. With you." Whit conjured up his sternest scowl. "I'm sure you won't mind."

Gunderson looked like he wanted to smack Whitman with something, preferably hard.

"Of course I don't mind. Don't block the desk, though. I do have customers to think of." He pointed toward two hard-backed chairs by the door. "You can wait there."

Whitman growled under his breath, earning a startled glance from Gunderson. Lorenzo grinned at Whit. "Fine. We'll wait over here."

The chairs, of course, were as uncomfortable as he expected, but he wasn't about to give the hotel owner the satisfaction of seeing his discomfort. After all, Whit was a trained soldier, not the pampered aristocrat everyone assumed he was.

He folded his arms and leveled a stare at the front desk, making sure Gunderson didn't forget whom he had just insulted.

Whit hoped they didn't have to wait long.

"Whitman, I remember something." Lorenzo startled him by jumping off the chair ten minutes into their wait.

"What did you remember?" Whit shifted on the seat, easing the pressure of the hard wood.

"In Belleville, I remember seeing the man with the bow tie. He talked to the man who attacked Sarah."

Whitman tried to absorb what Lorenzo said. "Are you telling me Abernathy talked to that dirty son of a bitch who hurt Sarah?"

Lorenzo nodded. "Yes, yes, I saw them talking outside the depot, a few minutes before Sarah appeared." He held up his hands. "I never saw her move that fast before."

"You can talk to Sarah about that later. Tell me exactly what you saw." Whitman wanted to shake the boy for not remembering earlier, but he didn't. Lorenzo might have found the key to figuring out what had happened to Abernathy.

Lorenzo sat down and pursed his lips, looking up as he apparently reviewed the memory in his mind. "I was around the corner, trying to figure out what had happened to Sarah. She'd missed the train that morning."

"Yes, I know. That was Mavis's fault. Continue." Whit fell so easily into his captain's voice. He needed to be careful.

"I saw movement in the depot and realized you were in there with Sarah. I was relieved and happy to see her. Two men were standing in the shadows, talking. The older man with the bow tie gave the dirty man something, but I couldn't see what." Lorenzo looked excited. "Then the man with the bow tie got on the train and Miss Ledbetter walked toward him, calling his name, I think."

Whitman couldn't believe he'd missed the connection. Abernathy must have known Mavis had already gotten rid of Sarah once. When he'd seen her in the depot, he had likely paid the sheriff to keep her in town.

It all made sense, but Whit still didn't understand why. Mavis had no money as far as he knew, but perhaps he was wrong. Maybe the older woman had saved every penny, enough to attract an old wolf to darken her door.

"So why was Sarah moving so fast? And how?" Lorenzo's questions pulled Whitman out of his thoughts.

"Talk to her about that, boy. I'm out to catch a murderer." Whit stood, determined to get past Gunderson to talk to Sarah. He had to find out exactly what kind of money or property Mavis owned.

That was the key to solving the mystery. He was sure of it.

Sarah compared the list with the hotel registry and found that fourteen of the men had checked in with wives. That left ten of them who could still be suspects.

Patrick was a sweet young man who was eager to help them solve the mystery. He was apparently an avid reader of mysteries and loved detective work.

She had more men than she needed, or knew what to do with. A first for the tough wench from the Spalding Plantation.

"Take a look at the list of ten men, Alfred. Do you recognize any of the names?" She peered at the list, hoping something would jump out at her.

"No, I'm afraid I don't. Perhaps your husband and Mr. Torreno have eliminated more names from the list. We can then narrow down the pool of suspects." Alfred stood and grinned down at her. "I don't remember when I've had so much fun."

Sarah had started out wanting to use the conductor for her own means, at any cost, in any way possible. Yet here he was, helping her save her neck and having fun at it. She felt a bit guilty, but Alfred was enjoying himself, a side effect she hadn't expected.

Sarah realized she held herself above most people, or at least outside of the same existence as them. There was never a time when she allowed herself to step out of that odd relationship she had with the rest of the world.

She was startled to realize she'd done it countless times on this trip.

"Sarah?" Alfred held out his hand. "Are you all right?"

She thought about how to answer, how to explain to him that she'd been turned inside out, upside down, and backward by her grand adventure on a cross-country train. Instead, she chose the simple route, and a half-truth.

"Yes, I think so. Let's go find Whitman." She accepted his help to stand, then smiled at Patrick. "You've been amazingly helpful. I can't thank you enough."

The freckle-faced young man smiled back. "Happy to help, Miz Kendrick. I hope you find him."

Together she and Alfred walked back to the lobby. Apparently just in time to prevent Whitman from pummeling Patrick's grandfather. The old man was a curmudgeon, to be certain, and had taken some hearty convincing to allow them to compare their list to the hotel register.

In the end, he had insisted only Patrick view the register, while Sarah called the names out to him.

"What's happening?" She hobbled as fast as she could toward them. "Are you all right?"

Whitman dropped his raised fist and stared at her. He blinked once and seemed to be unable to speak.

She touched his cheek. "Whit?"

He shook his head as if to clear it and stepped out of her reach. "Yes, I'm fine. Gunderson was just about to see the error of his ways when you arrived." He scowled at the hotel owner. "You're a lucky man."

Sarah took Whit's arm and led him away from the desk. "Are you trying to get put in jail for punching that old windbag? Believe me, he isn't worth it."

"What did you find out?" he asked through clenched teeth.

"We narrowed the list down to ten names. Let's go sit down and eat and compare them." She led him toward the dining room, Lorenzo and Alfred behind them.

Beneath her fingers, the muscles in his arm felt as tight as guitar strings. She'd never seen him so out of control, and it worried her although it shouldn't. As she'd told him before, they were adults and made grown-up decisions, accepting the consequences as they came.

The consequence of falling in love with a Yankee, however, would cost her dearly.

Supper turned out to be a wonderful meatloaf with mashed potatoes and fried squash. The good Southern cooking was exactly what Sarah needed. It made her think of home, which led her to think of Lorenzo. He was a sad-faced young man across the table from her.

She refused to get pulled into his fantasy of making her his woman. There were several reasons why they couldn't, not the least of which was a huge age difference and the fact she didn't, and wouldn't ever, love him.

Alfred took on the task of comparing the two lists, surprising Sarah. He was definitely a man who enjoyed food, yet he'd set aside his hunger to do work.

Sarah wondered if it was to help them or to satisfy his own curiosity. Either way, she was grateful. The nightmare of Mavis's murder investigation was peppered with the bright lights of a few people in town who believed their innocence.

"How does it look, Bannon?" Whit speared a forkful of mashed potatoes and chewed without taking his gaze from Alfred's bent form.

"So far, we're down to six men, and I'm not quite finished." He shot a small grin at Sarah. "I think we'll be able to give Sheriff Miller a short list of suspects to interrogate."

"Good." Sarah didn't add she thought the sheriff would need a short list. His investigative skills were obviously lacking.

"How are you eliminating the men from the list?" Whit kept chewing mechanically, not meeting Sarah's gaze.

"Ones who are traveling with wives, or those who didn't board the train until after the initial departure in Virginia, and any men under the age of thirty." Alfred pushed the hair from his forehead. "I believe we now have four suspects on this list."

Whit held out his hand and Alfred gave him the list. "Four? Really? That's incredible." For the first time that afternoon, Whit sounded almost normal.

"It's good detective work," Alfred preened.

"Thank you, Alfred." Sarah was truly grateful for his help, and for Patrick's and Lorenzo's. Alfred and Patrick didn't have any reason to assist them, but they did anyway.

Whit peered at the list as Alfred dug into his supper. Sarah wanted to snatch the paper out of her "husband's" hand, but thought it better not to, considering his odd behavior.

She didn't want to have to whack him with the cane to get the list either.

They ate in silence as Whitman apparently read the list about a hundred times. Sarah's patience was beginning to wear thin when Sheriff Miller appeared at the table.

"Well, this is a cozy group." He nodded at Alfred. "Bannon, I'm surprised to see you here with the Kendricks and, uh, this foreigner."

"We've been investigating Miss Ledbetter's murder." Alfred apparently couldn't keep his mouth shut about how excited he was to be a detective, at least for a day.

"That so? And how are you doing that?" Miller grabbed a chair from another table and sat down, straddling the seat and leaning on the back.

"Well, you see Mr. Torreno witnessed the man Mrs. Kendrick identified as Abernathy. We determined he had nefarious purposes for befriending Miss Ledbetter." He pointed at the list in Whitman's hands. "With the passenger manifest and the hotel register, we've narrowed down the suspects to four men."

Miller's face grew redder the longer Alfred spoke. While the conductor was excited to display his cranial power for the sheriff to see, the idea he'd been doing the sheriff's job apparently hadn't occurred to him.

"I suppose you're going to explain how and why you decided to investigate a murder in my jurisdiction?" The handsome sheriff speared Alfred with his sharp gaze.

Alfred sputtered and looked at Sarah. "I was helping the investigation, not taking it over, Sam. The fact is, I believed Miss Sarah when she said she was innocent. I thought it was my duty as an employee of the railroad to ferret out the murderer."

Sarah was proud of the portly conductor. He had stood up to a bully like Miller and spoke his piece.

"You believe she's innocent? What about her Yankee soldier husband?"

Sarah's blood froze in her veins. "What are you talking about, Sheriff? My husband is a banker from New York, not a soldier."

Her heart pounded so hard, her ears hurt. Yet when her gaze met Whitman's, it nearly stopped. In his green gaze, she saw the truth.

He *was* a Yankee soldier.

Chapter Fifteen

"Why, I don't believe it." Alfred Bannon looked as surprised as Lorenzo.

Sarah, however, looked as if Whitman had driven a knife in her heart. He had dreaded the day she would find out the secret he'd been hiding from her. Of course, she didn't know the other half of that particularly nasty secret.

Her face drained of color, and her freckles stood out on the pasty white skin. Her eyes, however, were the worst part. Sarah was completely and utterly in shock. Her mouth opened and closed, but she didn't speak. Then she looked away.

Whitman's heart stopped beating for a moment as her emotions hit him square between the eyes. He tried to catch Sarah's gaze, but after the initial look of shock and hurt, she didn't look in his direction again.

"You married a Yankee soldier and it don't bother you, a Southern gal such as yourself?" Miller peered at Sarah, earning a growl from Lorenzo.

"Do not be mean to Miss Sarah. She does not lie to you." Lorenzo needed to work on his intimidation tactics.

"Look, all of you, my job is to find out who killed that poor woman out behind the hotel. I appreciate your help— well, actually no, I don't—but that's beside the point." He pointed at Alfred. "You hand over that list and I'll take it from here. I am an elected lawman."

Sarah touched his arm. Her voice was hoarse and full of emotion. "Then find that man before he hurts someone else."

Somehow she'd find the right thing to say to the prickly lawman.

He looked into her eyes and nodded. "I'm not sure how you do it, Miz Kendrick, but you have a way of making folks believe you." He held up the paper. "I'll track down these four and bring them to the jail. You all meet me there in an hour."

Sarah rose with painful dignity and nodded to Alfred. "Mr. Torreno, please escort me to my room."

Whit felt the impact of her request all the way to his heart. She'd asked Lorenzo, the boy puppy who'd followed her scent from Virginia, to help her. Not Whitman. Not her supposed husband.

It was like a knife, even if it didn't have a physical shape. It sure as hell cut like one.

Miller speared him with one of his intimidating gazes. "If you promise to behave yourself, you can come with me."

Whitman was surprised by the offer. "What about your deputy?"

"He's taking care of a ruckus down at the Posy. He'll be along in a while. Meantime, why don't you use some of that bulk to find the man you say killed Miss Ledbetter." The sheriff's challenge was enough to make Whitman get to his feet, ready for battle.

If he could do nothing to heal the hurt he'd inflicted on Sarah, he could at least try to clear her name of the false murder charge. It wouldn't even begin to undo the lies he'd told her to conceal his army background, but he would do what he could. No matter what or who stood in the way.

"Let's go hunting." His grin was positively feral.

Sarah held her back straight and her head high as she walked to the hotel room. Their room, the one that held the bed she'd shared with a Yankee soldier.

Her stomach twisted into a knot so tight, bile coated the back of her throat. Since Whit hadn't denied the accusation, it meant the sheriff had been correct.

Whitman Kendrick was a Yankee soldier, the very epitome of all she hated.

The reason she was crippled.

The reason she could never escape her self-made prison.

The reason Sarah had grown into a bitter old spinster.

The reason her life had been ruined.

Lorenzo, bless his heart, held on to her arm as she stumbled near the end of the hallway. He'd been a steady presence in her life for seven years, since he was a scrawny teenager with a penchant for stealing.

Now she had to rely on him like an anchor in a sea of misery, confusion, and betrayal.

The more she thought about Whitman, the more she realized he had shown her the signs of his military background, but she'd refused to see it. Involuntarily or not.

His haircut was too short for the style of the day. The way he carried himself with that back ramrod straight and his shoulders squared spoke to training.

Hell, he probably was the right age to have fought in the Civil War.

That thought made the vomit rush up her throat, and she barely made it into the room before she dropped to her knees with a painful crash.

Tears mixed with regret as her heart broke into a thousand pieces on the floor of that hotel room.

Lorenzo was there to clean up her mess and comfort her as she cried for everything she'd lost, everything that had been taken from her, and everything she'd never have.

Sarah had finally allowed herself to grieve, and instead of grieving for the life she'd lost so long ago, she grieved for the life she couldn't have with the man she loved.

The Yankee soldier who'd run away with her heart and left her with nothing but ashes.

*   *   *

Whitman stood next to the very sheriff who wanted to convict Sarah of murder as they tracked down the four men on the list. Three of them were found easily, in either the dining room or their hotel rooms, and none of them even resembled Abernathy.

The fourth name on that list, Ethan Rebay, had to be the man they sought. The problem was, they couldn't find him.

After determining the man was not in the hotel, Miller suggested going back to the jail to meet everyone. It seemed the sheriff was beginning to believe someone else was responsible for Mavis's death.

A blessing and a curse.

When the case was solved, Sarah would be absolved of the crime.

When the case was solved, she could ride away on the train and leave him forever.

Whitman needed to talk to her, desperately needed to talk to her, but he'd be lucky if she even acknowledged his presence again.

As much as his heart ached, his head told him it was for the best. Sarah was the wrong woman for him in many ways. He already had a fiancée waiting for him in Kansas City. His life was going to begin anew in San Francisco.

The best ending for all of them was to have Whitman and Sarah go their separate ways for good.

Too bad his heart howled against the possibility.

Whit was not the type of man to be led by his emotions, but Sarah had knocked him out of that box he'd lived in and trampled him in the dirt. Somewhere along the way he'd fallen in love with her.

The very rawness of his reaction to the thought confirmed what he suspected. He and Sarah were polar opposites, yet they'd found the other half of their souls within each other.

And Whitman's past mixed with Sarah's had ripped them apart, painfully and irrevocably.

Whit rubbed his eyes, wiping away the stinging from the dust on the street. After all, there was no way a tough old soldier would cry over a woman.

It took Sarah half an hour to get off the floor, and another fifteen minutes to stop crying. Lorenzo tried his best to comfort her, but if she was honest with herself, she didn't need comforting.

She needed Whitman, but would never, ever have him.

He'd destroyed the trust and faith Sarah had in him by lying to her. There was no chance she'd forgive him for that.

Lorenzo handed her a cool cloth. "Wipe your eyes, *amore*. They are puffy."

"You know, flattery is not your strong suit." She pressed her face into the rag, grateful for its cold roughness. Her face felt hot and tight.

"I'm sorry. I'm only trying to help." He squatted next to her, alternately wringing his hands and peering at her.

"I know," she said through the cloth. "And I appreciate it, truly I do. You and I need to have a talk soon, about why and how you followed me, but for now, I just want to get through this evening."

Silence met her words, and when she looked at him, he'd pulled a few feet away, sadness filling his brown eyes.

"You know, Lorenzo, I used to think that was cute. The puppy-dog expression you wore around me. No matter what I did, I couldn't shake you. You were like a cocklebur on my back." She grew stronger as she spoke, recognizing the poor boy was about to feel the full wrath of her emotional agony. "Now you show up after not staying behind like I told you to, and you give me that same stupid look."

She tried to stand, but her legs had stiffened as she lay on the floor. Lorenzo helped her up without a word, further driving the nail of guilt into her heart.

"You are a good man, a young man who has no business being in love with a crippled mess like me. Find a young woman to marry and make babies with, but please, for God's sake, don't love me anymore." She picked up her brush and tried to comb out the snarls. The action made her eyes tear up yet again.

"I can't stop it, *amore*. You are my heart." Lorenzo got down on one knee. "I would have married you, Sarah, if I had known you wanted a husband."

She threw the brush at him, catching him in the forehead. "You stupid fool. I didn't want a husband. I wanted a new beginning to my life, but it seems I can't get away from my past, not from you and not from Yankee soldiers. I'm trapped, dammit. Do you hear me? I can't get out of this dark hole."

Sarah grabbed her cane and left the room, ignoring Lorenzo's protest and the pain shooting down her leg. It was no worse than the sheer agony in her heart.

Whitman paced the jail, checking outside every two minutes to see if Sarah was coming. He should have been there to help her, or carry her if need be. Walking could be dangerous for a woman crippled by damaged legs.

He looked outside yet again when Miller yelled at him.

"Jesus Christ, man, are you that henpecked?! I know she's a strong-willed woman, but hell, man, don't you have a pair of balls?"

Whitman wanted to let out a laugh, but it stuck in his throat. "In case you hadn't noticed, Sarah is crippled. A walk down the street isn't easy for her. I'm worried, not henpecked."

Miller snorted from behind his desk. "Coulda fooled me."

"Now let's not argue anymore, gentlemen," Alfred piped up from his perch in the corner on a rather ancient-looking wingback chair. "We're working together, remember?"

Whit ignored them, although what he wanted to do was knock the sheriff into next week. No one understood what he was going through except Sarah, and she wasn't even speaking to him.

He'd made an enormous mess of things and damned if he had any idea how to fix it. Fixing things had become his habit. He fixed everything he laid his hands on, or at least he thought he did.

His mother's stubborn refusal to speak to her family again hadn't been fixed by moving her to a farm in Maryland. In fact, it had done nothing but cause the rift between them to grow wider.

Maybe Whitman's skill at fixing things was limited to areas that didn't involve women. God knew he needed help in that area.

The door to the jail opened and Lorenzo stood there, alone. He glanced around at the three men. "Where is Sarah?"

Whit's heart dropped to his knees. "What do you mean, where's Sarah? I left her in your care, Torreno." He had the boy in his grasp in seconds. "If anything happened to her, I'm going to hold you personally responsible. Do you understand me?"

Miller appeared between them. "Now, Kendrick, don't hurt the boy. He's an innocent bystander."

Innocent? Not hardly. The man had lived in Sarah's boardinghouse. There was no way he was innocent.

Whitman let him down and stepped back a pace. "What happened?"

Lorenzo looked panicked. "She left the room five minutes before me. I-I was washing up, and when I left the room, she'd already gone."

Whit didn't believe for even a moment the boy had been washing up, but he did believe Sarah left five minutes earlier.

"Was she headed to the jail?"

"Yes, she was. Sarah is very angry and I tried to comfort her, but she does not want my comfort. She only wants you, you stupid Yankee bastard." Lorenzo might not have been fully grown, but his punch packed a wallop.

Whitman fell to his knees, his ears ringing and the coppery taste of blood coating his tongue. Miller did his job and restrained the boy, although what they probably needed was to just get the fight over with.

Later that would happen, after they found Sarah.

Whitman spat out a mouthful of blood and rose to his feet. "You and I have some unfinished business, Lorenzo. Right now, we're going to find Sarah. Then I'll either beat the tar out of you or kill you. The choice depends on whether or not Sarah is unharmed."

He nodded to the sheriff. "I'd say Abernathy, or Ethan Rebay, caught wind of our investigation and decided to take some leverage to ensure he could get out of town safely."

Miller nodded tightly. "I'm guessing you're right, Kendrick."

"Ethan Rebay!" Alfred stood, snapping his fingers. "That's it. Don't you get it? Ethan Rebay is the letters of Abernathy mixed up."

Whitman wanted to slap his own forehead. Of course it was. The man had left it right there for them to find and they'd missed it. Sarah might have to pay the price for their male stupidity. He made a promise to himself to never let her down again.

"Let's go find her then, and Ethan Rebay will regret the day he touched my wife."

Sarah should have expected the attack, but she was so involved in her self-pity, she wasn't on alert. A pair of arms grabbed her from the alley next to the hotel.

The man was strong enough to steal the breath from her, but not her will to fight. She tried to bring the cane up and hit him, but he kicked it out of the way, leaving her without her weapon.

"Son of a bitch!" Sarah threw her head back to break his nose, but he was ready for that too, moving out of the way. The only thing she got from it was a sore neck and a bump on her head from slamming into his shoulder.

"You'd best stop fighting, Mrs. Kendrick, or should I say Miss Spalding?" he hissed in her ear. "I know your secret, you know. Mavis was a talkative woman and she loved to spread gossip."

Without the protection of their fake marriage, both Sarah and Whitman were open for target practice by Sam Miller. She yanked at his arm.

"Let me go and we can talk." She struggled to stay on her feet as he dragged her into the alley.

The image of Mavis's bloody body raced through her mind and she fought against the panic that rose. She wouldn't end up a rusty stain in the dirt. Sarah was too strong for that.

"Sure we can talk. I'm going to leave town and you're going to help me." He pushed her up against the building. In the gloom of the meager light, she couldn't make out his face, but the voice was familiar.

It was definitely Abernathy.

"I remember you from the first day of the trip, you know." She fought back her fear and concentrated on surviving. "I showed hospitality to you and invited you to ride in my compartment. This is how you repay that?"

"As you know, Miss Spalding, time changes us all, as does the human need for survival." His voice had a Southern drawl, probably Georgia if she wasn't mistaken.

"Were you in the war, Abernathy? I know you're a Southerner. Why do you want to hurt me?" She tried desperately to get a good look at him.

He chuckled. "The war is over and so is the Southern way of life. I'm taking what I learned from those damn carpetbaggers and using it for my own gain."

Sarah hated carpetbaggers almost as much as Yankee soldiers. "I realize Mavis was as annoying as the day is long, but did you have to kill her?"

"Oh no, you're not getting a confession that easily. Now let's go. We're taking a buggy ride." He flipped her around, pressing her face into the wood building. Splinters lodged in her cheek even as her legs screamed in protest at the rough movement.

"You're not going to be trouble, are you, whore?" His hot breath gushed past her ear. "I heard about your boarding-house. Maybe you can show me some of your tricks. I hear you can suck a dick like nobody's business."

He pulled her arms up behind her back, then put his other arm around her neck and squeezed.

Sarah wanted to kill him. No, she made a promise she would kill him.

He dragged her down to the other side of the alley. Her heels dug into the ground, sending painful shocks up to her already aching legs. She tried to regain her footing, but he was walking too fast.

For the first time in a very long time, she wished someone was around to rescue her. No doubt one or both of them would be dead before the night was over.

Chapter Sixteen

Whitman was frantic. He'd never believed that particular emotion would overcome him, but it had. Right after they found evidence Sarah had been taken.

Her cane lay in the dirt, discarded in the rotten lettuce leaves and broken crates behind the hotel restaurant. She'd never leave it behind. It was not only her walking stick, but her weapon.

He knew the secret of the handle as well as he knew she'd never have let the cane go without a fight. Abernathy had her. Whitman knelt beside the tracks and determined she'd been shoved up against the wall, possibly beaten, before he dragged her down the alley.

When he rose, a small smear of blood caught his eye on the wall. He reached out with a shaking finger and touched it. The wet texture told him what he already knew.

It was fresh. It was Sarah's.

"He knew we were getting close." Whitman whirled to face the sheriff. "If you hadn't been after Sarah for Mavis's murder, this wouldn't have happened. Don't you know how to investigate a crime? You look at all the evidence, not the circumstantial shit any fool could see."

"Mr. Kendrick, take a moment to calm yourself. We won't find your wife without working together." Bannon might only be a train conductor, but he was persistent in his faith of others.

"Step back a pace." Miller held up his hands, palms out. "We won't find her if you intend to pick a fight with me."

"I'm not picking a fight with you. I'm letting you know that I'm angry as all hell and I intend to make you pay for your ineptitude if anything happens to her." Whit blew out a breath and tried to rein in his anger.

He wasn't helping Sarah by yelling at Miller. Right then, she needed him to keep a clear head and focus.

"I hope nothing happens to her, and that's the truth." Miller sounded sincere. "I like your Sarah. She's a hell of a lady."

Your Sarah.

If only that were true. Even if they found her in time—no, *when* they found her—she was already lost to him. The pain and fury he saw in her eyes already told him she would never forgive him for being who he was.

Or for not telling her the truth about it.

"Where does this alley lead?" Whit picked up her cane and started following the drag marks.

Miller was right behind him. "To Elm Street. Not much there but some houses, the laundry, and the livery."

Whit stopped and turned to look at the sheriff. "The livery?"

It only took seconds for that information to sink in. Whit started running, regardless of what was in the alley. If Abernathy had access to a horse or a carriage, they could have a huge head start.

Whit exploded out of the alley, unable to get his bearings. "Where is it?" He glanced behind him at the sheriff.

"There, on the right." Not surprisingly, Miller ran like the wind. He was a healthy man who probably spent a good deal of time chasing drunks and runaway horses.

Whitman was right on his heels, praying they would be in time to save Sarah.

*   *   o

Abernathy tied Sarah's wrist to the post while he saddled a horse. It was after he'd knocked the stable boy unconscious, of course. No one appeared to be safe from Abernathy's violence.

Sarah watched him, balancing herself on her left leg while her right leg protested even the slightest bit of weight.

She needed to find a way to disable the man, but he was much younger and stronger than she expected. In the light from the lantern in the stall, she saw what the wide-brimmed hat and perhaps theatrical make-up had hidden.

Abernathy was not much older than Whitman.

"You collect widows and spinsters to keep yourself flush with cash?" She didn't expect him to react, but he did.

"Shut up. I do what I need to survive. It's not my fault if they are eager for companionship and fall under the spell of a charming man." He bared his teeth at her. "Mavis was especially eager."

Sarah snorted. "I have no doubt. She'd never been in a man's bed before, and I'm sure she was trolling for a husband. Too bad you had to kill her and spoil her plans."

"Her plans meant nothing to me. I needed traveling money and she provided it, even if I had to kill her to get it. You'd be surprised to find out what she had hidden in a money belt under her skirt." Abernathy cinched the saddle tightly on the bay mare, then picked up the bit.

It did surprise her, actually, that Mavis had money, but it shouldn't have. She'd spent her life as miserly as they come, and when she sold her property, she likely had a stockpile of money.

Now Abernathy had it.

The glint of something in the hay caught her attention and she shifted to reach for it as slowly as she could. Abernathy had his back to her, fortunately.

When her fingers came in contact with cold, hard metal, she nearly smiled. It was a spur.

Sarah had a weapon.

*   *   *

Whitman crept around the side of the livery, keeping out of the line of sight. Miller was on the other side of the building.

They were going to hit Abernathy from both sides, and hopefully, before he hurt Sarah or escaped from the building. Whit wanted to tear the man apart with his bare hands, but he needed to make sure Sarah was safe first.

The inky blackness of the night hid his approach. The low murmur of a man's voice reached his ears. He strained to hear what was being said, but it was too far away to tell.

Whitman reached the back of the livery and checked the latch on the door. It was well oiled, a nice advantage. He opened the latch and eased the door open.

The voice grew louder through the opening and Whitman crept in, following the sound.

Please be all right, Sarah.

Sarah tucked the spur up into her sleeve. Her hasty departure from the hotel room meant her knife was back on the dresser, useless and forgotten and her cane was lost in the alley. However, the spur would give her the advantage she needed.

Abernathy was busy going on about how smart he was, how women were gullible and stupid, and how he'd made a fortune taking what they were willing, or unwilling, to give.

He obviously liked to hear himself talk, judging by the fact he told her everything about his crimes without her even asking.

That meant two things: he likely planned on killing her and she was running out of time.

Sarah gripped the neck of the spur, the rowel digging into her palm. When Abernathy turned, she was ready, or at least as much as she could be.

He pulled the brim down on his hat and put his hands on his hips. "How am I gonna get you up on that horse? You're a big cripple."

Cripple jibes hadn't bothered her in years, but he didn't know that.

"You don't have to be so mean." She sniffled dramatically. "I can't help the fact that my leg doesn't work. Some Yankee soldier tore it up."

"Poor baby. Did he tear up your cunt too?" His grin was anything but pleasant. "Don't think I forgot about your special skills, Sarah. Care to give me a little loving and maybe save your life?"

Sarah looked him in the eye and nodded. With his pants down, Abernathy would be vulnerable and she could use that spur to her best advantage.

Whitman heard what Abernathy said and had to bite his fist to stop the murderous rage that flew through him. The bastard was going to rape her.

Sarah was probably scared and angry, same as Whitman. The only thing he could do was throw himself into the fray to save her.

Perhaps if he died, she might forgive him for not telling her the truth about himself.

As he crawled through the dirt and hay, he heard what sounded like a slap, then clothes rustling. Whitman ignored the pain in his heart in favor of the rage in his blood.

He peered around the corner to see Sarah tied to a post in the stall, her hair full of straw and dirt. Her cheek was bloody, and her eyes, damn it to hell, were full of fear. A man stood in front of her, his trousers gaping open.

Whitman forgot how to think and just acted.

Sarah heard a bellow just before she thrust the spur into Abernathy's balls. He screamed in agony, falling back into the horse.

The mare neighed and reared in fear, and Sarah tried to make herself as small as possible.

A tug on her wrist made her look up into Whitman's green

eyes. His face was contorted into a mask of rage and fear. She hadn't seen that look since her brother, Micah, had tried to kill their mother, so long ago.

Whitman sliced the rope holding her wrist and yanked her out of the stall before the horse could kick her.

Abernathy wasn't so lucky. In addition to the rather vicious wound Sarah had dealt him, the mare had stomped him to death. He stared up sightlessly at the ceiling as the horse continued to yank at the reins, bloodying her mouth with the bit.

"Stay here," Whit said through clenched teeth.

"You all right, Miz Kendrick?" Sheriff Miller appeared beside her. "Your face is a bit cut up."

Sarah stared at him, surprised by his concern. "I'm okay."

She looked back at Whit as he struggled to calm the horse. He obviously had worked with equines before, likely in the army, considering the ease he had with the mare.

Through the ordeal with Abernathy, from which she had rescued herself for the most part, she hadn't been upset. She'd been angry and determined to survive.

Now that he was dead, and the sheriff there by her side, emotions started trickling through her, not the least of which was shock.

"Your husband was about ready to tear my head off." He frowned. "I don't think I've ever run into a man more devoted to his wife."

Sarah burst into tears.

Whitman finally led the mare from the stall and Abernathy's body. The poor man had been turned into a pile of meat by the horse's sharp hooves. Whit didn't even want to look at the wound Sarah had inflicted with the spur.

It sent a shiver up a man's spine.

The mare's neck shook as he led her to an empty stall. He spoke soothingly to her, even as his insides jumped and popped like an egg on a hot pan.

Soon the mare was safe in the stall and he could take a deep breath. Miller stood near the stall alone, staring down at Abernathy's body.

"So that's him, huh? Poor bastard."

"I can't vouch for how his face did look, but I can tell you, he was definitely the one who murdered Mavis. The man was a self-centered, pompous ass who took what he wanted from people, no matter what the consequences." Whitman grabbed a saddle blanket and covered the body. "If you've got a gravedigger, I suggest you find him quick. Nobody needs to see this."

"I've got to call Ben too. The doctor needs to examine the body. There's a wagon out back. If you help me hitch up the horses and move the body, I'll drive him over to Ben's house." Miller started to walk away.

Whit glanced around and realized Sarah was gone. "Where's my wife?"

"Gone. That Lorenzo fellow picked her up and carried her back to the hotel. Now let's get this mess out of here."

Whitman wanted to go to Sarah to see if she was all right, but he had an obligation to help Miller first. After all, the sheriff didn't need to believe either of them, but he had. It cost a murderer his life, but the accusations hanging over Sarah and Whit died with him.

Now they had to deal with the aftermath, including the visit of the deputy from Belleville in the morning. If Whit went to jail for punching the idiot, then so be it. At least Sarah would be safe and the train could continue its journey.

With or without Whitman Kendrick.

Sarah leaned into Lorenzo, his firm young body carrying her with ease down the street. He kept to the shadows, trying to shield her from any passersby or prying eyes.

Lorenzo was a good person, a devoted friend. He didn't ever hesitate to help her, no matter what the cost. The truth was, Sarah didn't deserve such a person as a friend.

Lorenzo deserved better.

When they arrived at the hotel, Patrick and Alfred were there waiting. They both exclaimed at her condition and went off to find medical supplies and clean water.

Sarah wanted to tell them not to bother, but her voice had deserted her. The events of the day had sapped her strength completely. She had survived so much, physically and emotionally, all she wanted to do was sleep.

After Lorenzo laid her down on the bed, she pushed him away.

"*Amore*, you must let me tend to you. There is dirt, blood, and hay. You need to be cleansed." He wrung his hands as he stood over her fussing.

"Go away. All of you go away. I want to sleep. Please just let me sleep."

Sarah closed her eyes and ignored the protests. Lorenzo finally seemed to understand that the sleep she needed was to heal, regardless of what was on the outside.

She needed to heal the inside first. The last thing she remembered was the snick of the door as it closed behind him. Then blessed sleep claimed her.

It was nearly an hour before Whitman made it back to the hotel. He was exhausted, filthy, and in no mood for questions. Patrick was still at the front desk and he wisely didn't ask Whitman anything.

"Where's my wife?"

"She's in your room, Mr. Kendrick. We tried to get her cleaned up, but she insisted on being left alone." Patrick looked pained by the prospect that he wasn't able to help Sarah, but he already had.

"Don't worry, son. With your help we caught the man who murdered Miss Ledbetter and hurt Sarah. Believe me, he won't be hurting any other ladies." Whitman let loose a bone-cracking yawn.

"Maybe you should go to sleep too, sir. I can have fresh water brought to the bathing room if you'd like."

For an extra fee, he could bathe in his own room, but Whitman knew it would wake Sarah. He'd make do with the bathing room.

"Yes, have the water brought in. I need to get clean."

If that wasn't the truth, he didn't know what was. Whitman's soul was stained with the muck and grime of all his sins, not the least of which was breaking Sarah's heart. He sat down in one of the hard wooden chairs and waited for the hot water.

He hoped the bath would help cleanse more than the dirt on his skin.

Chapter Seventeen

The morning sunlight pricked Sarah's eyelids, making her roll over to avoid the bright rays. She felt a stinging on her cheek and reached up to find a wound.

The day before came at her in a rush and she gasped at the enormity of it all.

Then she looked at her hands and realized she had dried blood, horse shit, and dirt all over her. There was even hay in the bed, and she'd slept in her wrinkled, dirty clothes.

Sarah wanted to pull the covers over her head and hide, but her own smell was enough to drive her from the bed. With a groan, she sat up and got her bearings.

She blinked and looked again. There in the middle of the room was a tub, with wisps of steam rising from the water.

Somehow they'd not only brought in a tub, but filled it without waking her. Sarah wondered if it was Whitman's doing, then stepped on the thought.

Her supposed husband was gone from her life from now on. She would no longer pretend to be married to a Yankee soldier.

After she peeled off her filthy clothes, she tried to climb in the tub but found she didn't have the strength. That's when she spotted the step stool.

Tears pricked her eyes again, this time for the thoughtfulness of whoever had left the step stool. Her legs ached so badly, she could hardly walk, much less climb.

With the most ungraceful gait known to man, Sarah got into the hot water and sank in up to her neck. It was sheer bliss.

Her aching, tired body trembled with the pleasure of the hot bath. It was exactly what she needed.

The door opened and closed behind her, but she ignored it. It didn't matter who saw her, as long as she could stay in the tub.

Strong hands rubbed her scalp, easing the ache in her head. Then he lathered up her hair and rinsed it gently, easing through the tangles as a mother would a child.

He handed her a cloth and soap, then left the room.

Sarah wondered if Whitman would ever speak to her again.

Then wanted to kick herself for hoping he would.

Whit stood outside the room and tried to calm his racing heart. The sight of Sarah naked in the water, beneath his hands, was enough to turn his dick into a steel bar.

He wanted to make love to her, to show her how much she meant to him. Her silence, however, let him know exactly how she felt about him. He needed to make her understand why he didn't tell her.

First he needed to see to her comfort. The train was leaving in an hour, later than normal per Alfred Bannon's orders. It seemed every man in town loved Sarah.

She had no idea how much faith and love she engendered in people around her. The sarcastic wit, the sharp tongue, and the cane were her defense mechanisms, but they couldn't hide the real Sarah Spalding.

Everyone else saw her and embraced her. Whitman had had the good sense to fall in love with her.

Now he needed to tell her the entire truth and hope like hell she would understand.

He headed for the restaurant to order breakfast.

*   *   *

Sarah lay in the tub clean and replete. The bath had been wonderful, but the water was cooling quickly. She had to get out, but the relaxing hot water had stolen her strength.

She tried to stand, but couldn't. Her pride prevented her from calling out to Whitman, so she sat there and tried to figure out how to use the towel and the bedpost to pull her from the tub.

The door opened and Whitman stepped in carrying a tray of food with a mouth-watering aroma. He displayed the same incredible masculinity that had called to her the first time she'd seen him.

"What do you want?"

He picked up a towel from the bed. "To help you get out of the tub."

"You are never touching my body again, soldier," she hissed, her hurt overriding her good sense.

"Too bad you can't stop me."

Before she could even tell him to leave the room, he scooped her up and deposited her on the bed, then handed her the towel.

"After you dry off, I want to rub some liniment into your legs. That ordeal with Abernathy yesterday probably caused serious pain." He spoke calmly as if there weren't a river of anger and pain flowing between them.

It didn't matter that he was right about her leg.

"Get out."

"I can't do that, and you know it. Your friend Bannon is holding the train until nine. That leaves us thirty minutes to get you ready and to the depot. I'm sure they won't leave without you, so let's get busy." He rummaged through her bag and she threw a pillow at him.

"I said get out."

He met her gaze, the green depths of his eyes reflecting as much raw emotion as she was feeling. "Let's just get this over with, okay? I want to help you, so let me. Then you can kick me out of your life for good."

He held up the liniment and walked toward her. Sarah had so many things she wanted to say to him, but she didn't speak again. His hands worked magic as he rubbed the horse liniment into her legs.

The bath had softened some of the stiffness, but he dug in, finding the knots that refused to go away. Whitman was like a maestro making her flesh sing for him. Sarah closed her eyes and tried to pretend it wasn't him touching her.

It didn't work.

When his hands left her legs, Sarah couldn't stop the sigh from escaping. Whitman, always the gentleman, was kind enough not to mention it. After all, she hated him and everything he stood for. A massage shouldn't change that.

She refused to allow it to.

Before she knew it, he began pulling on her underclothes, and she lay there and let him. Sarah wanted to tell him to stop, to get away from her, but she didn't. She would in just a minute or two.

In the meantime, he dressed her as he would a doll. His touch was as gentle as it was silent. Whitman didn't speak a word as he worked, allowing Sarah to control the situation.

He set her in the chair in the corner and gathered up all her things, putting them in her traveling bags. When he stood by the door, she noticed he'd placed her cane beside her.

Sarah wanted to wail at the heavens for allowing her to love such a man.

"There're a few things you don't know. I want to tell you everything before we leave the hotel." He took a breath and leaned against the door. "I was in the army for fifteen years."

She sucked in a breath. Although she knew he'd been a soldier, hearing his admission was enough to shock her. Again.

"The army shaped me into a man, something my mother and her family were unable to do. They tried to make me into something I wasn't with their money, into a banker who spent his days behind a desk playing with other people's money."

Whitman put his hands in his pockets, his gaze never meeting hers as he spoke. She knew whatever it was he had to say, it was worse than his admission of being a soldier.

"At eighteen, I left home and joined the army, against everyone's wishes. For the first time in my life, I felt as if I was making all the decisions instead of following everyone else's. It was liberating."

She knew what he was talking about, understood it at the deepest level. When she'd finally shaken free of her mother's ghost and opened the boardinghouse, she'd felt that freedom.

"I joined the army as a private, the lowest of low. I had to do whatever my commanding officers told me, no matter who they were or how crazy the orders were." He shook his head. "There wasn't much time for fun, but they still took some time to show me how low on the chain of command I was."

Whitman walked over to the window and looked out. "During the war, I did things I never want to remember, but can't ever forget. It turns men into animals, into base creatures intent on surviving no matter what they have to do." He blew out a shaky breath and Sarah knew the worst was coming. "We were stationed in Virginia, a hundred miles south of Washington, D.C. By then I was a corporal and was responsible for half a dozen men. Sergeant Booker found a plantation he wanted to use as a base."

Sarah's throat began to close up even as her heart pounded hard against her ribs.

Oh, God, no, please no.

"I pitched my tent outside and waited for orders. Booker went into the house with his three corporals and left the rest of us to fend for ourselves. That night at the campfire, he came back a bit bloody, talking of how he'd found a young girl to slake his thirst. Said he'd taught her a lesson."

Whitman finally met her gaze, and in the green depths, she saw the truth. Sarah couldn't breathe for the pain that roared through her. She didn't remember getting to her feet, but she was in front of him hitting and pounding on him as she screamed.

She didn't know how long she'd been hitting him, but she finally stopped and stared. His cheeks were red, his right eye was already beginning to swell, and his lip was split.

He accepted her hatred, her anger, and her rage without a word. She slapped him so hard, she broke blood vessels in her hand. Whitman still simply stared at her, then picked up her hand and kissed it where the finger was missing.

"I hate you."

"I know." He reached for her cane and handed it to her. "We've got a train to catch."

Sarah took a deep breath and tried to rein in her emotions. She accepted the cane, cursing the fact her hand shook—hell, her entire body shook. Whitman had taken every bit of her heart and left her with nothing but anger and regret.

Two tastes that did not go down easy.

Whitman felt like an empty shell, a man who had lost his soul and his heart. He knew telling Sarah would be hard, but he didn't know how hard.

Her rage had hurt, but the devastation in her eyes was even more damaging. His admission had cost them both dearly. It had cost them a future together, and every shred of love between them.

When they walked into the hotel lobby, Patrick was there with a big smile on his face. The freckle-faced young man handed Whitman a basket.

"Some breakfast for you." He held out a hand to Sarah. "We'll miss you, Miz Kendrick."

She took his hand and managed a smile. "Sarah, please call me Sarah. And thank you, Patrick, for everything."

"My pleasure, ma'am. I'm glad we were able to help." He nodded at Whitman. "Mr. Kendrick, take good care of her."

"She'll be in good hands, I promise." Whitman nearly choked on the words.

They wouldn't be his hands.

"Sheriff Miller is outside waiting." Patrick left them with one last good-bye for Sarah.

Whitman let her set the pace, knowing she was recovering from so much and not wanting her to suffer any more than she already had.

The door to the hotel opened and Sam Miller stood on the other side, a half grin on his face. "Thought I might have to keep the train in town another day."

"I'm sorry, Sheriff, it's my fault." Sarah stepped outside and murmured her thanks.

The sheriff met Whitman's gaze with a frown. "Everything okay, Kendrick?"

"Probably not, but we're more than ready to head out of town." Whitman couldn't summon a smile. "You speak to the sheriff from Belleville?"

"I did and it turns out the deputy who grabbed your wife was drunk. He didn't want to get in trouble so he made up a story for the sheriff." Miller shook his head as he walked beside Whitman and Sarah to the train depot. "Never considered the man was lying."

"People lie every day, Sheriff. It's an unfortunate fact of life," Whitman said. The passengers milling around the platform all stopped as they approached.

Whitman didn't know what was happening and apparently neither did Miller. "What's happening?" Whitman asked.

"I dunno. Let's see if Bannon knows." The sheriff ran ahead and onto the platform, pushing his way through the crowd.

As if Sarah didn't realize what she was doing, her arm slipped easily into his. He supposed the enemy she knew was better than the enemy she didn't.

The clapping started somewhere in the back, then built up through the crowd until it turned into a thunderous sound. Whitman wasn't expecting the greeting and obviously neither was Sarah.

Her hand tightened on his arm and she sucked in a breath.

Alfred Bannon appeared from the middle of the crowd with Miller at his side. Both men were clapping. "We just wanted to thank you for helping us solve a murder and get the train moving again." Alfred beamed at them.

They walked up the steps, Sarah moving slower than Whitman had ever seen her. He knew he was the cause and wanted to take her pain away, but he had no idea how.

By the time they made it to the train car, the other passengers had begun getting on the train. Alfred was waiting for them.

Surprisingly, he gave Sarah a hug and Whitman a hearty slap on the back and a handshake. "You two have made my life more interesting. I'll be keeping an eye on you the rest of the trip."

"Thank you, Alfred." Sarah nodded to him, her face pale.

"Let's get Sarah on board so she can rest. She's been through so much." Whitman set the bags down.

"Oh, of course, of course." The conductor moved aside with a smile. "Your compartment is cleaned and ready."

Knowing she'd protest, Whitman scooped her up in his arms for the last time and carried her onto the train. Sarah's scent washed over him, reminding him of what he'd already lost. He gritted his teeth against the wash of emotions.

When he set her on the seat, she grabbed his arm. Whitman met her gaze and saw what he didn't want to see.

A good-bye.

Sarah watched as Whitman stored her bags, then bowed to her as a gentleman.

"I'll be in the public car if you need me." He left without another word, leaving Sarah in a pool of misery.

Why did Whitman have to be a Yankee? A soldier? A member of the very platoon that had left her crippled?

She curled up on the seat and hugged her knees, rocking back and forth. Her mother had predicted what would happen. Told young Sarah time and time again about how unattractive, gangly, stupid, and so on she was. No man would want Sarah Spalding.

It was a blessing the soldier had crippled her, of course. Then she could have a valid excuse as to why she never married. It never occurred to Vivian Spalding that a man might want to marry Sarah because he loved her.

The war and its aftermath had destroyed so much, and now it seemed it reached out years later and snatched what could have been a happy ever after for Sarah. The compartment door slid open.

"Do you mind if I join you?" Lorenzo asked hesitantly.

"As long as you don't fart or snore, you can come in." Sarah found her sarcasm was still around.

Lorenzo smiled, his handsome olive-toned face lighting up like a Christmas tree. "*Grazie, amore.* I don't want to intrude on you and your husband."

Sarah's heart clenched and it took monumental effort not to scream at her friend. "He's not joining me in the compartment. Don't ask why or you won't be either."

Lorenzo held up one hand and sat down without another word. Sarah should be glad she wasn't completely alone, but yet, she also didn't want company. Self-pity was so much better when she was alone.

The train picked up speed and soon they were well on their way again. The miles flew past, leaving Sarah to wonder just what would happen when they arrived in Kansas City in a few days. Would Whitman simply leave without saying goodbye?

Or would he ask her to stay with him?

Whitman had never felt so numb, so completely drained of everything. All he wanted to do was sleep for a week, try to forget the crazy train wreck his life had become.

The public car was noisy, smoky, and it smelled as expected. Too many bodies, too many reasons for body odor. Whitman ignored it as best he could and garnered himself a window seat.

If the other passengers were surprised to see him there, they didn't ask him about it. He wasn't looking forward to explaining to Alfred Bannon why he wasn't in his compartment with his wife.

His wife.

If only it had been true. Whit could have avoided so much misery, but, of course, Sarah wouldn't have known about his army background and his deep, black secret.

Now she did, and now she hated him.

Whit had barely spared a thought for Melissa, the innocent fiancée waiting for him in Kansas City. He owed her an explanation, and an apology. He only hoped his wire to her about the delay on the train had reached her.

The wedding was supposed to be in two days which meant he'd arrive more than a day late. Perhaps that was the way it was supposed to be. He'd cause Melissa nothing but misery if he married her.

Or maybe the opposite was true. Perhaps she'd heal his broken heart and teach him to love again.

And perhaps pigs could fly.

Whitman closed his eyes against the noise and tried to find a place deep within himself to retreat. He couldn't be with Sarah, and he didn't want to be with a train full of strangers.

"Mr. Kendrick?"

Whit opened his eyes to find an elderly gentleman with wavy white hair, a monocle, and an impeccable suit. "Yes?"

"My name is Mortimer Carmichael. I own this railroad and I wanted to personally thank you for apprehending the man who murdered one of my passengers." He held out his hand and Whitman shook it, a bit reluctantly.

"My wife, that is, Sarah, was the one who stopped him, not me." He didn't want to lie to the man.

"I've already spoken to her and she assures me that you

were the hero. Please join me in my private car on your journey west. I insist." Carmichael smiled and gestured to the huge man behind him. "Portman will carry your bags for you."

Whitman had been looking for an escape from reality and Mr. Carmichael offered it to him. He'd be a fool to refuse.

"Thank you, sir, I believe I will."

Chapter Eighteen

Lorenzo helped Sarah off the train that evening. The sky was a beautiful painting of orange, pink, purple, and yellow as the sun slipped down. She should appreciate the bounty of nature before her, but sadly, she was still stuck in a rut of self-pity.

The hotel was nothing special, the desk clerk didn't greet her with a smile, and the evening passed with Sarah in her room feeling sorry for herself.

Life continued on for two more days, full of bland, colorless existence. Now that they were in Kansas City, Sarah knew it would be the last time she'd ever see Whitman.

She'd seen him a few times and he always tipped his hat and was achingly polite. Yet Sarah had ignored him, choosing instead to hide behind a wall of anger and resentment.

"You drive me crazy, you know?" Lorenzo had apparently decided he'd had enough. He threw up his hands and paced the compartment while she put away her book. "You are like a ghost. Nobody is there when I talk to you."

Sarah rolled her eyes. "You are so dramatic, Lorenzo. I'm just tired is all. I'll feel better the closer we get to Colorado."

"Ha! You lie and you know it. I thought perhaps I could help you forget him, but no, it not happen. You love him, Sarah." Lorenzo took a deep breath. "Don't let him go."

She knew it cost her friend a great deal to say that to her. He'd been wanting to keep her for himself for more than three years.

Sarah cupped his cheek. "You are so sweet, but you know there's no way I can keep him. He has a fiancée, and aside from that, he's a Yankee soldier."

Lorenzo proceeded to curse in Italian, vehemently, while Sarah watched openmouthed. "You are a fool. He loves you, you love him. What does it matter who fought for who? Love doesn't care."

He snatched her bags along with his own and stomped to the compartment door. When he turned to look at her, Lorenzo was actually glowering.

Sarah was so shocked, she meekly followed him out, her cane thumping on the platform.

When she saw the tiny woman in yellow embracing Whitman, Sarah wanted to crawl back onto the train and hide. All the blood drained from her face as she looked at what the future held for Whitman.

Melissa was a beautiful, petite brunette with a nice smile and ample breasts. Whitman smiled down at her and Sarah's ears rang.

"Come, *amore*, let's be away from here. You no listen to me anymore. I am crazy in the head." He tried to pull her away, but Sarah wouldn't budge.

She stared at Whitman, willing him to look at her. Finally he did, and Sarah regretted her impulse. Lorenzo had been right and Sarah had been a fool.

Whitman had loved her, but she'd thrown it away with hate and prejudice. Now he was going to start his life anew, deservedly so, and leave Sarah behind.

She limped over to him and held out her trembling hand. "I wish you good luck, good fortune, and a happy life, Mr. Kendrick." Her voice was thick with emotion, but she held her back straight, dammit.

Lorenzo appeared by her side and nodded at Whitman. "Good luck, *signore*. And to you as well, *signorina*. We must go."

"Good-bye, Sarah." Whitman squeezed her hand, sending a shiver up her arm. "I wish you nothing but happiness."

Sarah nodded, unable to respond. Tears pooled in her eyes when she turned to Melissa, the woman who would be the real Mrs. Kendrick.

"Take care of him or I'll come find you and kick your ass."

With that Sarah turned and left her heart on the train depot platform in Kansas City, along with an openmouthed woman. It was time to start living again.

Melissa stared at Sarah's retreating back. "Did she just say what I think she did?"

Whit managed a rusty chuckle. "You have to know Sarah to understand it, but yes, she did."

Sarah had just shown more class and dignity than any person he'd ever met. It had cost her dearly, but she'd said good-bye for good. Her actions told Whitman Sarah had gotten through the hurt and shock to a place where she could puzzle out her choices.

And she didn't choose Whitman.

He picked up his traveling case. "My trunk should be out soon. Why don't we sit down and talk? I have a lot to tell you."

Melissa smiled prettily. "Why of course, Whitman, whatever you say."

Whitman forced himself not to look back at Sarah or he'd never have the courage to face what he had to do.

They sat down on the bench and Melissa fluffed her skirt to cover her ankles. Then she folded her hands and looked up at Whitman. "I'm ready."

"It all began in Virginia when I boarded the train and found myself in a compartment with the woman you just met—

Sarah Spalding—and another woman named Mavis Ledbetter," Whitman began his tale.

Sarah didn't sleep a wink that evening, knowing that Whitman was somewhere in town with his new bride. She needed to start forgetting him instead of remembering him.

She threw back the covers and pulled on her dress. Damn, she needed a drink and a smoke.

The saloon in town was called Tootin' House, and she didn't really want to know why. There were men aplenty inside as well as the standard saloon girls working the room. The bartender was a bald, husky man with a patch over one eye.

He looked like a pirate, for pity's sake.

Sarah made her way to the bar and climbed onto the stool. Her leg had been better since Whitman's massage, but it appeared even her flesh required daily doses of his magic. Too bad she'd never get it again.

"Whiskey, and not the cheap rotgut you give these idiots. I want the good stuff." Sarah laid a gold eagle on the counter.

The bartender's bushy brows rows. "Yes, ma'am."

She slung back the whiskey, closing her eyes against the burn as it slid down her throat. "Damn that was good. Give me another."

The last person she expected to see in the saloon was Alfred Bannon, but he sat down beside her.

"Hello, Sarah."

"Alfred, what are you doing here?" She sipped the next whiskey, not wanting to get falling-down drunk when she had to get on the train in six hours.

"Same as you, I suppose. Finding an escape." He sighed and laid down a fifty-cent piece. "Beer."

They drank in silence and Sarah found herself relaxing for the first time in days. Alfred had turned out to be more than she expected.

"Do you have a family, Alfred?"

He shook his head. "Nothing but my job, unfortunately." He gave her a small smile.

"We're pitiful, aren't we?" Sarah found herself smiling back. "I had something wonderful and I threw it away."

"You weren't really married, were you?" Alfred peered at her.

"Legally, no, but in all other ways, yes." It felt good to admit that to someone.

More than good, it felt liberating.

"He loves you and I think you love him. What happened?" Alfred took a long gulp of beer and looked at her expectantly.

"We found out our pasts wouldn't let us have a future." Sarah tossed back the rest of the whiskey. "As simple and as complicated as that."

Alfred put his hand on hers. "I'm sorry, Sarah."

She nodded. "So am I."

They sat there talking for another hour, as the whiskey floated through her veins. Sarah knew she should go back to bed, but the stool was comfortable and the company was too.

"The train leaves early in the morning." Sarah motioned to the bartender. "I should get to bed." She realized it was likely two in the morning and the conductor was drinking beside her. "What are you still doing in the saloon?"

Alfred shook his head. "Kansas City is the last stop for me. I'm not working tomorrow. The train leaves Thursday morning for New York with me on board."

"New York? Alfred, that's wonderful." Sarah hugged him, glad for his good fortune. "You got your dream."

"Thanks to you and your hus—Mr. Kendrick. It happened that Mr. Carmichael, the owner of the train, heard about what I did from someone and he offered me the northern route yesterday." This time the smile lit up his face. "I am off to my own adventure."

Sarah wobbled a bit as she stood. "And a well-deserved adventure too. I'm so happy for you."

And she was surprised she meant it. Alfred had been a

stranger, a distrustful, strange portly man who threw suspicion on her a week ago. Now she considered him a friend, a
lifelong friend, and she was genuinely pleased for his good
fortune.

"Thank you." Alfred took her hand and squeezed it. "I
wish you only the happiness you deserve."

Sarah smiled sadly. "Me too."

"Let me help you to the hotel, Sarah." He held out his arm.
"It's the least I can do."

With her new friend at her side, Sarah made her way back
to her room. At least someone who'd been on the train had
come into good fortune.

Sarah headed for her lonely bed with her lonely heart and
into her lonely future.

As the train pulled into Denver, Sarah had butterflies in her
stomach. She didn't know what her reception would be with
Micah. It had been more than ten years since she'd seen him.

The memory of that day, the bloody day she'd lost not only
her mother but the remnants of her innocence, haunted her
dreams on occasion.

Micah had been wounded, both inside and out. From what
she found out from his wife, he wasn't expecting her. That
alone set off an entire colony of butterflies.

It was dark outside and she planned on waiting until morning before renting a buggy to travel the last three hours to
Plum Creek.

In the dark, Denver looked like every other city. Lorenzo
peered out the window and back at her.

"I will do what you ask, *amore*. Are you all right?" He'd
been a constant companion, a reminder of her past, but not a
painful one. Since she'd left Kansas City, and Whitman behind, Sarah had come to terms with her decision.

She didn't want to keep punishing herself for what she did
and didn't do. Alfred and Lorenzo had helped her realize the
present was where she needed to live.

As they got off the train, the cool mountain air felt good on her face. It was a welcome change from what she'd grown up with, a heavy air that never seemed to lose its moisture.

"Is nice, no?" Lorenzo stepped out beside her. "I think I will like Colorado."

Sarah smiled. "I think Colorado will like you." She took his arm and they walked down the sidewalk to the hotel. "The porter is going to bring my trunk later. In the morning I'm going to Plum Creek."

She didn't ask Lorenzo what he planned to do, and she wasn't going to ask him to come with her. It was time for him to make his own decisions.

"Do you want me to come with you to meet your brother?"

She expected the question. "No, I don't." Sarah stopped and touched his cheek. "You are an amazing friend and an extraordinary man. I wish you the best of luck in whatever you choose to do, but it won't be with me."

He closed his eyes and when he opened them, she saw he'd accepted her decision.

"Do you understand?"

"Yes, *amore*, but I will miss you." He pulled her close for a hug. "Will you spend the night with me?"

Sarah would have said yes if she hadn't met Whitman, but she had, so she couldn't be with another man. Probably not for a long time, if ever. "No, but I'll give you a kiss and buy you supper."

Lorenzo leaned down and kissed her softly. "I accept."

Arm and arm, Sarah headed to the hotel to have the last supper with an old friend. Then in the morning, her new life would begin.

She'd never felt so scared or so alone.

The carriage ride to Plum Creek was uneventful, fortunately or not. It was different from the wild journey in a carriage she'd made with Whitman.

She cut that thought off before it could go anywhere. Sarah

had spent a good deal of time thinking about Whitman and enough was enough. They'd both made their choices.

It had been before dawn when they left for the three-hour journey. She'd arrive before eight, her nerves and her courage on edge.

When the carriage stopped, Sarah looked outside at an average-looking small town. The streets were well swept and it had an air of pride to it. She was glad Micah had found such a place to live.

The door opened, revealing a blond man with a gleaming star on his vest. Although Sarah was still leery of any lawman, she gave this one the benefit of the doubt considering the bright smile on his face.

"Sarah Spalding?" He held out his hand. "Daniel Morton. I'm the sheriff here in Plum Creek."

"Pleased to meet you." She shifted to the side of the carriage and slowly made her way out the door, cane first.

Sheriff Morton was patient and helpful as she finally got her feet on the ground and stood. "You look like your brother, you know. I'd recognize those eyes anywhere."

Sarah tried to swallow, but her mouth had gone dry. "Does he live near here?"

"Yes, ma'am, just a five-minute walk." He glanced down at her cane. "But we can ride there if you'd like."

"Actually, no, I'd rather walk. I'm a bit stiff from riding. A walk would help work out the kinks." What she didn't tell him was that the walk would allow her to gather her courage.

He offered her his arm and they started walking down the street at a slow pace, which suited Sarah just fine.

It had been so many years since she'd seen Micah. So many things had happened to her in that time, she had no doubt he had many life-changing experiences too.

She was glad he'd survived, happy he'd found a woman to love and marry. Sarah was afraid he'd see her and all of his bad memories, his nightmares really, about their mother and what happened would color his relationship with Sarah.

"Are you cold?" Sheriff Morton must have felt her shivering.

"No, just nervous." She laughed shakily. "I'm afraid I don't know how my brother will react since he doesn't know I'm coming."

She'd come so far, endured a lifetime of joy, sorrow, and heartache, and yet she'd arrived safely almost at her brother's doorstep. Sarah wasn't used to feeling ill at ease and she found she didn't like it.

"Don't you worry about that. Eppie wouldn't have contacted you if she wasn't sure Micah would welcome you." Daniel patted her hand.

"Who's Eppie?" Sarah's grip grew tighter on the sheriff's firm arm.

"That's what we call Elizabeth—it's her nickname." Daniel pointed ahead to a huge house with a picket fence and swing on the front porch. "There's the house."

Sarah's heart began to pound as a figure on the porch stood up from the swing. She didn't even have a drop of spit in her mouth. It was as dry as the cotton fields from her past.

The figure walked down the steps and she could clearly see it was a man. In the dappled sunlight from the trees, she couldn't make out his face, but in her heart, she knew it was Micah.

Suddenly the trip seemed like a bad idea, a really, really bad idea. Sarah wanted to run, to hide, anything to avoid facing her brother again. A little girl poked her head up from behind the fence, followed by a yellow dog, and then they both disappeared.

"I think I'm going to vomit." She didn't realize she'd said it out loud until the sheriff chuckled.

"It's okay, Miss Sarah. There is nothing more important than family. I've heard Micah speak of you and it was always with love in his voice."

Micah reached the gate and stepped out on the sidewalk,

staring at them as they walked the last twenty feet. Sarah's heart was thundering as she finally saw her brother's face.

He had a scar from the saber wound she'd stitched, an ugly scar that marred his handsome face. However, his hair was the same, a little darker than hers but long too. It shouldn't surprise her, but it did.

Sarah didn't feel the tears sliding down her cheeks, but the sheriff pressed a handkerchief into her trembling hand. And then there she was, face-to-face with her brother.

He was a man, a full-grown man with wrinkles near his eyes and, amazingly, love in his silver gaze.

"Sarah?"

She nodded and then she was in his arms, surrounded by the one person in the world she had always loved. His scent surrounded her and she was awash in memories of Micah, the brother who was in her heart and her soul. The boy who became a man while she had grown into a woman.

Sarah pressed her face into his neck and sobbed. Their lives had been fraught with so many tragedies, so many obstacles, and so much darkness. It was so hard to believe they had journeyed through life apart and yet when they came together it was as if no time had passed.

He rubbed her back and waited while the storm of emotions wreaked havoc on her. She still could hardly believe she was there with Micah.

"God, how I've missed you." His voice was husky with emotion. "Sarah, honey, I can't believe you're here."

She could hardly speak, hardly form a thought other than relief and joy at finding Micah again.

"It wasn't easy," she managed.

"Nothing worthwhile ever is, right?" He picked up her cane and glanced at her curiously. "I'd say we have a lot to talk about."

She took the cane and nodded. "Yes, we surely do."

Then he smiled and gave her the most wonderful gift.

"Welcome home, Sarah."

*   *   *

Whitman stepped out of the restaurant in Kansas City and looked up at the sky. He figured Sarah must have made it to her brother's that morning and he was happy for her.

She'd been nervous about seeing him again, but Whit knew she'd be welcomed with open arms. Family always did—at least normal ones always did.

Whit couldn't call his family normal by any means, but he had a feeling Sarah and her brother would be just fine. He walked back slowly to the hotel, without really knowing where he was going.

In the morning, he was due to leave for San Francisco on the train west. He'd already purchased a house with the money he'd saved from his army pay. All he had to do was get on that train and begin his life.

Alone, of course.

He'd told Melissa he couldn't marry her. Whit was no kind of man if he'd let that innocent woman bear the burden of the ghost in the bed with them.

Sarah would never leave his heart—of that he was certain. She had been the woman he was supposed to spend his life with. Too bad he'd destroyed their relationship.

A light rain began to fall, which turned into a full-blown deluge by the time he made it to the hotel. He was soaking wet and miserable. He expected miserable to be the normal state of things once he reached San Francisco.

He'd been dreaming of Sarah, wondering how she was, what she was doing, and if she was all right. He had no right to ask, of course, or even to intrude on her life anymore.

But, damn, he wanted to so badly it made his stomach hurt. The train to Denver was leaving in an hour. He'd checked the schedule already, perhaps just to torture himself some more.

As he stepped into the lobby, dripping wet, a couple was just leaving. The woman smiled up at the man and he kissed her on the tip of her nose.

"Ready?"

"Whenever you are, honey." The man nodded to the desk clerk. "Thank you for your help. We're off to catch the train."

"No problem, sir." The redheaded desk clerk reminded Whitman of Patrick.

After the couple went out into the rain, Whitman started toward the stairs, then stopped and changed his mind. Instead he walked over to the desk.

"May I help you, sir?"

"What's your name?"

"Jimmy Finn." The clerk smiled. "Is there something I can do for you?"

"Where was that couple going?"

"The train to Denver. They were supposed to meet two days ago, but the man got held up because the train was delayed. I heard it was because of a murder." Jimmy sounded as if he was imparting gossip and lowered his voice. "They had to be in Denver by yesterday to buy their house, but instead of going without him, she waited."

Whitman stared at the young man, certain he hadn't heard the story right. "So they lost the house?"

"Yep, sure did. But they're as happy as a pig in a wallow. I don't understand love sometimes." Jimmy shook his head. "Folks will go through hell and back for it, though. Maybe one day it will happen to me."

Whit's heart shook off the cloak of misery and began to beat again. The boy was right. Love endured all things, even heartbreak and separation. True love forgave.

True love never died.

He ran up the stairs to his room and threw his belongings into his travel case. The trunk lay wide open, but he didn't have time for that. The train was leaving in an hour and he intended to be on it.

When he came back downstairs, Jimmy stared at him as if he'd grown two heads. "You okay, sir?"

"For the first time in days, I'm okay." Whit's smile was genuine. "I've got to get to Denver, but my trunk is upstairs. Can you see to it that it gets on the next train west to Denver?" Whit scribbled his name on a piece of paper and handed the boy twenty dollars. "This should be enough for the trunk and your trouble. Have it sent to Plum Creek, Colorado, in care of Micah Spalding."

Jimmy took the money and the note. "Yes, sir, I can do that." He cocked his head and studied Whit's face for a moment. "You in love, Mr. Kendrick?"

"More than you can ever know. Thank you, Jimmy!" Whit dashed out the door and ran through the rain toward the train station.

The rest of his life waited for him, and all he had to do was ask for it. Sarah was his love, his soul, his very heart that beat in his chest madly.

He couldn't spend the rest of his life wondering if she would say yes if he asked her to marry him. Regret would eat away at his soul if he didn't try.

By the time he arrived, he was dripping wet again, but Whit didn't care. He'd made the right decision—he could feel it in his bones.

He walked up to the depot clerk's desk and smiled. "One ticket to Denver please."

The gray-haired clerk looked him up and down from beneath bushy white brows. "I'd say it's raining out there, young fella."

"You'd be right." Whit counted out the money and handed it to the clerk.

"Is it a woman?" the old man asked as he filled out the ticket and gave it to Whitman.

Whit stared at the ticket in his hand. "The only woman."

"Ah, it's that way, is it? Good luck, son." The twinkle in the old man's eyes told Whit he knew exactly how he felt.

With a spring in his step, Whit went out onto the platform and started toward the train.

A voice from his past stopped him in his tracks, making his blood run cold.

"Is that you, Kendrick?"

Whit turned and saw the one person who had nearly destroyed the woman he loved.

Sergeant William Booker.

Chapter Nineteen

Sarah sat on the porch swing of Micah's house. She was shaking with relief, joy, and a hundred other emotions. He picked up a mug of coffee from the railing and she noticed his hand shook as much as hers.

At least she didn't feel like a fool anymore.

"How did she find you? It was Eppie, right?" He sipped the coffee and waited for her to answer. Micah had discovered patience in the years they were apart.

"I was living at the boardinghouse, what used to be the Spalding Plantation house, when I got a telegram."

The coffee cup stopped halfway to his lips. "Did you say you were living at the house? Our house?"

She could see in the silver depths of his eyes the question he didn't want to ask out loud.

"Mother died almost ten years ago. After that, I was lonely and desperate, as many people were. I met someone, a friend named Vickie"—she swallowed the lump at the thought of her best friend so far away—"and we concocted the idea of opening the house up as a boardinghouse."

He nodded. "It's big enough, that's for sure."

"Exactly. Too many women and girls were out there alone and unprotected. We decided that together we could make a home for all of them." She managed a small smile. "We were pretty young and full of big ideas, but damned if it didn't work."

Sarah hadn't meant to let the curse slip out, but if Micah was surprised by her cursing, he didn't show it.

"Eppie found you there?"

"She did. When the telegram came at first, I wasn't even going to send a reply." She studied her hands, unwilling to meet his gaze. "I thought you didn't want anything to do with me, especially after what Mother did to you."

Micah sat beside her and took her hands, frowning at the missing little finger. He rubbed the spot with his thumb.

"Ah, honey, you were the only sunshine in my life as a boy. I would never, ever blame you for anything that bitch did. I loved you, and I still love you." He tipped her chin up. "You are one of the strongest people I know. I can't believe you made it all the way to Colorado alone."

Although she thought she was done crying, one tear slipped out. Micah had to mention her journey, didn't he? She hoped it would be at least a few hours before she thought of Whitman again.

"It wasn't an easy trip, was it?" He put his arm around her shoulder. "But you made it. I hope the cane isn't a result of the trip, though."

Sarah shook her head. "That story is for another day. I can't handle too much telling all at once."

Micah kissed the top of her head. "I understand, sprite."

Sprite.

She had forgotten the nickname. He'd called her that because she resembled a wood sprite, with her gangly arms and legs, and her long wavy hair. Micah would tease her about growing pointy ears.

God, it was so long ago, the memories tasted bittersweet to her.

"Are you happy, Micah?" She felt comforted by the sway

of the swing, the warmth of his body, and the knowledge she had finally made it.

"Yes, I'm happier than I ever thought I could be, or was allowed to be." He let out a long sigh. "I'm guessing you know exactly what I mean."

Sarah thought of what she'd lost along the way from Virginia, her heart being the biggest. Whitman had frustrated, annoyed, and fascinated her. The big dumb Yankee had wormed his way into her heart and she doubted he'd ever leave.

Yet he had. He'd left her on the train without ever asking her if that was what she wanted. Of course, she probably wouldn't have been able to tell him at the time.

However, she knew now. She also knew Whitman was another woman's husband now, and she could never have him again.

"Yes, I do know what you mean." She closed her eyes and counted to five to try to hold back the damn emotions that kept rearing their ugly heads.

Could she get through one day without crying?

Apparently not.

"Do you want to meet my family?" He smiled down at her.

"I would love to meet them." She knew that he had a daughter, figuring the girl she saw at the fence was one and the same, and that he and Elizabeth were to be married soon.

Micah helped her to her feet, then handed her the cane. "Is this something you need a doctor to work on?"

Sarah smiled sadly. "No, I need magic."

He chuckled softly and led her into the house to meet the family he loved. As she stepped over the threshold, Sarah felt as if she was finally coming home.

Whitman stared in disbelief at Booker. He was the same big, hairy man, but different. Gray streaked his beard, and he had a much bigger belly, if that was even possible. Yet his eyes were just as cold as, if not colder than, Whit remembered.

"Booker?"

"Yep, it sure is. Fancy seeing you out here in Kansas City."
He pointed at the case. "Where you headed?"

Whitman's stomach somersaulted and landed with a thud.
"Are you on the train to Denver?"

"Nah, I got a job at a mine in California. A cousin of mine
got it for me. I've been living hand to mouth for a while, making my way west. The train don't leave until tomorrow morning, though." He loudly sucked back snot, then spat a wad of
phlegm on the wooden platform. "How about you?"

"I, uh, just mustered out of the army actually." Whit was
faced with the possibility that Booker might end up somewhere near Sarah, and he couldn't let that happen.

"Really? Are you fucking loco?" Booker was loud enough
to garner attention from nearly everyone around them.

"It was a good steady job, Booker. I worked in Washington
most of the time." Whitman straightened his shoulders. "You
need to show some respect to both the army and your fellow
passengers, Sergeant."

Booker leaned in close, the fetid smell of his breath nearly
overpowering. "I ain't in the fucking army no more, Kendrick.
Don't be calling me nothing but Booker."

There were many crimes Booker was guilty of, not the least
of which was raping and mutilating Sarah. Whitman had a
choice. He could get on the train and forget about the man,
find Sarah, and make her his wife. Or he could have Booker
arrested by the local army outpost, put in the brig, and tried
for twelve-year-old crimes.

Whitman stared at the man who had shaped the lives of
both him and Sarah until he made a decision.

"I can only hope you suffer the same type of suffering you
have inflicted during your lifetime. You're a miserable excuse
for a human being and I'm sorry I ever saw your face. I'd wish
you good luck, but I wouldn't mean it. Rot in hell, Booker."
Whitman started to walk away, leaving a sputtering bastard
behind him.

"You ain't got no call to say things like that, lousy son of a bitch." Booker continued to curse and shout at him, but Whit kept walking.

The battles he fought in life had always been thrust upon him. This time, Whitman chose not to fight one.

Instead, he chose to fight for the woman he loved.

Sarah snuggled into the soft quilt and sighed. It had been an amazing day of getting to know Micah's Eppie and Miracle. The love in their eyes when they looked at one another had made her heart ache.

It seemed their path hadn't been smooth either. Sarah gathered that some folks didn't take kindly to their marriage or their beautiful daughter.

Yet they had persevered and fought for what they wanted and loved and, in the end, won the battle. Sarah was happy for her brother and wondered if she'd ever find a man she loved as much as Whitman.

Of course, in her heart, she knew there would never be another man besides Whitman. She rolled over and stared at the curtains in the window. The guest room was at the top of the stairs in the enormous mansion.

Micah had told her softly that his friend Madeline had given it to them as a wedding gift. For a moment, Sarah wished she had a friend like that. Then she thought better of it. Rich friends usually expected too much from a person.

Sarah preferred her ragtag, poor friends, who only had their love and affection to give and receive. She hoped Lorenzo was all right in Denver, and Vickie and the girls in Virginia.

As Sarah drifted off to sleep, she thought of Whitman and how he looked when he was above her, making love to her. Her body thrummed with arousal almost immediately and she cursed aloud.

It seemed Whitman would haunt her mind, heart, and body. He had become part of her. Goddamn, but she loved him.

She'd never be able to let him go.

* * *

Whitman could hardly wait to ride to Plum Creek. It was still dark when he went to the livery in Denver to buy a horse. The young man working there looked at him as if he were crazy.

"You want to buy a horse *now*?" The boy had sandy-blond sleep-tousled hair and wore a pair of overalls with no shirt.

"Yes, I want to buy one now. Are all of these for sale or are they boarded?" He started walking down the stalls looking for a sturdy mount.

"Um, some of them is owned, and others is what we rent to folks." The boy rubbed his eyes and yawned. "Mr. Foster will be here at six. You got to wait til he gets here to buy a horse."

Whitman glanced at his pocket watch. That was an hour away and he could hardly stand the wait. "Can I rent one then?"

"I suppose. I do that all the time for Mr. Foster. Where you headed?" The boy yawned again and scratched his head.

"Plum Creek, and I need directions too."

"That's about three hours from here, due north."

Whit was dismayed to find there were no good horses in the barn. Half of them were swaybacks, the others too small or old to ride. What did he expect in a livery? He was pleased to find a nice-looking buckskin in the last stall. "Is this gelding for rent?"

"That there is Mr. Foster's personal horse. He ain't never for rent."

"Hell's bells. Where does Mr. Foster live?" Whitman couldn't wait even one more minute to be on his way. Knowing Sarah was only a few hours away made him nearly crazy.

He had to find her, to apologize and grovel at her feet. Whit had to tell her he loved her. He'd never done that and he'd regretted that fact ever since he'd left her train compartment.

However, Whit refused to live with regrets anymore.

"Up the hill a ways at number forty-two." The boy pointed. "He ain't gonna be happy if you wake him up, though."

Whit grinned. "He will be when I pay him twice what his horse is worth. Saddle this one up—I'll be back."

With an energy he hadn't felt in years, Whitman ran up the hill to number forty-two and Mr. Foster.

Whit wasn't going to wait for his new life to begin.

A man emerged from the shadows and stepped toward Jeremy. The boy shrank back, afraid of the man, as he hadn't been by the stranger who wanted to buy Mr. Foster's buckskin.

"Boy, where is that man going?" the man's voice was harsh and rough.

"P-plum Creek." Jeremy swallowed, but his mouth was so dry it made his tongue stick to the roof.

"Where's that?" The stranger came closer, revealing himself. He was hairy, with a beard and crazy, cold eyes.

"Th-three hours n-north." Jeremy began to shake and prayed he wasn't about to piss his britches. The stranger scared him like a bogeyman.

"You got a horse for rent?" The stranger peered into old Tink's stall.

"That one there is. He's an old bay, not too fast but he's s-sturdy." Jeremy wanted to run, but he had no idea why. The stranger hadn't threatened him or even hit him.

But he was afraid. Damn afraid.

"How much?"

"T-two dollars a day."

"For that you'd better suck my dick, boy." Two dollars fluttered in the air in front of Jeremy's face. "Saddle him."

As he ran to do the man's bidding, Jeremy focused on not getting attacked or worse.

After he had the horse saddled, the stranger took hold of Jeremy's jaw and squeezed. Nasty onion breath gushed out of the man's bearded face.

"If'n you tell the other man I was here or I'm headed to Plum Creek, I'll come back and gut you. Understand, boy?"

Jeremy nodded, too frightened to speak. It wasn't until after the stranger rode off that he realized he had pissed his britches after all.

But he was alive and he planned to keep it that way.

Mr. Foster was more than glad to get a hundred dollars for his buckskin. Whitman walked back with the man as he chattered away, pleased with his early morning sale.

When they arrived back at the livery, the buckskin was saddled and ready, but the boy was nowhere to be found.

"Well, you just be on your way then, Mr. Kendrick. It was a pleasure doing business with you."

"Thank you, Mr. Foster." Whitman led the buckskin out of the barn. "What's his name?"

"I called him Horse, but you can call him whatever you want."

"How do I get to Plum Creek?" It would be a shame to get lost on the way to propose marriage.

"Take the road north out of town. Follow it until you reach the fork by the big mossy rock. Can't miss it. Take the right fork, and Plum Creek is about ten miles from there."

"Thank you again." Whit turned to leave.

"Good luck, Kendrick. I hope your lady is worth it." Mr. Foster, a big barrel-chested man with a balding head, went in search of his errant stable boy.

"Oh, she's more than worth it. She's worth everything."

Whit mounted with the ease born of a man who spent many years in the saddle. When he was astride the gelding, the horse whickered and tossed his head.

"Me too, boy. I'm ready to ride. I'm going to let Sarah name you. Then I'll buy her a carriage and you can be her wedding gift." Whitman smiled as he kneed the horse into motion.

Within hours, he'd see Sarah again. His stomach jumped right along with the rest of his body. The anticipation was enough to make him light-headed.

Was this what love did to normal men?

No wonder he'd shied away from it most of his life. If it hadn't been for a sarcastic sharp-tongued Southern belle, he'd never have discovered the joys and sorrows of love.

Then again, he'd never have found love, and that would have been a real tragedy.

It was a beautiful spring day, perfect for a ride into the Colorado countryside. Tall evergreens towered over the ground from the mountains. The views were absolutely breathtaking.

Whit could understand why Sarah's brother decided to make his home there. Of course, in the winter, there was probably quite a bit of snow.

He could feel the thinness of the air as he rode and was doubly glad he'd been smart enough to carry water with him. But he'd forgotten the food, so within an hour, his stomach began to rumble.

None of it mattered, though. He was close enough to Plum Creek that he could almost smell her rose-scented skin. Or maybe that was the flowers on the side of the road.

For the most part, his journey was uneventful. However, every once in a while, Whitman thought he heard hoofbeats, but they were faint. It sounded as if someone else was on the road with him on the way to Plum Creek.

When he got to the fork in the road by the big mossy rock, Whit went right, as Mr. Foster had instructed. His heart beat a steady rhythm as he rode the last ten miles to Sarah.

To his heart, his soul, his woman.

Sarah sipped at the strong coffee and moaned as it slid down her throat. "This is the best coffee I've had in a long, long time. Delicious."

Eppie, Micah's fiancée, smiled at her. She had the most beautiful brown eyes set in a flawless light cocoa skin. Their daughter, Miracle, was a blend of both of them, but she had her mama's chocolate brown eyes.

The little girl was eating a biscuit and staring at Sarah over the breakfast table. "You're the sad lady."

Startled by the girl's insight, Sarah could only nod. "Yes, I am sad, but I'm happy to be here with you and your daddy and mommy."

"Daddy used to be sad, but Mommy fixed him."

Sarah smiled at the girl's precociousness. "Mommy is very talented."

Eppie hid a grin behind her hand. "Go take care of Daisy now, Miracle. She's probably hungry too."

Miracle popped the last of the biscuit into her mouth, then jumped up from the table. She hugged Eppie around the middle, then whispered at her mother's belly.

When she turned to Sarah, Miracle launched herself into her arms and hugged her neck. "Love you, Aunt Sarah."

Sarah was overwhelmed by the child's sweet honesty and open, loving behavior. The sweet innocence of a child's love was as refreshing as it was welcome. Sarah needed it. She hugged her niece back and kissed her forehead. "I love you too, Miracle."

"Gotta take care of my doggie." With that the girl skipped out of the kitchen, her braids swinging.

Sarah met Eppie's gaze, which was full of motherly pride. "She's amazing."

"I know, and I thank God every day for her." Eppie shook her head. "Someday I'll tell you the story of how she came to be and why she's called Miracle. Micah tells me it's my story to tell, but it's really his."

Sarah was more than curious to hear that story, but she understood how hard it was to open up to someone, especially when they'd really just met.

"Why did she whisper at your belly?"

Eppie smiled. "She tells me there's a little brother growing in there and she has to tell him secrets."

Sarah could hardly believe a girl of three could be so smart and so insightful. Then again, she could believe it—Miracle was Micah's child.

"Good morning." Micah walked into the kitchen, freshly shaven and looking more content than Sarah could ever hope to be. He kissed Eppie and patted her belly. "My son okay this morning?"

"Micah, you foolish man, you're as bad as your daughter." Eppie rolled her eyes.

He laughed and kissed her again. Sarah sighed quietly with envy over the closeness they shared. She'd turned into a complete sap after meeting Whitman. Her hard edges had softened and even her cursing had lessened. Damn, he'd ruined her for good.

Micah turned to Sarah. "Do you know a man named Whitman Kendrick?"

Sarah's heart slammed into her ribs. Her entire body began to shake. "Yes, I do."

Her voice was rough with emotion.

Micah gestured with his head. "Well, he's at the door with a hangdog look on his face and asking for you. Do you want me to send him packing?"

Sarah rose to her feet as quickly as she could, what with all the shaking and the crippled leg and all. "No, don't send him packing."

As she limped out of the kitchen and into the hallway, Sarah thought of a million reasons why Whitman was in Plum Creek, then dismissed all of them.

The only one that mattered was what was in her heart and what she hoped was in his.

When she got to the door, her palms were so sweaty she could hardly turn the knob. As the door opened, Sarah's stomach dropped when there was no one there.

"Whitman?" she whispered.

He stepped in her view from the left and somehow Sarah threw herself into his arms. Whitman caught her and murmured her name over and over against her neck.

He smelled so good, felt even better, and he was there. Thank God, he was there.

Sarah found herself crying—*again*, for pity's sake—as her heart beat against his. The thumping vibrated through her, making her realize anything that happened before she met Whitman meant nothing at all.

It didn't matter that he was a Yankee and she was a Southerner.

It didn't matter that he had been in the army.

It didn't matter that she hated Yankee army men.

What mattered was that she loved him and he was there in her arms.

"Sarah, sweetheart." He held her so tightly she could hardly get a breath.

"What are you doing here, Whit?" She finally got hold of her runaway brain and extricated herself from the embrace.

His green gaze locked with hers. "I came here because somewhere between Virginia and Kentucky I fell in love with a sharp-tongued Southern belle. She turned me on my head, beat me with her cane, and taught me what it meant to live again."

He got down on one knee and looked up at her. "I came here to tell her that I love her with all my heart and to ask her to marry me."

Sarah pressed a hand to her chest. She'd wished for a man who would love her, and here he was, on his knees, asking her to marry him. Her mother had been so wrong. There was someone for her.

"Well, I've already had practice at being Mrs. Kendrick." She smiled and cupped his chin. "I think I'll say yes."

He whooped and picked her up, whirling her around the porch until she thought she would show Kendrick just how strong the coffee had been that morning.

"Something I should know, sister?" Micah's voice stopped the mad spinning, thank goodness.

Whitman set Sarah gently on her feet and held out his hand

to Micah. "I've just asked your sister to marry me. With or without your permission, but I think I'd prefer with, of course."

Micah raised his brow and met Sarah's gaze. "A Yankee?"

Sarah shrugged. "We can't always choose who we fall in love with, Micah."

He smiled. "Well then, you have my blessing." Micah finally shook Whitman's hand. "But you'll have to get used to Southern cooking, because we make real food to eat."

Sarah swatted at her brother even as the men laughed. She'd never felt so happy, so amazingly delirious in her life. Joy sang through her veins as she slipped her hand into Whitman's.

Yes, this was it. She was finally home.

Chapter Twenty

Whitman sat cross-legged on the floor with Miracle as she introduced him to her dolls. He'd never played with children, but Sarah's niece was an amazing little girl who hugged him immediately upon meeting him.

Sarah watched him from the settee, her silver eyes calm for the first time since they'd met. Whitman still couldn't believe she had said yes to his marriage proposal.

Of course, she hadn't told him she loved him, but that was okay. He was patient enough to wait.

She wouldn't have agreed to marry him if she hadn't loved him. Sarah had no fondness for Yankees, after all, so she had to have true feelings for him to want to be his wife in earnest.

"Picnic with me?" Miracle was looking up at him with those fathomless brown eyes.

"You want to go on a picnic?"

"Uh-huh. Mama and Daddy goin' to town and I don't wanna go." She climbed into his lap. "Picnic with me?"

He glanced up in time to see Sarah hiding a grin.

"As long as Aunt Sarah comes on the picnic with us."

"I can't go traipsing around to a picnic site. For pity's sake, Kendrick, I can barely hobble to the necessary." She hadn't changed, thank God, and Whitman loved her all the more.

"Then let's do it in the yard. We can lay out a blanket under the trees and have a picnic."

"Yay!" Miracle stood up and danced around him. Her childish joy was infectious and soon Whit was dancing with her, much to Sarah's delight.

Eppie poked her head in the parlor and stared at them with a grin playing around her mouth. "She's convincing, isn't she?"

"Amazingly convincing." Whit laughed a bit sheepishly, then held out his hand. "Picnic, Miss Spalding."

Sarah frowned but accepted his help standing. Miracle picked up her cane and handed it to her aunt.

"You need magic." Miracle touched Sarah's right leg. "Make you all better."

With that the girl went skipping off singing about picnics. Sarah met Whit's gaze and he was surprised to feel a tremble in her hands.

"She's a very special child."

Whitman had already come to that conclusion and was glad to hear he wasn't crazy. "She'd have to be, considering how special her aunt is."

Sarah swatted at his shoulder. "You're just trying to get in my drawers."

Whit threw back his head and laughed. He felt so free, so alive, and so blessed.

Nothing would stand in the way of their new life.

The picnic spot was chosen after careful consideration by Miracle and her dog, Daisy. Apparently the pooch had a special sense about picnics.

Whitman and Sarah watched from the kitchen as the girl and dog wandered around the yard examining grass, rocks, and sniffing at everything. Of course, Daisy did most of the sniffing.

"What do you suppose they're looking for?" Sarah asked.

Whitman shrugged. "I don't know, but maybe she'll tell us when she finds it."

Sarah chuckled. "I would've expected her to be special and love being outside. I always did."

He wrapped his arms around her waist and pressed into her. "Mmm, maybe later we'll find our own special spot."

Sarah's pulse picked up and her nipples peaked at the nearness of his body. It had been a week—too long—since they'd been together.

She missed him in every way possible, but especially in her arms. They made their own magic then.

"You'd best be careful, Kendrick, or you'll light a fire you might not be able to douse."

He laughed against her neck. "I sure as hell would have fun trying, though."

Sarah turned her head and captured his lips in a quick, but hot kiss. "Me too."

The back door banged open and Miracle came running in with Daisy at her heels, startling Sarah and Whitman.

The girl looked up at them. "Hide." Her voice was full of fear.

She ran down the hallway, her shoes nearly sliding on the shiny wooden floors. Sarah felt a frisson of fear snake through her. She met Whitman's gaze and he looked as worried as she felt.

"What do you suppose scared her?"

"I don't know but we need to find out." Whit opened the door and peered out. "Stay here."

Sarah snorted and followed him out the door. "What makes you think I would stay put?" She made her way down the small set of stairs, thankfully without falling on her head.

Micah and Eppie had left fifteen minutes earlier, so no one was around but Sarah, Whitman, and a frightened little girl.

Whitman was halfway across the backyard when a shadow darted between the carriage house and the trees.

"Did you see that?" she hissed.

"Yes, now get back in the house, woman. Now."

"I'm not going anywhere." Sarah could protect herself. Whit should know that after all they'd been through.

There was no way she'd allow herself to be hurt again. Beneath her hand, the cane was warm against her skin. The deadly knife in her sleeve was comforting. Sarah was armed and ready for whoever or whatever threatened.

Whit was at the edge of the trees before Sarah reached him. He disappeared into the gloom, the leaves and sticks cracking beneath his boots.

She stopped and listened and heard a second set of feet in the woods.

"Whitman, look out!" She started toward where she'd seen him as fast as her crippled damn leg could carry her.

The sounds of a struggle bounced around the trees. By the time Sarah reached where she'd seen him, the sounds had stopped. The silence made every hair on her body stand on end.

"Whit?"

As expected, he didn't answer. Blood rushed around in her veins as she readied for whatever battle was about to be hers. Someone had come to steal her life away from her and she wasn't going to let it happen.

If Whit had been killed, then whoever it was would soon join him.

Sarah pulled the top from the cane and it made a swoosh of metal as the ten-inch-long blade was revealed. With her other hand, she slid the dagger from its pocket in her sleeve.

"Come on then! Let's get on with it!" she called to the trees. "Afraid of a crippled woman?! Do you have a pair of balls or not?!"

A rustling noise came from her left. She watched as a figure appeared in the shadows of the trees, pulling something behind it.

Then she realized the something being dragged was Whitman. Another man had him by the arm and was pulling him through the leaves with no regard for the sticks and rocks beneath them.

Sarah checked her balance and tightened her grip on the weapons.

When the man came closer, the world shifted beneath her feet. There before her stood the man who'd raped her, crippled her, and cut off her finger.

Her heart stopped beating for just a moment.

The sheer terror of being beneath the man returned, and it felt as if she'd run into a brick wall. It stole her breath and turned her back into a seventeen-year-old girl hiding in the cobwebs of the root cellar.

The very last person she expected to intrude on her life was this man. This poor excuse for a human being who found pleasure in hurting others.

Sarah grew dizzy with lack of air but she was finally able to suck in a lungful. She knew the man was waiting for her to speak, but her voice was still stuck in her throat.

He was as big as she remembered, gap toothed and ugly but dirtier, with a full, greasy beard and a big stomach. The one thing that definitely hadn't changed, however, were his eyes. They were as cold as death.

"Go away, bad man!" Miracle called from somewhere in the house.

"Come down here and I'll teach you a lesson, you little shit!" The man rubbed a bloody spot on his temple. "That little bitch threw a rock at me."

Miracle's courage gave Sarah the time and the boost to find her own.

"Get out of here before I kill you."

The idiot had the audacity to laugh. "Kill me? Listen, missy, I just about split your man's head in two. I don't plan on leaving before he's dead."

He kicked Whitman in the ribs and Sarah heard a sickening crack.

"I'm going to give you one more chance to leave, and then I'm going to enjoy killing you." Sarah didn't even recognize her own voice.

The threat on Whitman's life, and on sweet Miracle's life, had pulled the fear that had been lingering deep down inside Sarah and thrown it aside.

It was time to fight.

"What's your name, sugar? I feel like I know you."

This time it was Sarah's turn to laugh. "You have no idea who I am, do you?" She pointed the dagger at him. "You came to hurt Whitman, didn't you?"

He kicked Whitman in the back. "Hurt him? Nah, I came to kill him." His smile would probably scare the fur off a squirrel.

Sarah knew Whitman's life was in her hands. There was no one else around to help her except herself. She had to be stronger and more agile than she'd ever had to be.

"Well, isn't that too bad. I'm going to kill you instead." Sarah bared her teeth and readied herself for battle.

The stranger circled around her, watching her. She somehow found the balance she needed to keep turning as he walked. Sarah's heart was beating so hard, she was afraid it would burst from her chest.

"You don't look strong enough to kill a bird, much less a man like me."

"You're not a man, you're an animal. Makes you easier to take down." Her jab hit home, judging by the red flush that spread across his cheeks.

"You've got a smart mouth."

"I've got a smart brain too. Better to defeat you with, you disgusting piece of dog shit." Sarah felt better with each word that burst from her mouth.

"I'm going to enjoy watching you suck my dick with that smart mouth." He lunged toward her and Sarah had only moments to react.

She whirled to the right and sliced at him as he went past

her. A blossom of red appeared on his shirt and Sarah growled in triumph.

She didn't celebrate long, however, because he regained his balance and grabbed her arm. Sarah pulled the dagger up and stabbed his shoulder.

He howled and punched her so hard, she saw stars. Yet she didn't fall.

"You bitch." He punched her in the stomach and she sliced him in the neck.

Blood sprayed everywhere, including in Sarah's eyes. She stumbled as he launched himself on her. His hands wrapped around her throat as she struggled for breath.

His weight kept her pinned to the ground as rocks dug into her back. The blood temporarily blinded her, but she could still see him in her mind's eye.

The bastard had tried to strangle her before, so long ago, and she'd fought until she'd passed out. Not this time, however. This time one of them would die.

Whitman came into consciousness after a scream echoed through his head. His body screamed in protest when he rolled over. It felt as if he'd been stomped by a horse.

He heard another scream and realized it was Sarah. Whitman got to his knees and shook his head, willing away the spots. That proved to be a mistake when he almost passed out again.

A grunt and a man's shout brought him back to the here and now. Sarah was in trouble.

Whitman looked up and tried to focus on the two figures struggling in front of him. A spray of blood told him it was a deadly battle and someone was losing.

With a mighty groan, he got to his feet and staggered over in time to see a man drag Sarah to the ground as he choked her. Whit fell to his knees and realized he wasn't going to be able to save her.

He crawled to her, desperate to save the woman who owned his heart. "Sarah," he croaked.

The man on top of her rolled off and Whitman howled in agony. He'd killed her. God, that son of a bitch had killed his Sarah.

Tears rolled down his cheeks as he crawled across the dirt to her. Sarah was covered in blood and lying there as still as death.

Whitman's heart was torn asunder with the knowledge he'd been in the dirt on his knees while she'd been murdered. When he got closer, he realized the man was Booker.

"No!" Whitman screamed when he realized his run-in with the former sergeant was what brought the man to Colorado.

To exact revenge.

To murder Sarah.

To take everything from Whitman.

Whitman reached her and tried to wipe away the blood from her face. She'd fought hard and hadn't given up easily. Booker was a big man and obviously too much for a woman with a damaged leg.

He pulled her limp body into his arms and rocked back and forth. Sobs of agony were torn from deep inside him as he grieved for the woman he loved.

"She needs magic." Miracle's voice broke through the haze of grief.

Whitman tried to focus on the girl but he was still seeing double. "What?"

"Give her a magic kiss, Uncle Whit." Miracle patted his cheek as if he were the child.

Whit stared into the girl's brown eyes. "A kiss?"

Miracle shook her head. "She wake up with a magic kiss."

He realized the child was seeing enough blood and gore to scar her for life. "Go back in the house, Miracle. You shouldn't see this."

Miracle stood up and put her hands on her hips. "Give her

a magic kiss." Her insistence finally made it through Whitman's fuzzy, grief-filled thoughts.

He looked down at Sarah's bloody face and touched her
lips. That's when he saw her lids flutter.

Give her a magic kiss.

Whit held his breath as he leaned down and pressed his lips
to hers. For a moment, it was as if he were kissing her dead
body, but then, God shone down upon him and her lips
moved beneath his.

She opened her eyes and looked at him. "Whitman, you
look like somebody beat the shit out of you."

He laughed and hugged her close, ignoring the pain thrum-
ming through his skull and his ribs.

Sarah was alive!

"Told you. Magic kisses are special." Miracle turned to
look at Booker's body. "Bad man dead now."

With that, the amazing little girl went back in the house,
leaving Whitman in the dirt next to a bloody dead bastard
and with a very alive woman in his arms.

"I thought you were dead," he whispered brokenly.

She snorted. "I'm too tough to die. That bastard never
knew what he was up against. My blades are sharp enough to
cut off someone's head."

Whitman laughed through his tears. "Are you hurt?"

"No, just bruised from the fall. He tried to choke me, but I
cut his throat and he bled to death first." She touched the
back of his head gently. "Are you all right?"

Whitman nodded, then hugged her again. He'd almost lost
her again, this time to a murderous bastard instead of his own
stupidity.

But no more. The last demon to inhabit the blackness of
their past was now truly dead.

Life would begin again for Whitman and Sarah.

*   *   *

After the sheriff had left with Booker's corpse and Eppie had tended to Whitman's wounds, there was a collective sigh of relief in the house.

Eppie convinced Sarah and Whitman to take a bath. There was a modern bathing room in the house, which had running water pumped in.

Whitman had used them in New York and Washington, but it was a special treat for Sarah. She had wiped most of the blood from her face and hands, but her clothes were stained with it.

She allowed Whit to carry her up the stairs, although she knew his ribs hurt and he wouldn't take no for an answer.

Sarah was still amazed they were both alive and had come out of the deadly confrontation with wounds that would heal.

Now they needed to heal the wounds on the inside.

The bathing room had white and blue tile and an enormous claw-foot tub. Whit set her down on the stool and closed the door. He had a bandage wrapped around his head, which gave him a look of mystery. At least that's what Sarah told him anyway.

He waggled his finger at her. "Now you sit right there while I get the bath ready."

"Yes sir." She saluted and made a face at him.

While he ran the hot water, Sarah watched. True to her word, she didn't move from the stool. Her body ached in places she forgot about. A bath would be heavenly.

As the tub filled, Whit pulled off his shirt, revealing a rainbow of bruises on his chest. She sucked in a breath and gestured for him to come closer.

When he was near enough, she reached out and kissed the bruises she could. He touched the top of her head and sighed.

"Magic kisses."

She smiled against his skin and looked up at him. "How about you undress me too, oaf?"

He knelt down in front of her. "As you wish, my lady."

Whit took off her clothes slowly, kissing her exposed skin as he went. Sarah had never felt more cherished or more loved. He stood her up to remove her skirt and drawers, leaving nothing but her hair to cover her nude body.

He was eye level with her legs when he looked up at her. "Magic kisses."

When his lips touched her ropy scars, Sarah couldn't contain the tears. She'd cried so much the last week, she was surprised there were any left, but they arrived just the same.

Whitman had been all she hated, resented, and avoided. Now he was everything she loved, wanted, and needed.

He stood and shucked his trousers, then scooped her into his arms. "Your bath is waiting."

Whit lowered her into the tub slowly and the warmth of the water enveloped her sore, tired body. The tub, built for two, was even large enough to fit Whitman.

He climbed in behind her and soon she was surrounded by heat and man. Two tantalizing combinations.

Whitman had silently bathed her long ago in Kentucky, apologizing to her with his hands, letting her know he cared for her well-being.

This time it was so much more. It was a symphony of soap and hands, massaging, soaping, and rinsing until her skin squeaked beneath his strong fingers.

He played with her nipples until they ached, then left them to land his hands between her legs. The day had begun with sadness and it was ending with love and sex.

She couldn't have asked for anything more.

He spread her legs as far as they'd go, then dipped his fingers into her pulsing pussy. He found her eager clit easily and began circling it, teasing her.

The other hand dipped lower and two of his fingers slid into her. She gasped as tingles raced up her skin straight to her nipples.

"God, you feel good."

"Mmm, so do you, kitten." He nibbled at her earlobe. "When I first met you I thought you hissed like a cat. Now I know you purr like one too."

Sarah arched into him, eager for the pleasure he gave her. His cock was hard against her back. She wanted to taste him, to bite him, to feel him enter her.

He fucked her with his fingers while he played her clit like a musical instrument. Faster and harder until she came, splashing water and pressing against his staff behind her.

Stars swam behind her closed lids as his hand gentled, bringing her back to earth.

"If you don't fuck me now, I'll never forgive you."

Whit chuckled against her ear. "God, I love you, woman."

She harrumphed and shifted against his cock. "I mean it. Now, Whitman."

"As you wish, my lady." He stood, the water sluicing from his nude body. His erection stood tall and proud above his firm balls.

She couldn't help herself. Sarah turned around quick enough to grab the base of his staff and pull him into her mouth.

He groaned and braced himself against the wall on his left. "Jesus Christ."

"No, I told you before, it's Sarah." She laved the head, paying close attention to the underside, tickling him with her tongue. "You taste good, Yankee."

He managed a croak in response.

Sarah chuckled, pleased to have the large man at her mercy. It was empowering, it was amazing, it was incredibly arousing.

She squeezed the base as she lowered her mouth, alternately nibbling and licking as she went. A slow, excruciating pace designed to make him wild.

He groaned and shook beneath her touch.

"Feel good?"

"You know it does," he gasped. "I thought you wanted me to fuck you."

Hearing him talk dirty to her just made Sarah that much hornier. She quickened her pace, loving the feel of the steel encased in satin in her mouth. He started moving with her, fucking her mouth, and Sarah felt his balls tightening beneath her hand.

If she didn't stop, the fun would be over for a while, and she wasn't ready for that yet.

With one last suck, and a lick on the head, she released him. He fell back against the wall, sucking in a breath like a bellows.

Whit opened his eyes and met her gaze. "Damn, you are incredible."

She grinned. "I know. Now let's get dried off so we can get down to business."

"Give me a minute to get my breath back."

Sarah laughed and reached out to run a finger down his still rock-hard erection. "Don't take too long."

Whit jumped out of the tub and grabbed her, splashing more water all over the room. "Your brother will probably know what we were doing."

"I don't care. He's an adult. And besides, they have a three-year-old child and aren't married." She shivered. "Now let's get dried off so we can get heated up."

Within minutes, they were both dry and wrapped in fluffy towels. Whitman peeked out the bathing room door and then looked back at her.

"All clear." He picked her up again and walked toward the guest room.

Luckily for them, they reached the door without seeing anyone. Sarah turned the knob and they ducked in.

Whitman set her on her feet and pulled the towel off her. Her nipples instantly pebbled just from him looking at them.

"Looks like I'm being called." He set her on the edge of the bed and dropped to his knees so her breasts were at eye level.

Sarah shivered in anticipation as he spread her legs and

nestled closer. He cupped her breasts and ran his thumb back and forth across the nipples.

"That feels good." She smiled. "Your mouth would feel better."

He leaned forward and captured one nipple in his hot mouth and she closed her eyes. His other hand crept down between her legs and lightly teased her clit.

Whitman bit and sucked at her until she thought she'd come just from his mouth. She took a much needed breath when he moved to the other breast.

"How am I doing?"

"I'll let you know in about ten minutes."

He chuckled just before he licked the other nipple and his fingers plunged into her. Sarah grabbed his shoulders and hung on as her body thrummed in tune with his touch.

Lick, bite, suck. Lick, bite, suck.

Sarah yanked at his hair. "I need you. Now."

He gave her one last bite, then leaned down to lick her pussy from top to bottom.

"You taste delicious, kitten." He lapped at her again. "Hot and spicy."

Much as she wanted him to lick her, she needed him inside her more. Later they could play in bed all night.

"You'd best climb up on this bed." She lay back and scooted to the side to make room for him.

"Oh, but my kitty needs to be petted." He lapped at her again.

Sarah's legs spread open wider, of their own volition. "Please, Whit." She didn't intend to beg, but damn if it didn't come out of her mouth.

"Please what?" His rough tongue licked her throbbing pussy.

"I don't know. Just something, now." She grabbed her own nipples and pinched as his mouth returned to her.

Whitman sucked her clit, then bit it while his fingers slid in and out of her wetness. She could hardly contain the scream building inside her. In all her experience, she'd never felt such pleasure, such ecstasy at a man's hands.

As Sarah was mere licks away from coming again, he stopped and kissed her pussy. "Beautiful."

When he rose above her, she opened her eyes again and met his gaze.

"Love you, kitten."

She forgot to breathe as he thrust into her, hard and fast. This, *this* was what she needed. He felt so damn good, sliding in and out.

Theirs was a mating, a base, primal mating of two souls forever fused into one. Sarah scratched at his back as he plunged into her, touching her womb, filling her.

Whitman leaned down to kiss her, capturing her mouth in a wild kiss, a clash of tongues that mimicked his cock inside her.

She felt her orgasm building near her toes, and it traveled through her body like the train that had carried them to Colorado.

When it arrived, he swallowed her scream as she received his. He poured his seed into her waiting body, bonding them together, bringing them the peace they needed.

Sarah's tears were finally ones of joy instead of sorrow. She had been healed by the stubborn jackass Yankee who had wormed his way into her cracked heart.

He had healed her with his magic.

Sarah Spalding was once again whole.

Epilogue

Whitman sat on the front porch with Sarah drinking coffee. The nightmare over, they were ready to talk about the future.

"Do you still want to go to San Francisco?" She took a sip of the hot brew. "Damn, Eppie makes good coffee."

Whitman smiled. "She does know how to brew it just right."

"You didn't answer my question." Sarah poked him in the shoulder. "San Francisco?"

He met her gaze. "I bought a house there months ago and it's still mine. However, we can live wherever you want. I don't care where, because as long as we're together, I'm home."

Sarah could get used to that. It might take some time, but she would. "It's cold here. Especially in the winter."

"Yes, it surely is. Colorado is a snowy place." He cocked one brow at her. "Southern girl doesn't like cold, right?"

She humphed. "No, I don't. Is San Francisco cold?"

He shook his head. "Nope. It is usually foggy in the mornings, then sunny and warm in the afternoons. It rains in winter instead of snow, and it's beautifully set with the ocean on one side and a bay on the other."

She nodded, picturing the city in her mind. "It sounds beautiful."

"It's not nearly as beautiful as you, kitten." He kissed her hand.

"Flattery will get you in my drawers every time."

Whit laughed and kissed her hard. "I love you, Sarah."

She stared at him, knowing she needed to respond, realizing it meant she'd have to make the final step in becoming a whole person.

"I love you too, Whit."

His smile was worth every second of pain she had endured the last two weeks. He was amazing, handsome, smart, funny, and he was hers.

"When are we going to get married?" She snuggled under his arm.

"We can do it here or wait until we get to San Francisco." He kissed the top of her head.

"Then my family can't attend unless they travel there too." Sarah had a sudden thought and sat up to meet his gaze. "Whitman, what about your family?"

He looked away. "What about them?"

"Your mother is alive, right?"

"Yes, she is. She lives in Maryland on a small farm." He glanced down at Sarah. "She and I haven't always seen eye to eye."

Sarah smiled wryly. "I figured that out already. You know, we all have things to say and do that we don't want to. But I want to help you fix whatever is broken between you and your mother."

He rolled his eyes. "You can't, so leave it be."

"No, I won't. You need to write her a letter and tell her how you feel and what's happened." She cupped his cheek. "We can't move on until you do, and you know it."

Sarah sat up and handed him her cup to rise. She had something she had to do too. "I'll leave it to you to decide what you want to do."

Whitman looked up at her, a scared little boy hiding in his green gaze. "Sarah, there's so much hurt there."

"I know, but I have faith in you." She took her cane and her cup and turned to go into the house. "I have to tell the story to my brother face-to-face. At least you can do it on paper."

He managed a grin. "Love you."

She blew him a kiss. "Love you too, Yankee."

After Sarah left, Whitman stared out at the street as the leaves moved with the breeze. It was so peaceful, so idyllic, it was hard to imagine there had been death there the day before.

He knew Sarah was right. There was much to be said to his mother and it needed to be done. He was thousands of miles from his mother, but it felt as if she was right next to him.

Whitman stood and went in search of pen and paper.

Sarah hobbled into the house and found Micah in the parlor alone. He smiled when she came into the room, but his smile faded when she closed the door.

"What's going on, sprite?"

She sat down on the settee next to him and took a deep breath. "Whitman and I are moving to San Francisco."

"I'll miss you, but we can visit, Sarah." He took her hand. "Now that we've found each other, there's nothing to stop us from being together as a family."

Sarah nodded and swallowed the lump in her throat. "We'll leave after your wedding, of course, and get married in San Francisco. But first, I need to tell you my story."

Micah nodded, his silver gaze steady. "And I'm ready to hear it."

Sarah held her brother's hand and thanked God she'd found him again. "I'll start with the story of how I came to use a cane."

Together yet apart, Sarah and Whitman healed the wounds from their past and looked toward their future. Magic, it seemed, had saved them after all.

If you like this book, you've got to try
ETERNAL HUNTER, the latest from Cynthia Eden,
in stores now from Brava . . .

She reached into her bag and pulled out a check. Not the usual way things were handled in the DA's office, but . . . "I've been authorized to acquire your services." He didn't glance at the check, just kept those blue eyes trained on hers. Her fingers were steady as she held the check in the air between them "This check is for ten thousand dollars."

No change of expression. From the looks of his cabin, the guy shouldn't have been hesitating to snatch up the money.

"Give the check to Night Watch."

At that, her lips firmed. "I already gave them one." A hefty one, at that. "This one's for you. A bonus from the mayor—he wants this guy caught, fast." Before word about the true nature of the crime leaked too far.

"So old Gus doesn't think his cops can handle this guy?"

Gus LaCroix. Hard-talking, ex-hard drinking mayor. No nonsense, deceptively smart, and demanding. "He's got the cops on this, but he said he knew you, and that you'd be the best one to handle this job."

Erin strongly suspected that Gus belonged in the *Other* world. She hadn't caught any scent that was off drifting from him, but his agreement to bring in Night Watch and his almost desperate demands to the DA had sure indicated the guy knew more than he was letting on about the situation.

Could be he was a demon. Low-level. Many politicians were.

Jude took the check. Finally. She dropped her fingers, fast, not wanting the flesh on flesh contact with him. Not then.

He folded the check and tucked it into the back pocket of his jeans. "Guess you just got yourself a bounty hunter."

"And I guess you've got yourself one sick shifter to catch."

He closed the distance between them, moving fast and catching her arms in a strong grip.

Aw, hell. It was just like before. The heat of his touch swept though her, waking hungers she'd deliberately denied for so long.

Jude was sexual. From his knowing eyes. His curving, kiss-me lips, to the hard lines and muscles of his body.

Deep inside, in the dark, secret places of her soul that she fought to keep hidden, there was a part of her just like that.

Wild. Hot.

Sexual.

"Why are you afraid of me?"

Not the question she'd expected, but one she could answer. "I know what you are. What sane woman wouldn't be afraid of a man who becomes an animal?"

"Some women like a little bit of the animal in their men."

"Not me." *Liar.*

His eyes said the same thing.

"Do your job, Donovan. Catch the freak who cut up my prisoner—"

"Like Bobby had been slashing his victims?"

Hit. Yeah, there'd been no way to miss that significance.

"When word gets out about what really happened, some folks will say Bobby deserved what he got." His fingers pressed into her arms. Erin wore a light, silk shirt—and even that seemed too hot for the humid Louisiana spring night. His touch burned through the blouse and seemed to singe her flesh.

"Some will say that," she allowed. Okay, a hell of a lot would say that. "But his killer still has to be caught." Stopped, because she had the feeling this could be just the beginning.

Her feelings about death weren't often wrong.

She was a lot like her dad that way.

And, unfortunately, like her mother, too.

"What do you think? Did he deserve to be clawed to death?"

An image of Bobby's ex-wife, Pat, flashed before her eyes. The doctors had put over one hundred and fifty stitches into her face. She'd been his most brutal attack.

Erin swallowed. "His punishment was for the court to decide." She stepped back, but he didn't let her go. "Uh, do you mind?"

"Yeah, I do." His eyes glittered down at her. "If we're gonna be working together, we need honesty between us."

"We need you to find the killer."

"Oh, I will. Don't worry about that. I always catch my prey."

So the rumors claimed. The hunters from Night Watch were known throughout the U.S.

"You're shivering, Erin."

"No, no, I'm not." She was.

"I make you nervous. I scare you." A pause. His gaze dropped to her lips, lingered, then slowly rose back to meet her stare. "Is it because I know what you are?"

She wanted his mouth on hers. A foolish desire. Ridiculous. Not something the controlled woman wanted, but what the wild thing inside craved. "You don't know anything about me."

"Don't I?"

Erin jerked free of his hold and glared at him. "Few things in this world scare me. You should know that." There was one thing, one person, who terrified her—but now wasn't the time for that disclosure. No, she didn't tell anyone about *him*.

If she could just get around Jude and march out of that door—

"Maybe you're not scared of me, then. Maybe you're scared of yourself."

She froze.

"Not human," he murmured, shaking his head. "Not vamp."

Vamp? Thankfully, no.

"Djinn? Nah, you don't have that look." His right hand lifted and he rubbed his chin. "Tell me your secrets, sweetheart, and I'll tell you mine."

"Sorry, not the sharing type." She'd wasted enough time here. Erin pushed past him, ignoring the press of his arm against her side. Her body ached and the whispers of hunger within her grew more demanding every moment she stayed with him.

Weak.

She hated her weakness.

Just like her mother's.

"You're a shifter." His words stopped her near the door. She stared blankly at the faded wood. Heard the dull thud of her heart echoing in her ears.

Then the soft squeak of the old floorboards as he closed the distance between them.

Erin turned to him, tilted her head back—

He kissed her.

She heard a growl. Not from him—no, from her own throat.

The hunger.

Sure, he made the first move, he brought his lips crashing down on hers, but . . . she kissed him right back.

Fall in love with a hero who's
HALF PAST DEAD. Go pick up the collaboration
from Zoe Archer and Bianca D'Arc today!

S he knew it now without a doubt.
   She wasn't alone.

Fighting the sudden lump of fear in her throat, Cassandra pressed herself against the granite slab. Not for protection, but to better see whoever, *whatever*, prowled in the darkness. She held her breath, waited.

There, again. A justified chill of fear scraped down her neck. Someone was sliding from shadow to shadow, movements so swift, so silent, anyone who wasn't trained to spot such subtlety would have missed it. Who could it be? Another Heir of Albion, like Broadwell? It couldn't be a Blade, for Cassandra had been unable to send a telegram to let them know Broadwell's whereabouts. Someone else, then.

Something else. The shadows gathered, shaping themselves into the form of a man gliding from darkness to darkness— tall, long-limbed, powerfully built. Twenty feet away. At a slight sound, he turned to investigate. His eyes literally glowed. Hollow and white, unearthly.

Cassandra stifled a gasp. Oh, it was one thing to read about and study magic. Entirely different to sense it, *see* it.

Whatever this . . . man . . . was, he moved with unearthly speed and stealth. She could not see his face as he shifted back into the shadows, more subtle and elusive than any human or animal. *What was he?* Before she could study him further, he melted into darkness, disappearing.

For several moments, Cassandra peered into the night, straining for another sense of him. Yet he was gone, absorbed into the fabric of shadow like a half-remembered dream. Cassandra, trying to refocus, turned back to keep her vigil on the tavern.

The unknown man stood right in front of her.

They both started, neither expecting the other.

Her pistol came up immediately.

Ambient light from the tavern revealed his face, the glow of his eyes vanished, and her fingers around the trigger slackened in shock. The tall man also started again, as shocked as Cassandra.

It could not be. Yet it was. She took a step forward, lowering her weapon, hardly daring to believe what she saw.

"Sam?" Her voice was a stunned whisper. "Samuel Reed?"

"Cassie."

Oh, God, she knew that voice. Knew it as well as she knew the deepest recesses of her own heart. A low, masculine rumble, much deeper now than it had been ten years ago, but it was him. Sam.

"Cassandra now," she said automatically as she grappled with understanding. Nothing made sense. It could not be that Sam was the creature she had just witnessed prowling through the darkness. "What the blazes are you doing here?"

Sam emerged slightly from the darkness, wariness evident in the guarded movement of his long, lean body. He'd been only eighteen the last time Cassandra saw him, verging into adulthood. Now there was no debate. Sam had grown up. He was, positively, a man. She noted it in the breadth of his shoulders, his broad chest, and powerful limbs. Even in shadow, even dressed in clean but slightly threadbare clothing, she could see it. Sam had left boyhood long ago. This man radiated potent strength, barely restrained.

Cassandra stared up at his face and felt another jolt of shock. The softness of youth had vanished entirely. Sam's face . . . there was no other way for her to describe it . . . it was *hard*, a collection of sharply chiseled planes that made no allowance for leniency. Bold jaw, tight-pressed lips, sharp nose, and forbidding, dark brow. Too severe to be handsome, but undeniably striking. Such a change from the boy he'd been.

"I should ask you the same damned question," he growled. "You shouldn't be out. Alone." He moved, as if to reach for her, but his hand stopped, curling into itself and falling to his side instead.

Fear suddenly danced along her neck. His voice was rough, almost menacing. But that was ridiculous. This was *Sam*, her brother Charlie's best friend, the boy she'd known—and adored—almost her whole life. Ten years ago, he and Charlie both bought commissions, joining the army and serving in the same unit together, as they had done everything together. Including—

"For a lady," Sam growled, "you're pretty damned free with that gun."

She glanced down at the weapon in her hand, then tucked it into her skirts. Proper young women did not carry pistols. Certainly not during the day, and most assuredly not in the middle of the night while lurking in deserted stonemason yards.

"Pistols are all the rage this season," she said. She could not tell Sam anything about her mission, bound by a code of silence, as well as for his own protection.

Although, she amended, gazing at Sam, he seemed perfectly capable of protecting himself. If forced to use only one word to describe this man, the word she must choose would be lethal. She'd never met a man who held such dangerous intent in his body, including the most seasoned Blade field agents. He did not even offer a veneer of a smile at her attempt at humor.

"Nothing good brings a woman out at night," he rumbled. "Some kind of assignation, then. A husband? Lover?" He raised a brow.

Cassandra wondered what kind of lover necessitated having a gun. "I might not be the same girl who collected spiders in jars," she said, "but I'm not the sort of woman who arranges moonlight trysts." However, she wasn't a maiden anymore. She'd seen to that a few years ago, though she wasn't about to tell Sam.

Truthfully, she did not know what to say to Sam. She'd so often dreamt of this moment, how she would greet him upon his return. She had even contemplated something as frivolous as the dress she would wear. It would show him she was no longer a girl with dirt under her fingernails, but a grown woman, with a grown woman's desires. And he would see her as if for the first time, a slow smile of wonder illuminating his face, and realize that what he had been searching for had been at home all along. Her nails, too, would be clean. She curbed the impulse to check them now—for often, after touring factories and inspecting conditions, her fingernails did get dirty. But that was a minor detail compared to seeing Sam again.

Her dream of their reunion had ended two years ago, but she remembered it vividly, an imprint of abandoned hope burned into an afterimage on her heart.

Yet this . . . fierce, dangerous man . . . was entirely unlike the Sam she'd longed for, resembling him only in the most superficial way. He burned with a deep, profound coldness that seeped into her own bones.

She realized that it *had* been Sam, stalking the darkness. Moving with an eerie fluidity. More at home within the realm of unnatural shadow than light and life. But how could that be possible?

"I've no idea who you are anymore." Sam's voice glinted like a knife in the darkness.

"That feeling," she said, "is mutual."

Truthfully, she had no idea who he was. Or, her mind whispered, *what* he was. She tried to push that thought away, but it would not be staved off.

Unfamiliar, this terror. Something clammy and frightened uncoiled in her stomach as she stared up at his impassive face. The changes wrought in Sam went beyond the shift from youth to maturity, from civilian to veteran soldier. Yet she did not know what, exactly, was different, was deeply, profoundly not right.

A burst of noise careened out of the tavern. Both Cassandra and Sam shot alert glances toward it, but no one exited the building. As Sam continued to rake the tavern with his gaze, Cassandra could feel the waves of anger and purpose emanating from him, palpable as frost. The gentling of his expression was gone. Nothing gentle in him now.

Sam had been a soldier, a major, the last she'd heard, and still held himself with a soldier's vigilant, capable presence. He wore civilian clothes, yet carried, she saw at that moment, an officer's sword and wore tall military boots. The war in the Crimea ended two years ago. What had become of him since then?

"This makes no sense," she said. "I was told. . . ." Her words dried as he swung his gaze back to her. Even in the weak light from the tavern's windows, she saw his eyes were the same palest blue, edged in indigo, only now his eyes did not dance with humor or mischief. They were . . . *haunted*.

"I was told," she began again, "that you were dead."

He stared at her with those anguished, cold eyes. And said, "I am."

Here's a sneak peek at Donna Kauffman's
HERE COMES TROUBLE,
out next month from Brava!

The hot, steamy shower felt like heaven on earth as it pounded his back and neck. He should have done this earlier. It was almost better than sleep. Almost. He'd realized after Kirby had left that he'd probably only grabbed a few hours after arriving, and he'd fully expected to be out the instant his head hit the pillow again. But that hadn't been the case. This time it hadn't been because he was worried about Dan, or Vanetta, or anyone else back home, or even wondering what in the hell he thought he was doing this far from the desert. In New England, for God's sake. During the winter. Although it didn't appear to be much of one out there.

No, that blame lay right on the lovely, slender shoulders of Kirby Farrell, innkeeper, and rescuer of trapped kittens. Granted, after the adrenaline rush of finding her hanging more than twenty feet off the ground by her fingertips, it shouldn't be surprising that sleep eluded him, but that wasn't entirely the cause. Maybe he'd simply spent too long around women who were generally over-processed, over-enhanced, and overly made up, so that meeting a regular, everyday ordinary woman seemed to stand out more.

It was a safe theory, anyway.

And yet, after only a few hours under her roof, he'd already become a foster dad to a wild kitten and had spent far more time thinking about said kitten's savior than he had his own host of problems.

Maybe it was simply easier to think about someone else's situation. Which would explain why he was wondering about things like whether or not Kirby was making a go of things with her new enterprise here, what with the complete lack of winter weather they were having. And what her story was before opening the inn? Was this place a lifelong dream? For all he knew, she was some New England trust fund baby just playing at running her own place. Except that didn't jibe with what he'd seen of her so far.

He'd been so lost in his thoughts while enjoying the rejuvenation of the hot shower, that he clearly hadn't heard his foster child's entrance into the bathroom. Which was why he almost had a heart attack when he turned around to find the little demon hanging from the outside of the clear shower curtain by its tiny, sharp nails, eyes wide in panic.

After his heart resumed a steady pace, he bent down to look at her, eye-to-wild-eye. "You keep climbing things you shouldn't and one day there will be no one to rescue you."

He was sure the responding hiss was meant to be ferocious and intimidating, but given the pink nosed–tiny–whiskered face it came out of, not so much. She hissed again when he just grinned, and started grappling with the curtain when he outright laughed, mangling it in the process.

He swore under his breath. "So, I'm already down one sweater, a shower curtain, and God knows what else you've dragged under the bed. I should just let you hang there all tangled up. At least I know where you are."

However, given that the tiny thing had already had one pretty big fright that day, he sighed, shut off the hot, life-giving spray, and very carefully reached out for a towel. After a quick rubdown, he wrapped the towel around his hips, eased out from the other end of the shower, and grabbed a hand towel. "We'll probably be adding this to my tab, as well." He doubted Kirby's guests would appreciate for a bath towel one that had doubled as a kitty straitjacket.

"Come on," he said, doing pretty much the same thing he'd done when the kitten had been attached to the front of Kirby. "I know you're not happy about it," he told the now squalling cat. "I'm not all that amped up, either." He looked at the shredded curtain once he'd de-pronged the demon from the front of it, and shuddered to think of just how much damage it had done to the front of Kirby.

"Question is . . . what do I do with you now?"

Just then a light tap came on the door. "Mr. Hennessey?"

"Brett," he called back.

"I . . . Brett. Right. I called. But there was no answer, so—"

"Oh, shower. Sorry." He walked over to the door, juggled the kitty bundle and cracked the door open.

Her gaze fixed on his chest, then scooted down to the squirming towel bundle, right back up to his chest, briefly to his face, then away all together. "I'm—sorry. I just, you said . . . and dinner is—anyway—" She frowned. "You didn't take the cat, you know, into—" She nodded toward the room behind him. "Did something happen?"

"I was in the shower. Shredder here decided to climb the curtain because apparently she's not happy unless she's trying to find new ways to terrify people."

He glanced from the kitten to Kirby's face in time to see her almost laugh, then compose herself. "I'm sorry, really. I shouldn't have let you keep her in the first place. I mean, not that you can't, but you obviously didn't come here to rescue a kitten. I should—we should—just leave you alone." She reached out to take the squirmy bundle from him.

"Does that mean I don't get dinner?"

"What?" She looked up, got caught somewhere about chest height, then finally looked at his face. "I mean, no, no, not at all. I just—I hope you didn't have your heart set on pot roast. There were a few . . . kitchen issues. Minor, really, but—"

"I'm not picky," he reassured her. What he was, he realized, was starving. And not just for dinner. If she kept looking at him like that . . . well, it was making him want to feed an entirely different kind of appetite. In fact . . . He shut that mental path down. His life, such as it was, didn't have room for further complications. And she'd be one. Hell, she already was. "I shouldn't have gotten you to cook anyway. You've had quite a day, and given what The Claw here did to your—*my*—shower curtain—I'll pay for a new one—I can only imagine that you must need more medical attention than I realized."

"Don't worry about that, I'm fine. Here," she said, reaching out for the wriggling towel bundle. "Why don't I go ahead and take her off your hands. I can put her out on the back porch for a bit, let you get, uh, dressed."

Really, she had to stop looking at him like that. Like he was a . . . a pot roast or something. With gravy. And potatoes. Damn he was really hungry. Voraciously so. Did she have any idea how long he'd been on the road? With only himself and the sound of the wind for company? Actually, it had been far longer than that, but he really didn't need to acknowledge that right about now.

Then she was reaching for him, and he was right at that point where he was going to say the hell with it and drag her into the room and the hell with dinner, too . . . only she wasn't reaching for him. She was reaching for the damn kitten. He sort of shoved it into her hands, then shifted so a little more of the door was between them . . . and a little less of a view of the front of his towel. Which was in a rather revealing situation at the moment.

"Thanks," he said. "I appreciate it. I'll go down—*be down*—in just a few minutes." He really needed to shut this door. Before he made her nervous. Or worse. I mean, sure, she was looking at him like he was her last supper, but that didn't mean she was open to being ogled in return by a paying guest. Especially when he was the only paying guest in residence.

Even if that did mean they had the house to themselves. And privacy. Lots and lots of privacy. "Five minutes," he blurted, and all but slammed the door in her face.

Crap, if Dan could see him at the moment, he'd be laughing his damn ass off. As would most of Vegas. Not only did Brett happen to play high stakes poker pretty well, but the supporters and promoters seemed to think he was also a draw because of his looks. And no, he wasn't blind, he knew he'd been relatively blessed, genetically speaking, for which he was grateful. No one would choose to be ugly. A least he wouldn't think so.

But while the looks had come naturally, that whole bad boy, cocky attitude vibe that was supposed to go with it had not. Not that he was shy. Exactly.

He was confident in his abilities, what they were, and what they weren't. But confidence was one thing. Arrogance another. And just because women threw themselves at him, didn't mean he was comfortable catching them. Mostly due to the fact that he was well aware that women weren't throwing themselves at him because of who he was. But because of what he was. Some kind of quasi-poker rock star. They were batting eyelashes, thrusting cleavage, and passing phone numbers and room keys because of his fame, his fortune, his ability to score freebies from hotels and sponsors, and, somewhere on that list, probably his looks weren't hurting him, either.

Nowhere on that list, however, did it appear that getting to know the guy behind the deck of cards and the stacks of chips was of any remote interest.

And there lay the irony.

GREAT BOOKS,
GREAT SAVINGS!

When You Visit Our Website:
www.kensingtonbooks.com

You Can Save Money Off The Retail Price
Of Any Book You Purchase!

- **All Your Favorite Kensington Authors**
- **New Releases & Timeless Classics**
- **Overnight Shipping Available**
- **eBooks Available For Many Titles**
- **All Major Credit Cards Accepted**

Visit Us Today To Start Saving!
www.kensingtonbooks.com

All Orders Are Subject To Availability.
Shipping and Handling Charges Apply.
Offers and Prices Subject To Change Without Notice.